My Sister's Killer

Helen Bridgett

Book 3 – Professor Maxie Reddick Files

Ruby
FICTION

Stories that inspire emotions!

www.rubyfiction.com

Published 2023 by Ruby Fiction
Penrose House, Crawley Drive, Camberley, Surrey GU15 2AB, UK
www.rubyfiction.com

A CIP catalogue record for this book is available
from the British Library

EPUB ISBN: 978-1-912550-84-5
PRINT ISBN: 978-1-912550-85-2

PRINTED AND BOUND BY AMAZON

For friends and family – always an inspiration.

For the real
Jean Carruthers!
Hope you enjoy it
[illegible]

Acknowledgements

Maxie's sister was killed in the 1990s, and it was quite a shock to realise that was over thirty years ago – I don't know about you, but that certainly feels like yesterday to me. As I've researched what was happening back then, I've loved being able to step back in time and reminisce about my own youth!

Police procedures have inevitably changed since the 90s, but I was lucky enough to have a friend who was and still is part of the police force. I'd like to thank Iain MacPhie for his help in understanding how processes might have worked during the original investigation and also Carole Hodgson for clarifying how school records might have been kept. You've both been absolute stars!

I know Maxie has some very loyal readers, and in this book I've used a few of their names as a thank you – in particular, Jean Carruthers who takes a starring role as our cold case investigator. Jean, I hope you enjoy the book!

Finally, I'd like to thank everyone at Ruby Fiction for helping me realise a dream. I have loved writing this series and it simply couldn't have happened without all your support. In particular I'd like to mention my editor, cover designer and the Tasting Panel readers who made publication possible: Lisa Vasil, Alan Roberton, Zoe Rippon, Carol Fletcher, Cheryl Woodbridge, Janice Butler, Shona Nicolson, Donna Morgan, Karen Mace, Dimitra Evangelou, Brigette Hughes, Lynda Adcock, Jenny Mitchell, Julie Lilly, Carol Botting, Bee Master and Lorna Baker.

Chapter One

Saturday 16 September, 1995

The phone rang once. Susan stirred in her bed; she hadn't meant to fall asleep – not while her little sister Maxine was still out with her friends.

The phone rang twice. This was their signal – three rings meant Maxine was on her way home and was calling from the phone box by the bus stop.

The third ring. Susan began to relax into her pillow but then the phone rang for a fourth time.

This wasn't the norm. Maxine was supposed to put the phone down after the third ring – that way she didn't have to keep any change for the call and Susan didn't have to get out of bed to answer it. But the phone kept ringing.

Annoyed, Susan swung her legs from the warm bed onto the floor, traipsed across her room squinting as she switched on the main landing light. She thudded down the stairs, shouting at the phone, 'Okay, okay I'm coming.'

A draught blew in from the hallway and Susan could hear rain lashing down outside. She shivered as she picked up the receiver.

The operator asked if she would accept a reverse charge call and letting out an exasperated sigh, Susan said yes. Maxine's voice was far louder and chirpier than it should have been at that time of night. It meant she'd probably gone on somewhere after the pub and had most likely been drinking too much. Her little sister had graduated sixth form that summer and having shocked everyone with the A-level grades she'd somehow managed to obtain, was off to university any day; right now though Maxine was enjoying her freedom and partying hard at every opportunity.

'You got me out of bed,' said Susan. 'Where are you and what happened to three rings?'

'Sorry,' sang Maxie sounding the complete opposite of the word. 'But I lost my key so I need you to leave the door on the latch.'

'What? And just let any axe murderer waltz in?'

'It's chucking it down.' Maxie laughed. 'Axe murderers are very much fair weather people – they don't want to risk the rust.'

'How long will you be?' asked Susan.

'The bus is due soon – so twenty minutes tops – it'll be fine, honestly.'

‘Okay,’ sighed Susan. ‘But you owe me big time for this and remember to lock it properly when you get in.’

‘Scout’s honour.’

With that Susan put the phone down and walked over to the back door. The raindrops pelted against its glass pane as Susan opened it and she wondered once again why Maxine would want to be out in this. She adjusted the latch so it wouldn’t lock and closed it, placing a pair of boots just behind so they’d scrape on the floor when the door opened and she’d hear when Maxine came in. No matter what her sister had promised, Susan knew the last thing on Maxine’s mind would be locking the door properly when she eventually got home.

As she ran back up the stairs, Susan couldn’t help but smile at the thought of the axe murderer looking out at the rain and deciding not to risk the rust. Maxine had a knack of making her laugh and it was almost impossible to stay angry with her. Almost. Susan got back into bed and snuggled down, pulling the still warm blankets around her and burying her head in the pillow. She now had to stay awake until Maxine was safely back. Their rather strict parents were taking a very rare weekend break and the two girls were making the most of it. Susan had been put in charge but although she was a year older than her sister it didn’t mean she held any sway and as Susan had held a party on the Friday, Maxine had decided that Saturday was for her. She had gone straight out to the local pub with her friends; it had a great jukebox and was more like a club so they’d be dancing all night. Susan had lent Maxine her black ankle boots and lacy tights, threatening certain death if either weren’t returned in perfect condition. She had made Maxine promise to get the last bus home and if she was good to her word, their mother would know nothing about the party or the night out.

Despite her best efforts, Susan felt her eyes grow heavy and her body relax into the cosy embrace of the bed. She pulled her hands into a fist, digging her nails into the palms of her hands to try and stay awake but soon enough, the grip loosened and Susan knew she wouldn’t be awake for much longer. Telling herself she was being too big-sisterly and Maxine was old enough to make sure the door was shut, Susan let every muscle in her body relax and drifted off.

A loud bang dragged her back into the land of the living. Although her ears had woken up, her eyes hadn’t yet opened and sticky remnants of sleep glued her eyelids together. There was another noise, not as loud as the first and this time it seemed to be directly below her – in the living room. What was Maxine doing in there? Had she drank so much she was stumbling around the living room? Susan had only just cleared the place up after the party and now Maxine was making another mess when she should have come straight up to bed. Susan untangled her arms from the blankets and rubbed her eyes. She really didn't want to have to get up again so first of all she tilted her head to try and hear what was going on. Another sound – what on earth was it? Furniture being dragged? Then the sound of glass tinkling.

'Oh please tell me you're not raiding the drinks cabinet,' muttered Susan imagining a drunken Maxine sneaking some of their parents' spirits as she'd actually done with her best friend before last night's party.

Whatever her sister was doing, Susan resigned herself to the fact that she had to get up and march Maxine back to bed. As she pulled back her covers to the now bitingly cold room, she blew out clouds of breath in front of her. Their parents had a rule about central heating – it went on from November to March and then you simply had to wear more layers. It didn't matter that this summer had been a wash-out and September had certainly not delivered the mellow fruitfulness usually associated with the month but instead more days of non-stop cold rain.

Susan got up and pulled her dressing gown tightly around her. She didn't want to wake her eyes any more than she had to so didn't put on the light but instead held the banister and walked slowly down the staircase. Her dressing gown cord dragged wearily on each step and as she got halfway down she stopped. There was another sound from the living room.

'Maxine?' she called out. 'What on earth are you doing?'

The sound stopped and a floorboard creaked as steps walked towards the living room door.

'If you're at the Drambuie, Dad will be able to tell,' continued Susan as she stomped down the remaining stairs.

The living room door edged open and Susan could see a small torchlight pointed downwards at the carpet. She felt the hairs on her arms stand on edge and knew this wasn't her sister.

'Who's there?' she called out, trying to sound braver than she actually felt. 'You'd better get out now. I'm calling the police.'

Susan pictured the phone in her parents' room and the safety of a door between her and whoever was in the house. She turned to run upstairs.

When the teenage Maxine Reddick eventually got home, the memory of that last Oasis track still playing in her mind, she found the back door wide open and her sister in the cold silent hallway – dead.

Chapter Two

Present Day

'When we started, we were one of the only podcasts around but nowadays everyone and his dog has one.'

Craig Johnston passed his co-host a sheet of paper showing the steadily declining audience figures for their own show, *Criminal Thoughts*. Professor Maxie Reddick glanced at them seeing that last night's edition had achieved an all-time low and shrugged.

'So what do we have to do to get people listening again?' she asked, handing the sheet back.

Craig was a crime journalist and Maxie a professor of Criminology at the local university. They'd started the podcast with the intention of looking beyond the headlines – tackling issues in depth whether through exploring criminal psychology or the latest policing statistics. They were often controversial in their conversations and had no problems getting decent guests to appear but the numbers didn't lie and it was obviously not enough.

'It's all about solving true crimes or holding one of those reality courtrooms at the moment,' Craig said. 'There's less interest in *why* people do what they do – we seem to have stopped caring about that.'

'So they want to hear less from experts and get more opportunity to give an opinion.'

'Isn't that the way of the world right now?' asked Craig. 'We're all experts in everything, including medicine.'

Maxie smiled ruefully. 'So it seems – although you really wouldn't want me doing open heart surgery on you.'

'Oh I don't know – there's probably a YouTube video you can follow.'

Maxie's phone rang – it was DS Andrew Dawson. She answered and asked Andrew to hold for a moment while she said goodbye to Craig. 'I'll think about those figures and what we can do to reverse them,' Maxie told him as she pressed down on the arms of the chair and pushed herself up, hobbling out of the studio.

On her last case, Maxie had taken a hard fall and badly sprained her ankle. That was only six weeks ago so it was hardly surprising that it still ached but there was nothing she could do about it. Correction – she could do something about it. She could take the rest and do the exercises that the physio had recommended but there always seemed to be something more interesting on her plate. She loved the teaching and research that her day job entailed, really enjoyed the debates for the podcast and became engrossed in any task assigned to her by the local police force. They were all far more interesting than some stretches. Even seeing DS Dawson's name light up her phone gave her cause for excitement – wondering what case they needed her for next.

Maxie and the local DCI, Heather McAlister had set up the Applied Criminology Unit – ACU – to enable collaboration between the force and the university. As Professor of Criminology, Maxie's role was to undertake research which would help the police force do their job as effectively as possible. Nowadays, McAlister tended to take a back seat and Maxie's normal day-to-day liaison was DS Andrew Dawson.

'Hi there,' Maxie said into her phone as she limped down the corridor. 'Sorry about that, I've spent my Sunday at the studio dissecting our numbers but I'm just leaving. What can I do for you?'

She listened and shook her head sadly as Andrew spoke. 'Oh that's awful,' she said. 'All murder is horrific but when anyone attacks someone vulnerable … Look, I've got some prep for next week's lectures but I can do that tonight. Are you at the station? I can get a cab and be there in half an hour.'

The door at the end of the corridor opened and Andrew burst through with his phone still attached to his ear. 'No need, I guessed where you'd be,' he said, still speaking into the phone even though he was only a few feet away.

Maxie laughed at him and also speaking into the phone told him she was hanging up. She did her best to keep up with the detective as he turned back towards the exit explaining the case as they walked.

'There isn't much information yet,' said Andrew. 'We got a call from the Belvedere Care Home saying they found a man lying at the edge of their lawn. They checked and found that he wasn't breathing so called it in. The team are there now securing the scene.'

'Someone they didn't know? So not one of the residents?' Maxie prompted.

'No, thank goodness,' Andrew said. 'I know I shouldn't feel this way but it was a relief when I found out it wasn't one of the elderly.'

'I know what you mean,' said Maxie. 'So why do you need me to be involved in this case?' Maxie was already working on several other research studies through the ACU and wouldn't normally take on any more.

'Not sure yet but I thought it might fit into that topic you mentioned a while ago – perception versus reality,' he said. 'You know any crime against the elderly gets so much coverage people think it happens all the time.'

'Too true,' Maxie said as she headed towards Andrew's car.

'You don't have the Jeep with you?' he asked?

'It's just back from being repaired after I hit that bollard. But the clutch is really too heavy for my ankle while it's in this state. I know I should swap it for a little automatic but I never seem to have the time. Let's go.'

Once inside his car, Andrew and Maxie discussed cars that she should take a look at. The Jeep had been her fantasy car since she was a teenager but it felt cumbersome right now and the reason she'd hit that bollard was that her aching ankle had slipped when she should have been braking. While Maxie was sure that her ankle would recover completely sooner or later, a smaller electric automatic would probably be better for her and the environment.

'There are some very trendy ones,' Andrew was saying. 'Your students would be salivating if you turned up in a BMW i8 or a Tesla Model X with those gull-wing doors. In fact, never mind your students, I'd be salivating.'

'Sounds very messy – all that drool.' Maxie grimaced. 'But I would appreciate some help if you fancy touring the showrooms one day?'

'Just say when.'

Andrew indicated right and drove into the driveway of what would have been a large manor house at some point in its life. After they'd parked up, they took a walk around the house to find the scene of the crime. The grounds were very tidy and paved with wide walkways for maximum accessibility. Bright coloured crocuses were peering through well-tended beds and their tiny hints at cheerfulness looked completely at odds with the frenzy of the police cordon and suited-up forensic team at the edge of the garden.

'It doesn't look like a place where violence should happen does it?' asked Maxie, turning her collar up against the February chill as they turned to go back to the main door at the front of the house.

'I could say that about any domestic I've ever attended. And then once it's happened even the most tranquil spot will from then on always be "the place where they found that lad".'

They entered the building and a receptionist directed them along the corridor where the Care Home Manager was waiting for them in her office. At one level, Maxie had been expecting someone meek and mild mannered but the woman Andrew and Maxie shook hands with was nothing like that; very efficient looking, about fifty, slender and with a neat easy to maintain short cropped hairstyle. She wore trousers and a polo neck jumper with a name badge – Jacqueline Morton. When she introduced herself, Jacqueline answered a question about the history of the home and said that she'd had a career in hotel management before taking up this position.

'I would have thought you'd need a clinical background for a post like this,' said Andrew.

'Not at all,' Jacqueline said, clearly annoyed by any suggestion that she might not be qualified for the job. 'We have fee-paying guests who need to be fed, rooms and grounds that need to be serviced, utilities that need maintaining and a budget that needs to run a positive cash-flow at all times. Our medical team look after health issues but if this place were to have a boiler breakdown or profit loss, they wouldn't be much use.'

'You're responsible for everything that people take for granted,' said Maxie hoping to get the conversation to a more amiable tone. 'And the house really does look fabulous.'

Jacqueline nodded a truce and invited them both to sit on the sofa in the corner of her office. It was a large room which would probably have originally been a parlour. A set of French windows looked out onto the rear of the garden where officers were combing through the neat hedgerows. She poured them each a coffee from a pot that was ready and waiting for them on a tray, then placed her hands on her lap, waiting for their questions.

Andrew took a quick sip of his coffee and began, 'What can you tell us about the victim? Did you know him?'

'I didn't,' replied Jacqueline. 'As I said during my call and to your constable, the postman found him when he arrived this morning. He delivers early and the residents who have rooms which overlook that section of the grounds would most likely not have opened their curtains by then. Even if they had, most of them have such poor eyesight it would probably have looked like a pile of clothes blown in by the wind. We're close to one of those charity recycling bins and are always clearing up the rubbish that people don't bother to dispose of properly.'

'And what happened next?' Andrew prompted.

'I asked my chief nurse to take a look and she confirmed that he wasn't breathing. The postman had to get on with his round so we covered him with a tarpaulin, I took his details, called 999 and then, as there was nothing else I could do, got on with serving breakfast.'

Maxie nodded her understanding and admiration. She felt a wave of respect for this woman who let everyone do their own job and seemed to know how to focus on what she could influence. She could probably learn a lot from Jacqueline.

'So neither the postman nor the nurse recognised him?' asked Maxie.

'I didn't say that,' Jacqueline clarified. 'You asked whether I knew him and I didn't. However, my nurse thinks she *may* know him – *may* because obviously he was in a bit of a mess. If our conversation is now over, I will ask her to come in.'

Without waiting for an answer, Jacqueline stood up and walked over to the door, opened it and called, 'Would someone fetch Crystal please?'

She turned back towards Maxie and Andrew. 'She'll be with you very shortly, now if you'll excuse me, I have some crisis management to attend to.'

And with that Jacqueline left the room.

Andrew picked up a biscuit from the plate that hadn't been offered to them and topped up their coffees. 'That's us put in our place,' he said before taking a big bite.

'No – she's right,' Maxie said. 'Her job is to keep this place running smoothly and there'll be so many calls to field now – media, relatives, her boss. And the residents will be worried too – what if our victim had intentions to harm them but was stopped before he could?'

'That's what I was thinking,' Andrew said. 'We need to know why he was here. Hopefully this nurse will be able to shed some light on that.'

As they waited, Maxie found herself deep in thought – wondering whether Andrew was right and whether this case might also be of interest to the podcast audience. Why crimes against the elderly – which were thankfully very rare – attracted a higher level of attention than those against middle-aged people. Why do those twenty years or so make you newsworthy?

Her thoughts were interrupted as the door opened and a young woman in a nurse uniform walked in. She introduced herself as Crystal and took a seat opposite Andrew. Crystal was a complete contrast to her boss Jacqueline – small, cuddly with dark curly hair, huge colourful earrings and a big smile. Whereas Jacqueline's demeanour said "efficient", Crystal's said "caring".

'Can you tell us what happened?' asked Andrew.

'I was in the dining room preparing for breakfast and Mrs Morton called for me, said the postman had found someone in the garden – she wanted me to check on him. My heart was beating like crazy because I thought it might have been one of our residents who'd got out somehow and fallen,' said Crystal beating her hand against her chest as she spoke. 'When I got a bit closer I saw that his clothes were too young for our guests and there was a lot of blood. I reached for his hand and tried to find a pulse but I couldn't. And he was cold. I didn't stay with him long in case I messed up the scene but we did call an ambulance as well as the police just in case I was wrong … They couldn't find a pulse either. It's so sad.'

Crystal dropped her head and clasped her hands in her lap looking genuinely devastated by the morning's events.

'Mrs Morton said that you may have recognised him – was he a friend or visiting someone here?' asked Maxie.

'I don't know,' she said. 'I think I recognise him but I could be wrong – his face was … there was lots of blood – but I think he goes to The Rose and Crown. I think I've seen him there.'

Chapter Three

Crystal took Andrew and Maxie to the dining room and all three looked out at the garden where the crime scene team were still at work.

'Was anyone else in here at the time?' asked Andrew.

'Albert Younghusband,' replied Crystal. 'He's a resident but gets up at the crack of dawn and likes to help us. I generally let him put the cutlery out.'

'And do you think he may have seen anything? Would he be able to answer questions accurately?' asked Andrew.

'I'm not sure,' said Crystal. 'He does have mild cognitive impairment and sometimes he's referring to things that happened years ago. Besides, you'd have to get permission – Mrs Morton doesn't like to spring any surprises on our guests or worry them unnecessarily.'

Andrew nodded his understanding but said that he would still like to speak to Albert and the other residents with that permission. They took another look around the room then thanked Crystal and walked out to the crime scene.

'What can you tell us?' Andrew asked the lead officer.

'Male, probably late forties to early fifties, beaten across the back of the head which caused him to fall on that low level wall,' the officer replied. 'It was that impact that very likely killed him but we'll confirm that for you. We've contacted the postman and he confirmed Mrs Morton's account. Says he was doing his round at the usual time – 6.30 or so and came across the body. He saw no-one else around, didn't recognise him and didn't touch the body.'

'Any ID on the body?'

'No, but there was a phone. We'll see what we can get off that.'

Andrew left the officer to get on with his work and made a note of the victim's clothing, build and hair colour. It would be a loose description to take to The Rose and Crown but better than nothing.

'I'm going to see if anyone knows him at the pub,' he said to Maxie. 'Do you want to come?'

Maxie told him that she couldn't – she really had to do that prep work. Andrew offered to give her a lift but Maxie shook her head. 'I have Furness Cabs on speed dial while the car is out of action,' she told him. 'I'd hate them to think they'd been replaced.'

Andrew drove off while Maxie stood in the care home reception waiting for her cab. Although she had been very relieved the victim wasn't a resident, as Andrew had said, that reaction also bothered her; why should we be more concerned about certain demographics? She knew from both personal experience and academic research that empathy levels impacted public response – the more empathy created, the greater the public appetite to help. Her taxi appeared and once belted in the back, she decided to get the driver's opinion.

'If I were to tell you that an old lady had been mugged in there, what would you say?' she asked.

'Oh no, she hasn't has she?' The driver looked at her in the rear-view mirror. 'I'd say whoever did it deserved a public whipping and I'd be the first to step up to it.'

'And what if I said it was one of the gardeners who'd been mugged?' continued Maxie. 'Would you whip the culprit then?'

'That's different innit,' he said. 'An old lady can't protect herself. It's like kids – I'd whip anyone who hurt a little kid.'

Maxie knew this was a classic example of perceptions of vulnerability, at work. The public tended to believe certain demographics – women, the old and very young – were more vulnerable and therefore crimes against them were somehow worse. Of course the media contributed with their coverage; it was rare to see a middle-aged male victim on the front pages – unless of course he was a teacher or serviceman – someone "worthy" of public sympathy. This would be a great subject to kick off one of tomorrow's lectures and might even be a subject to get the podcast ratings up. Maxie sighed and silently berated herself for thinking of ratings before the poor victim.

The following day, Maxie was quietly contemplative on the cab drive to the university. Although already a month old, the term still held a sense of excitement and anticipation. Students who'd only started in the autumn had now found their bearings and were rushing around campus knowing they belonged while those facing their final year knew that something they loved would be ending way too soon. Maxie inhaled this buzz and with a sense of purpose she stood tall, ignoring the constant twinge of pain in her ankle and headed straight for the lecture theatre where a group of students sat, staring at their phones and waiting for her to arrive.

‘The role of empathy in crime narratives,’ said Maxie assertively, resulting in a frenzy of students putting away their devices and looking up at her. ‘Who would like to tell me about its importance or otherwise?’

The students shuffled to attention and one girl raised a hand. Maxie nodded at her to speak.

‘Where empathy is higher,’ said the student, ‘positive behaviours are enhanced. So with regard to crime, the public are more likely to come forward with information or report suspicious behaviour before an offence is even committed.’

‘And the more you connect with a person,’ added another student, ‘the more you relate to them – maybe because you know someone like that – then the more involved you get emotionally.’

‘Can anyone give me examples?’ asked Maxie.

‘That case last year, with the student who was attacked,’ called out one person. ‘I totally related to that because I walk home on my own all the time.’

‘And the twelve-year-old boy who was stabbed,’ said another student. ‘That’s the same age as my little brother.’

Maxie listened as a wave of stories emerged. The student views confirmed every piece of academic research – increase the empathy and you increase the call to action.

‘I’m hearing that you relate to the victims,’ said Maxie. ‘And indeed crowdfunding campaigns to pay for funerals or requests for volunteers to search areas always get more response when there is empathy but what about intervention? What would make you intervene to stop a crime?’

An awkward murmur started as students began talking amongst themselves; Maxie let it flow and then cleared her throat loudly to get their attention back. ‘Anyone?’ she asked.

‘You’d have to be sure that you wouldn’t make matters worse,’ offered one student. ‘Or get hurt yourself.’

‘You weigh up the risk don’t you? If you were in a group it would be easier,’ said another. ‘And you can intervene by calling the police or pulling the emergency cord on the train – you don’t have to try and break up a fight. I don’t think I’d tackle a gang with knives, personally.’

This got a murmur of agreement.

‘What if the person being threatened on the train was elderly?’ asked Maxie. ‘Like one of your grandparents?’

Maxie noticed the energy in the room became charged.

'I wouldn't stand by and watch anyone's grandma being attacked,' said one.

'Me neither,' said another. 'There'd be something you could do – anything. If the attacker was after money, I'd give them mine and tell them to do one.'

Again the students seemed to endorse this course of action. As they settled back down and quiet filled the room, a voice piped up, 'Has all this got something to do with the attack at the old people's home yesterday, Professor?'

Maxie looked up at the young man who'd spoken. He held his phone up and removed an earbud.

'There was a feature on *Secret Sleuth*,' said the student. 'There's a picture of the police cordon and you walking in the grounds with that detective.'

Any attempt at continuing the lesson would have been futile as everyone in the lecture room, including Maxie, picked up their phones and accessed the report.

'Okay, let's look at this together,' said Maxie plugging her tablet into an HDMI cable and projecting the video onto the main lecture room screen.

The video footage had been taken from the outside perimeters of the care home but clearly showed the crime scene examiners at work, as well as Maxie and Andrew arriving. The voice-over promised more details later; they obviously hadn't been able to establish who had been hurt or how. Maxie sighed with relief as the short report ended.

'Yes,' she said turning back to the students. 'That's where I was yesterday and that's what got me thinking about empathy – why we feel more engaged or even responsible if the victim is somehow vulnerable.'

'Will you be looking at this on your own podcast?' asked one of the students. Maxie replied that she probably would.

'Looks like *Secret Sleuth* has beaten you to it,' said the young man who'd first told the room about it. 'You'll have to find a decent angle.'

He was smirking and Maxie felt her hackles rise. She wanted to blurt out that the podcast didn't even know anything about the victim but she took a deep breath and calmed herself. 'I certainly will,' she said smiling and faking a little good humour. 'Is this *Secret Sleuth* popular? Anyone know who's behind it?'

The conversation that ensued told her that it was quite new, a very popular show and that even if her students did know who produced it, they wouldn't tell her.

'It would hardly be a secret then would it?' said one making the obvious point.

Maxie spent the rest of the lecture outlining the academic research behind the discussion they'd had. She'd always found that her students could relate better after they'd talked about their own experiences. She noted that they nodded enthusiastically as she went through a five-step model of bystander intervention.

'You notice the situation, label it as a problem, decide that you're going to take action, decide on that action and then execute it,' she said. 'Your decision to take action is heavily influenced by empathy and as you've said the action you decide on is often based upon the perceived personal risk.'

After setting their assignment, Maxie watched the students file out and as the final one was out of view, she picked up her phone to see if *Secret Sleuth* had posted any further updates. Maxie was relieved to see they hadn't but was annoyed at herself for being bothered about it. Her job was to assist the police and to teach Criminology – the podcast was a side interest and nothing more.

'That's rubbish and you know it is,' Maxie said to herself as she made for her office. 'You don't want to lose listeners to some Johnny-come-lately.'

Once behind her desk, Maxie popped in her earbuds and listened to another two or three episodes of *Secret Sleuth.* She decided they were quite superficial in their analysis but they leant heavily on the emotional. They seemed to feature lots of interviews with people who had opinions but very little expertise – the exact model Craig had mentioned. Nevertheless, it reassured Maxie that the producers of this show had no access to the police and right now, she had to focus on helping to establish what had happened. She was about to dial DS Dawson's number when her phone rang – the man himself was calling.

'You must be psychic,' she said. 'I was just about to call you. By the way, have you heard of a podcast called *Secret Sleuth*? They were filming at the care home while we were there.'

'Can't seem to stop people filming at crime scenes no matter how hard we try.' Andrew sighed. 'Sometimes it comes in useful – rarely but you never know.

'Anyway,' he continued, 'I was just calling to see if you'd be coming back to the scene this afternoon? We've found a weapon that looks as if it could have been the one used on our victim.'

'What is it?' asked Maxie.

'A cricket bat,' he replied. 'Mrs Morton has said that it could very well be one of theirs; they do organise cricket games in the summer and she's asked their entertainment officer to come in to the station and take a look at it. But it's a fairly standard one so could have been brought in by the attacker.'

'Entertainment officer? There's a cast of thousands at that home isn't there?' said Maxie. 'I bet it's not cheap to stay there. I tell you, when my day comes, I want a home with an entertainment officer and a cocktail waiter.'

'Well if you ever felt like retiring, I could actually see you as a cocktail waiter in a care home – getting everyone singing along with the assistance of a few piña coladas.'

Maxie laughed and pictured the scene herself. 'You know what? I could imagine myself doing that too. And when my generation get to the care home stage, we're not going to be happy with a cup of tea in the afternoon. We've spent our lives having wine o'clock – we won't want to stop.'

'I'll drink to that,' said Andrew. 'Anyway – are you coming back over?'

Maxie looked at her commitments and knew she couldn't in all conscience leave the university until late afternoon so told the detective that she could get there around six.

'And did you find out who the victim was?' she asked.

'Tell you all when you get here,' Andrew said.

Chapter Four

‘So where was it found?’

The evening had turned icy and Maxie was standing in the freezing cold of the care home garden, under the glare of the crime scene lights, looking at a photograph of a fairly ordinary cricket bat that had been bagged up and sent to the labs for processing.

‘Over there,’ replied Andrew. ‘By the bins that Mrs Morton mentioned.’

‘So whoever did this dumped it on their way out.’ Maxie hugged herself tightly, shivering as she spoke. ‘Possibly panicking and running from the scene?’

‘Could be. They may not have intended to injure him so badly and when he hit the rock on his way down, fled as quickly as possible. Or they just didn’t want to be seen walking down a street with a cricket bat so this bin was pretty convenient.’

‘What’s down that alleyway?’ asked Maxie pointing to the narrow path that led from the bins.

Andrew suggested they walk it and picked up a torch from one of his guys. Together they passed the area where the bins had been upended by the investigation team, and onto a path, once-tarmacked but now fairly neglected. A frost was beginning to form on the weeds that grew through splits in the surface and litter clung to branches of trees.

‘Not exactly lovers’ lane is it?’ said Maxie as she pushed aside a discarded burger carton with her foot then grimaced as an open sachet of ketchup spilled out.

The alley led to a quiet street with a bus stop a few yards down. It wasn’t well lit but enough for the detective to be able to switch off the torch. Instinctively both Maxie and Andrew looked up to see if there were any visible CCTV cameras. There weren’t.

‘I wonder if he knew there weren’t any cameras down here?’ asked Andrew.

‘Maybe he jumped on a bus to get away – they might have a record,’ suggested Maxie but they both looked at each other and shrugged, knowing it was unlikely.

They strolled a little further along to a crossroads.

‘The Rose and Crown is down that direction,’ said Andrew. ‘It’s not really walking distance so let’s go back and get the car.’

'You mean it's not walking distance at the pace I go these days,' Maxie said as they turned back.

'How are the physio exercises going?' Andrew asked.

'The same way that all exercise tends to go with me.'

'You do know that it won't get any better if you don't do them.'

'So they keep telling me.' Maxie was aiming for a jokey tone to end this conversation. 'But then *they* also say that time heals everything don't they? So I thought I'd opt for the time rather than exercise option.'

'Hmm – I'm not convinced. Look at it this way,' persisted Andrew, 'if you don't do the physio, you might end up with a limp for the rest of your life and it would be like a permanent reminder of that waste of space, Orlando.'

Maxie stumbled on a piece of split tarmac and Andrew shot out a hand to steady her. She cursed the timing as it confirmed everything the DS had said. She certainly didn't want to be reminded of the man who'd caused this injury but she equally didn't want to talk about it right now.

'So tell me what you found out about the victim?' she said.

'Changing the subject?'

'As quickly as possible,' she confirmed.

Andrew shook his head in mock despair as they turned back into the alleyway towards the care home. 'They think he sounds like one of the regulars but the barman on duty when I called in couldn't give me a name – that's why we need to head back,' he said. 'He had no ID on him so we haven't been able to find or notify any next of kin yet. I don't want to dig too deeply on this before letting his family know. I can't have that podcast finding out before we do.'

'That's unusual isn't it? Coming out without ID? No wallet? So you're thinking it was stolen?'

'We found no wallet but he did have a phone. If he pays for everything by phone, he wouldn't necessarily need one. Until we unlock the phone we won't know. I suppose a theft gone wrong is a possibility but there've been no reports of any other local muggings so if he was a random victim then it's atypical of the area.'

'Unless he turns out to be the first of many.'

'I hope not,' Andrew said. His phone rang and during the short call he asked that an interview be arranged as soon as possible.

'News?' asked Maxie at the end of his call.

'The entertainment officer has confirmed that the cricket bat looks like one of theirs but they buy them at the big sports shop in town – they're nothing special. I'm getting him in tomorrow when hopefully we know who our victim is.'

They'd reached the care home car park and leapt into Andrew's car. As they drove, Maxie was lost in her own thoughts; not knowing the identity of the victim made her uncomfortable. She hated the idea of someone lying on a slab when their family didn't know. Was someone planning what to make him for dinner? Were there children waiting for him to help them with their homework? She gave a little prayer that *Secret Sleuth* hadn't discovered his name as she really couldn't imagine a worse way of finding out that a loved one had died.

The pub was part of a chain but styled to look like a country inn. It had a painted white exterior with sage green window frames and flower baskets that couldn't possibly be real at this time of the year and on closer inspection, Maxie saw that they did indeed house high quality artificial blooms. Maxie inspected a bright purple anemone and briefly wondered what it would cost to deck her own balcony out in these – she was woefully useless when it came to gardening. They parked and walked into the pub where the light was almost as dark as it had been outside due to the low ceiling and low wattage wall sconces. Maxie imagined these were probably also part of the standard décor of a new building pretending to be old.

A barman looked up as they entered and disappeared behind a door, returning shortly afterwards accompanied by another man who walked towards them with his hand outstretched. 'Afternoon, I'm Ken – the landlord here,' he said pleasantly. 'I understand you were asking about someone who might be one of our regulars.'

'That's right,' replied Andrew. He told Ken that a man had been found injured at the care home and gave him a description. 'It was one of the nurses who told us he drank here.'

'Was he wearing a kind of smock with a hood – like an anorak that walkers might wear? Red?' asked Ken and when Andrew nodded he continued, 'It does sound like one of our quizzers: George – he comes in with a team every week. Hang on for a second, I've got one of their numbers in my phone.'

He called out to the barman who grabbed a mobile phone from under the bar and brought it over. Ken flicked through it and then held out a number to Andrew. 'This guy is more or less the captain of their team and he'll have George's details.'

Andrew took down the information and turned away to make the call.

'You said he's a quizzer,' said Maxie. 'I presume that means he's a real enthusiast? Does he do well?'

'Oh yeah,' Ken said. 'Him and his team go to a few of the local pub quizzes and it's always them or this other team that win. They're really competitive. I know that the captain sets them all homework if you like. One has to learn all the US states, the other has to know all the kings and queens – that kind of thing.'

'Do they win very much money?' asked Maxie.

'You could probably get around £30 a night,' Ken said. 'So it pays for your night out but they don't drink much in case they lose their focus.'

'Sounds a bit serious.' Maxie laughed.

'Oh you don't want to mess with a quizzer,' Ken said with a smile. 'Or it's …' He drew his finger across his throat and laughed.

When Maxie didn't join in, Ken's smile dropped and he appeared to be trying to read her expression. 'You said he'd been hurt,' said Ken. 'It's more than that isn't it? It's serious.'

Maxie nodded but told him that she had no more details and their first priority was to confirm it was George and then find his family.

Ken rubbed his face in shock just as Andrew finished his call.

'He's going to come down to the station tomorrow after work,' he said to Maxie and then turned to Ken. 'Thanks for all your help. I hope it goes without saying that you should talk to no-one about this until you hear from us.'

'Of course,' replied Ken still looking very shaken. 'I hope I'm wrong and it's not George.'

'We'll let you know.'

'Oh,' said Maxie as Andrew turned to leave. 'Did you have a quiz on Saturday night?'

'No, they're generally held on quiet nights – why?' asked Ken.

'I was just wondering if George would be likely to have any winnings on him,' she said.

'Our quiz is on a Thursday but I think The Red Lion might have had a one-off – to compensate for the money we lose during Dry January and all that. The team might have gone there.'

They thanked the landlord and left. Once outside, Andrew told Maxie that during the call he'd had with the quiz team captain, he'd given a very good description of the clothes George usually wore, down to white Nike trainers with a splodge of dark green paint near the toe. 'The type you use to paint the fence,' he'd said.

'So the odds are that it's him.' Maxie sighed.

'Yep. And if it is, he's single but apparently has a long-term partner. The quiz captain has given us George's address so I'll send a team round in the morning to see if we can find out her details. She sounds like the nearest we have to a next of kin.'

Maxie bundled herself into the passenger seat for the drive home. Although she loved being part of any investigation and helping to get justice for people, she hated this part. When the victim was lying friendless and alone, when a house that wasn't expecting visitors was about to be ransacked, when somewhere – a loved one was about to get the worst news possible.

Chapter Five

The following day, Maxie had no lectures after lunch so as soon as she could, she made a mad dash to the station just as the interview with the quiz captain was starting. He leapt up and reached out to shake Maxie's hand very vigorously as they were introduced. She thought he looked extremely excited to be involved and that was confirmed with his first words as they sat down in the interview room.

'I'll do anything I can to help,' he said. 'George's been on the team for nigh on four months now so I regard him as a friend. So do the rest of the lads and I can assure you, we'll be here when you need us.'

DS Dawson thanked him and asked him to confirm his name, address and relationship with George.

'Peter Rogerson, 25 Welbeck Avenue,' he replied. 'The team and I go to two or three of the quizzes around here – the wife says it keeps us all out of trouble. Anyway – last autumn, we were sitting down to start in The Rose and Crown and I noticed this guy sitting on his own following along. When the winners were announced, we'd come first but this bloke, all by himself, came in third. So when I got up to collect our winnings I congratulated him and invited him to come and sit with us for a pint. Turned out he'd just moved here from London and hadn't really got to know anyone yet.'

'Do you know why he'd moved up?' asked Maxie. 'What he did for a living?'

'He had his own business,' Peter said. 'Sales or something; anyway, we said he was welcome to join our team and he did. We've met up pretty much every week since and he's a real asset – a whizz at the photo rounds and science questions.'

'Thanks Peter, and can you tell us anything about his personal life?' asked Andrew. 'You gave us his address – and you said he has a partner?'

'Yeah, I sometimes dropped him off at his place after the quiz. I've never met her but he said she was a nurse.'

'A nurse?' said Andrew with a slightly anxious tone. 'Do you know which hospital she works at? And her name?'

Maxie guessed that Andrew was worried that the man's next of kin would find out about his death at work and she knew he would desperately want to avoid that. Peter was shaking his head. 'I'm sorry – I can't remember if he mentioned her name. To be honest, we talk quizzes, footy, politics sometimes but not family really. I don't think I've even seen a photo of her but then I don't go around showing people photos of my wife – you know what I mean?'

Andrew nodded and checked his watch. 'Thank you for coming in, Peter,' he said standing up. 'I'm going to let you get back to your family while I see if the team at his house have found out the name of his partner yet. I wouldn't want her finding out what's happened on the grapevine.'

'No, of course,' Peter said. 'Well you know where I am, happy to come in when you need me – unless you want me to help search his house?'

Andrew quickly turned down the offer of help and called an officer to show him out of the station.

Maxie couldn't help but smile when Peter was out of sight. 'I can't understand why you turned down that offer of help. Surely Peter and the team would be invaluable?'

'Yeah, I'm sure. Anyway, it wouldn't take a team,' Andrew said rolling his eyes at her. 'I went there this morning but the place isn't exactly homely. I left forensics to see if they could find any evidence he still lived there.'

They walked down the corridor towards the tech team. 'Any news?' asked Andrew.

'There's a bank account that he pays the rent from so we're getting those details through,' one of the techies said, 'and we got into the phone but there's hardly anything on it, certainly not any kind of payment app. A couple of numbers but that's it.'

'Any of them a women's name?' continued Andrew.

The techie shook his head.

'What about a pet name?' asked Maxie. 'Bunnykins or something – we're looking for his girlfriend.'

'Nothing – just three or four male names.'

The techie handed the phone over to Andrew and he scanned the very short contacts list, showing it to Maxie – the names included Peter Rogerson and from the messages, the others looked very much like the quiz team. Andrew thanked them and headed to his own desk where an officer approached him. 'Anything from the house yet?' asked Andrew.

'Just what you saw boss,' said the officer. 'He definitely stayed there but looked as if he'd just moved in – no photos, nothing.'

'I have to see it,' said Maxie. 'This is sounding very odd.'

'You're right there. I don't like the sound of this at all.'

Andrew drove them both to the flat which was a fairly ordinary affair in a modern building; nothing flash but perfectly respectable.

'And he rents this?' asked Maxie although she already knew the answer from the notes she'd read.

'Yes,' Andrew confirmed. 'The agent said he took it on for six months with the option to renew. He's been here since October – so the full four months that Peter mentioned.'

'There's not much to show for that time is there?' Maxie observed, walking around the scarcely-furnished flat, pulling open empty drawer after drawer. 'Whatever sales this guy did, it didn't seem to involve any paperwork or computers. There's something very wrong here – he doesn't look as if he planned on staying.'

'I know,' Andrew said. 'Even that decluttering woman – Komodo? – would have more in her house than this.'

Maxie snorted with laughter. 'I think she's called Kondo but full marks for having heard of her at all.'

'My ex used to watch her videos but then seemed to ignore her advice – especially when I told her that my collection of vintage *Q* magazines did bring me joy so she couldn't throw them out.'

'And my wine bottles bring me joy – or they do when they're half-empty,' added Maxie.

They both stood quietly looking around the living room as if waiting for a secret cupboard to reveal itself. Around them the team continued to work. 'I don't think we're going to be much help here,' said Andrew. 'If we're going to find anything, it's going to be very small – a memory card or similar.'

The last time Maxie had searched for a memory card she'd found it at a graveside. The brother of the man buried had wanted to keep it close to him. She wandered into the bathroom, looking at the small number of toiletries that had already been examined by the police. Andrew was right: this search needed specialists now.

'Got something,' shouted someone from the other room.

Maxie exhaled with relief and ran towards the voice. Andrew was standing in the bedroom with a member of the search team holding up a small remote key fob.

‘What do you think it’s for?’ she asked.

‘Well I’ve got something similar for my garage,’ Andrew said. ‘It was in the seam of the curtain.’

‘Accessible but hidden,’ said Maxie. ‘Good place – I wouldn’t have thought of that.’

‘Me neither,’ said Andrew. ‘Let’s get back, try and find out where this is for then work out who on earth this guy is and what he’s playing at.’

‘Lead the way.’

Both Andrew and Maxie were fairly silent on the drive back to the station. After twenty minutes or so, Andrew turned and asked, ‘You’re very quiet, what’s whizzing around that mind of yours?’

Maxie frowned a few times as she got to grips with her thoughts. ‘He’s strange,’ she replied. ‘On the one hand the details he gives people – in sales, just moved from London – they’re so generic they’re the kind of thing you’d say if you wanted to keep yourself to yourself …’

‘And on the other hand?’

‘He joins a quiz team where people will want to get to know him. If you want to remain truly anonymous then why not just stay indoors or drink on your own?’

‘We know he’s not on the missing person register so maybe he’s just divorced – left the family home, doesn’t want the ex to find him but does want to start again somewhere,’ said Andrew.

‘And being in sales always sounds slightly dodgy,’ added Maxie. ‘Although that doesn’t mean they’re all crooked – it’s the same with consultants – far too ambiguous.’

‘It would make my arrest rates much better if I could just charge people on the basis of their jobs,’ said Andrew. ‘I’d just have to turn up at conferences and say “Oi, all you consultants – I’m afraid you’re nicked”. Although as technically that describes you, I’d have to arrest you too.’

‘Oh I’m bound to have broken some law at some point in time,’ said Maxie. ‘But it doesn’t feel right does it? And does this partner even exist? No photos, no number on his phone.’

‘Well we’ll run everything through the databases and see what we get. We have the bank account so that may reveal something more.’

‘Which is better than a poke in the eye,’ Maxie said, getting a shake of the head from Andrew in response.

The investigation team were still hard at it when they got back to the incident room in the early evening.

'Any news?' Andrew asked as soon as he walked through the door, and while shuffling his arms out of his jacket.

'The bank account is registered to a George Fairview and has a regular amount going in and a few direct debits out,' replied the officer. 'The strange thing is that he pays a salary in every month – with cash but it's only bills and rent that goes out.'

'Who on earth pays cash these days?' asked Maxie.

'Only dodgy professions in our experience, Professor.'

'If he's in sales,' said Andrew, 'I'm starting to guess what he's actually selling.'

Maxie watched as Andrew's team busied themselves with analysis and online searches. She knew there was very little she could offer them at this stage. It was getting late and she'd promised Craig that she'd think about an angle for the podcast and get it back to him as soon as she could. It was important to her as the venture wasn't just a vanity project – it had been set up to help recruit new students to the university. If potential undergraduates started to see the podcast as boring or dated then that would reflect on their status in the academic market – and whether she liked it or not, it was a market and they were trying to sell a dynamic, relevant course.

'I think I'll head home and do some work,' she told Andrew. 'Call me if you need anything at all.'

Once ensconced at her dining table, Maxie looked again at the podcast's listening numbers and then reviewed the *Secret Sleuth* footage. It hadn't been updated since the earlier photographs but had attracted a number of comments. She knew as she read them that to compete and grow her own channel, she needed younger voices.

'It takes the young to recruit the young,' she murmured to herself as she began typing out an email to her co-host.

"Why don't we let my students do a take-over of the podcast? They have an understanding of the academic issues but they talk about things in a far more personal way – they're direct and honest. They'd also want to beat Secret Sleuth *so would do whatever it took!"*

She hoped the guy who'd practically goaded her during the lecture might volunteer and have to put his money where his mouth was.

If Craig wasn't keen on that idea, Maxie thought about getting some of the students in and replicating the discussion of bystander intervention that they'd had in the lecture. They could probably get a debate going about who the public would help and who they wouldn't.

After a couple of hours, she rose from her desk and felt a rumble in her stomach. It had been an exhausting day and was way past dinner time but as she'd rushed to the station at lunchtime, it meant that she'd had nothing since breakfast. Maxie dug out a loaf of uncut bread and sliced herself a very large chunk. From the fridge she pulled out half a block of cheddar then plonked the two ingredients together on a wooden chopping board and sat back down ready to devour them. 'A poor man's Ploughman's,' she said to herself.

She had just enjoyed the first mouthful when her intercom buzzed; it was Andrew asking to come up. 'You can't stay away can you?' she mumbled, wiping crumbs from her lips as she let him in.

As Andrew crossed into her hallway, he exhaled deeply and said nothing. He walked past her towards the living room.

'Andrew?' said Maxie following him. 'What's the matter? Have you found something?'

'I think you should sit down,' came the reply. Maxie noted that Andrew sounded rather subdued and did as she was asked.

'You're making me nervous,' she said. 'Just spit it out, whatever it is.'

'Maxie …' He was taking his time and Maxie watched as his Adam's apple rose and fell in his throat. 'I'm sorry but I don't think I'm able to involve you in this case.'

'Why? What's going on?'

Maxie knew the only reason she would be excluded from the case was personal involvement and she flicked through the mental filing cabinet in her brain trying to quickly work out what that involvement could be. She hadn't recognised George Fairview and knew no-one at the care home.

'We've found a partial fingerprint on the murder weapon …' He was speaking slowly and carefully so Maxie knew he was allowing each word to sink in.

'Those prints were on our database. We don't have a name attached and they appear only once … in relation to a cold case from the 1990s.'

Maxie swallowed and the room around her started spinning. Even sitting down she felt a dizziness rock her. Her throat ran bone-dry and she stumbled to the kitchen and the sink for a glass of water. She tried to take a sip but almost choked on it. She knew what was coming next and yet it seemed to take an age for Andrew to confirm it. He stood beside her and put his hand gently on the small of her back as he spoke.

'That case is the burglary at your parents' house and the death of your sister.'

Chapter Six

A frenzy of freezing-cold nerve endings ran through Maxie's body from top to bottom. Then her legs started to give way and she was about to stumble but Andrew caught her and steadied her until she nodded that she was okay. They said nothing for a few moments as Maxie tried to process her thoughts but there was nothing. Nothing was happening in her brain; it was as if it had stopped working, as if the shock had shut it down.

Although she talked about that period of time, Maxie had stopped reliving it many years ago and had stopped feeling anything – until now. It was like being thrust back through the years and forced to acknowledge the worst days of her life. She'd always felt responsible for Susan's death – and it was made worse by the police being convinced she knew more, that she was hiding something. She should have fought harder back then – forced the police to find out what had really happened. In her eyes, they didn't really try at all.

In the near thirty years that had passed, Maxie had given up hope that she'd ever know the truth. Watching cops solve cold cases on TV annoyed her intensely as she knew that clues from the past resurfaced far less frequently than these shows would have the public believe. And yet here it was, happening to her. She'd often imagined this moment and envisaged feeling angry, hysterical and determined to put the guy behind bars forever but she felt none of these things.

Maxie's body felt so numb that she actually had to pinch her wrist to be sure she wasn't hallucinating. Her head felt heavy, as if now rammed with so much responsibility, the weight of it would cause her neck to snap. As her sister's had.

Tears started to form and Maxie felt her breathing deepen. She wasn't going to be able to stop herself, so she didn't. She sobbed and sobbed. Andrew pulled her close and held her but said nothing, simply allowing her to release all the grief.

Eventually Maxie pulled away from him, and taking a handkerchief from her pocket, wiped her eyes and blew her nose. She looked at Andrew and nodded her thanks. 'I don't know what to say,' she whispered. 'I feel that I should but I just don't.'

'It's okay,' Andrew said. 'You don't have to say anything. Would you like a cup of tea?'

Maxie snorted with laughter and as she'd only just stopped crying; it was a messy snort which had them both laughing. 'It's such a cliché isn't it?' she said when she'd recovered. 'Tea – but yes, actually I think I would like one.'

Andrew busied himself making the tea while Maxie simply stared out of the window. He passed her the mug and she held it close to her chest, letting the warmth sink in.

After a few moments she took a sip and sighed. 'It's the taste of comfort isn't it? What would we do without tea?'

'Drink more wine?' Andrew said with a gentle smile.

'I might just do that later,' said Maxie.

They both moved to the dining table and sat in silence until Maxie took a deep breath and started talking. 'It was the sixteenth of September 1995 – the year I graduated sixth form and high school,' she said. 'I had my A-level grades and knew I'd be out of Barwick soon – I couldn't wait. Susan had graduated the year before but opted to stay at home, save some money and do teacher-training at the local Higher Ed college.

'I did so many things wrong that night,' continued Maxie still staring out of the window. 'I was high on life and I thought nothing could touch me. I couldn't understand Susan wanting to live with my parents while she studied but she was a home-bird. She'd still be in Barwick if she were alive, teaching in our old school no doubt. It's horribly ironic that staying safely at home was the thing that killed her.'

Maxie looked at the remnants of her supper which were particularly unappealing to her now. She pushed the chopping board towards Andrew. 'Help yourself,' she said. 'I doubt you've eaten today either and it's fairly fresh out of the fridge.'

'I can't imagine eating anything,' he said.

'Me neither,' Maxie said. 'That's why they call it the grief diet isn't it? The only time I ever remember losing weight is after Susan – but it's not one I'd recommend.'

Andrew put his hand on top of hers but she pulled it away. 'You need to get home,' she said, sitting up straight and hoping that she looked as if she was pulling herself together. 'Thank you so much for coming round but you have a crime to solve in the morning and I need you to find out who did this more than ever.'

'Do you want me to call anyone?' he asked. 'You should have someone with you.'

Maxie shook her head; it was way too late to call anyone and she needed to process the news first. Besides who would she call? Not her parents at this hour and not her son; Karl hadn't known Susan – to him she was just a grainy photo from the nineties. She was never his aunt though she would have been a brilliant one.

'No,' she said realising Andrew was still staring at her. 'I'd just like to get some sleep now. It feels so strange – I lost her years ago and yet tonight it feels as if I've lost her again. I don't know how I'm supposed to react – happy that I might find out what happened or sad that it won't bring her back.'

She glanced up at Andrew who nodded but looked slightly uncomfortable. She smiled and gave him an appreciative rub on the arm. 'So just leave me to process this,' she said walking him towards the door. 'And I'll call you in the morning.'

Andrew left, saying that she could call him at any hour if she needed to. Alone again, Maxie walked to her bedroom then lay down on the bed; she hugged a pillow close and cried herself to sleep.

To her astonishment, Maxie slept for seven deep hours but far from feeling refreshed when she opened her eyes, she had a banging headache and felt as if she'd been in the ring with a heavyweight boxer all night. She decided immediately that she wasn't going into work – she really needed to think things through. Edging her legs to the side of the bed, she bent down and rubbed her injured ankle; it had stiffened up as she'd slept. Andrew had been right, she couldn't let it go on like this – she had to do something about it.

The news had brought unforeseen emotions to the surface. Not just grief but realisation of a truth – her sister was gone but she was not. She was lucky enough to still be alive and yet here she was, taking her health for granted. She had to take better care of herself. Her aging parents would not be around forever but she planned on being here quite some time. Her son Karl might marry one day, might have children and then her family would restart. She wanted to be a fit, fun gran not a hobbling old one. Maxie stood up and winced as she put weight on her foot.

'By the end of this term I will stand without pain,' she vowed to herself. 'And I will also know what happened to Susan.'

She shuffled into her slippers and headed to her wardrobe, digging around at the bottom for an old boot box which contained a diary of

Susan's, her broken jewellery box and some old photos. She'd collected these from her sister's room when her mother had decided that it was time to clear it out. The police had searched through all Susan's things anyway – so it all felt dirty – even then.

Wiping a layer of dust off the boot box, she took it into the kitchen, emptied the remnants of last night's meal into the bin then sat down, spreading the contents of the box over the table. Maxie hadn't looked at the diary for decades and remembered feeling extreme guilt just opening that first page. To her relief she'd found it was just an appointments schedule rather than an outpouring of teenage angst. She put it to one side and as she began picking through the snapshots, memories of her childhood came flooding back and she found herself smiling. Her own dress sense, her hairstyles and her make-up were pretty dreadful as she'd favoured a grunge look. Susan however was always on-trend when she was a teenager and had some great jewellery that Maxie was regularly in trouble for "borrowing".

They'd been chalk and cheese – the rebel and the head girl. In the year Susan died, Maxie had taken her A-levels and no-one expected her to do well as she simply hadn't studied as much as Susan had. But the younger sister was naturally clever and to her parents' surprise, aced them. Maxie mused that Susan would have been amazed at her sister's academic progress – a professor of criminology. Susan would never have predicted that for her. She had been the one at teacher training back then while Maxie had at one time seen her future in the police force – but Susan's death changed that. After the failed investigation, Maxie knew she simply couldn't join a force that was so bound by procedure.

However soothing she found it, looking at old photos wasn't helping so Maxie pushed them aside and googled the date that would be forever etched in her memory – September 16, 1995. Pages of facts about that day sprung up in front of her within seconds; if only searching had been as easy back then. If half the technology now taken for granted had been around then perhaps things would have been different – but there was no point in thinking like that. She had to work with the facts as they were. She scrolled past details of which singer had been top of the charts and which celebrity had been outed as gay back then. It had been scandalous news at the time – at least some things had changed for the better.

Maxie found the headline she'd been looking for – the case that had prevented her sister's death being looked at properly – at least in her mind. Three children had gone missing and after two days of combing every inch of the area, the police had found two bodies. The whole force and hundreds of volunteers were in a desperate search to find the final child and to find her alive. The parents had made heart-wrenching pleas for help and it seemed like the whole of Lancashire had answered their call. In the midst of this fear and panic, Susan had been found dead in her own home.

Maxie and her parents had been as anxious about the missing children as anyone but now they were more concerned about what had happened to their own daughter.

As a young woman, Maxie had always had an interest in crime and had begged the investigating officer to DNA test everyone they knew but it was expensive and if they were going to use it anywhere, it would be to catch the killer of those children. Resources were stretched to the point of breaking and so, after a superficial investigation, an open verdict was declared. The case they presented was that Susan had disturbed a burglar and been pushed down the stairs, and there were no leads to follow.

They had investigated only one other possible turn of events – a row between the sisters leading to a scuffle on the stairs and a heavy fall.

Neither could be proven and Maxie thought back to the despair and devastation she'd felt when she realised she was being questioned about pushing Susan. She knew she was to blame at one level, after all she'd been the one out partying and she'd forced Susan out of bed in the middle of the night to open the door and leave it unlocked. But that was all she did – she swore to her parents that she hadn't hurt Susan and they said that they believed her.

The narrative from that night was that a tragic incident had occurred – but every time her father uttered the words "if only" Maxie expected her own actions that night to be somewhere in the sentence.

She put her elbows on the table, dropped her head into her hands and closed her eyes. Reliving the mistakes of the past wasn't going to help but how on earth was she going to sweep it aside for long enough to think logically about all of this? She had to try and look at it as if it had never been personal, as if it was any other investigation.

She went back to the photos and separated any that contained pictures of the interior of their house or their friends at the time. Susan had kept most of the same school friends when she moved onto college and Maxie couldn't remember many of their names but someone would. She hadn't moved that far from their childhood home and guessed that a few people in these photographs were probably living in the same town today. She picked up one particular picture that showed Susan with her best friend, Rebecca. She had to start somewhere and interviewing those close to her sister seemed the logical place. If only she could remember Rebecca's surname then she might at least be able to enter it into a search engine or Facebook. Maxie lay the picture on the table in front of her and stared at it.

'Rebecca, Becky, Becks,' she said out loud, willing the girl's surname to free itself from the dusty recesses of her mind. 'What do I remember about you?'

The long, teased hair, black eyeliner and Guns N' Roses T-shirt worn by the teenager in the photo suddenly brought a smile to Maxie's lips. 'Axl Rose,' she exclaimed. 'You loved your rock music, much to Susan's dismay.' Maxie remembered the girls playing records in Susan's bedroom and comparing the lyrics of Susan's favourite – The Housemartins, with "Welcome to The Jungle". Susan had said the rock band were just flavour of the month and would be forgotten about within a few years.

'Sorry Susan, but thirty years on and Slash is still going strong although the Housemartins disbanded.'

Her doorbell rang and Maxie stood up straight, wondering who could be calling so early. Her ankle niggled but she tried to ignore it and seeing DS Dawson on the intercom with a slim folder and a tray of coffees, she buzzed him in. Maxie checked her watch and saw that it was just past 8 o'clock – Andrew was obviously on his way to work.

'I guessed you'd be up and saw the living room light on,' he said, passing her a brown paper bag that was tucked underneath the folder. 'And I didn't come empty-handed. How are you doing?'

'Getting there,' Maxie said, leading him through to the kitchen where she took plates from a cupboard. They sat at the dining table as Maxie retrieved two Danish pastries from the paper bag and Andrew put down the coffees. He picked up some of the pictures.

'Going down memory lane?' he asked, accepting a plate from Maxie.

'Something like that.' Maxie nudged her coffee against his. 'To answers.'

'Answers,' echoed Andrew, taking a sip.

'So what do you have for me?' asked Maxie. 'I can't imagine you've found out who the fingerprint belongs to overnight?'

Andrew shook his head. 'No I have read the file from back to front though. The print was recovered from inside your old house. It was fairly fresh when recovered so whoever it belongs to was there in the twenty-four hours prior to Susan's death.'

Maxie knew if he'd read the file then he would have realised that an awful lot of people were in their house during that period. The sisters had decided to have one night each where they could do as they liked – Maxie was heading to the pub on the Saturday and Susan was holding a party on Friday. It wasn't supposed to be a big affair but it had got out of hand. The police had testified that the party was one of the main reasons the investigation had come to a dead end. And they'd actually used that expression in court.

'I was just thinking,' she said, trying to stay positive. 'If the owner of that fingerprint was in my house in 1995 there are three possibilities: they were our friends – in which case they're in their late forties or fifties now; it was the intruder – who let's say was early twenties – so they're fifty to sixty; or it was a friend of my parents and if that's the case, then they're seventy at least so it could be a resident or visitor to the home.'

'Or a care worker there,' added Andrew. 'I have a team questioning everyone at the home and they will get all those prints.'

Maxie picked up her phone and looked at the photos of the cricket bat she'd taken. She increased the size of the image, seeing a close-up of the edge with its smudges of blood and of the handle where they'd found that crucial print. This one item, this run-of-the-mill object, knew something about her history that she didn't.

'Why don't you tell me who you belong to?' she said to the picture. Maxie ran her finger down the image hoping that something would leap out and speak to her, but of course it didn't.

'I won't be able to tell you any more than what I've said,' said Andrew. 'You know I can't involve you on the care home case but if you trust me, I'll do everything I can to find out who owns that fingerprint. Although you need to be ready for more disappointment – it might not have anything to do with the death and we might never know any more than we do now. Can you cope with that?'

'I could say yes just to reassure you,' she said, 'but you'd know that I was lying. Besides which – I would have excused myself from the case anyway. I'll have another investigation ongoing soon.'

Andrew frowned at her, puzzled.

‘A cold case,’ said Maxie standing up and tidying away the breakfast. ‘I’m going to get Susan’s case reopened and find out what happened to my sister.’

Chapter Seven

Maxie rang the university and said that there'd been a family bereavement so she needed to take the day off to be with her mother. There were remnants of truth in that – she did need to tell her parents what had happened and let them know that she'd be investigating Susan's death. She wasn't sure how they'd react; her sister's funeral had been an awful event. Maxie had watched as her mother tried to stay strong and thank people for coming to pay their respects while her father simply fell apart. He dropped to his knees as the crematorium curtains closed over the coffin and cried out her name. He had to be held back from rushing up to grab it. He was a big strong man and seeing him reduced to that was something Maxie would never forget.

Susan's death changed all their lives. Maxie didn't take up her place at university but instead escaped her parents' grief by heading off to Asia for a year. When she came back ready to study, she found her parents heading for divorce. Her mother remarried and rebuilt her life up in the Lake District but her father lived in a small flat, spending all his time in his allotment making the plants his closest companions.

Mid-morning, Maxie called her mother's number and very quickly heard her cheery response. 'Maxine – to what do I owe this pleasure? It's not a Sunday,' she said, referencing the fact Maxie usually made her regular update calls at the weekend.

Maxie gently told her what had happened and explained that she'd be following up, and opening a cold case investigation. At the other end of the line, her mother sighed. 'Are you sure this is wise?' she asked softly. 'Isn't it best to leave the past resting peacefully?'

'I can't, Mum,' Maxie replied, quite surprised by her mother's response. 'I have to know what happened and this might be the chance to find out.'

'It wasn't your fault – I know you've always blamed yourself but it wasn't your fault. We never, ever blamed you.'

Maxie felt a lump form in her throat. 'I think Dad did,' she whispered.

'Oh sweetheart of course he didn't, he just couldn't cope with it all. He blamed me for wanting to go away for that weekend and himself for not putting a chain on the door but *never* you.'

Maxie remembered her dad fitting their home with security worthy of Fort Knox after Susan's death. If anyone knocked on the door after dark, he wouldn't let either woman answer it and he always kept a garden spade in the hallway ready to defend his family if he needed to. The atmosphere was claustrophobic in that house and Maxie had been glad to escape.

'I know I won't be able to change your mind,' her mother continued. 'But please, please don't tell your father. Not yet and certainly not by phone. If you find anything, we can go together and talk him through it.'

Maxie was happy to agree to that and to keeping her mother up to date.

The small town of Barwick where Maxie had grown up was about a forty-minute drive away. It lay on the outskirts of the forests of Bowland and it had inevitably changed over the years. The small town square was much the same but the new estates that had sprung up around the old town heralded a new generation and hence the old greengrocers had now become a vape shop.

She had no option but to take the Jeep for this journey but took it slowly as she drove to the house she'd lived in but as she looked at the ordinary whitewashed detached building all she saw was a place of sadness and death. She gave herself a slap on the leg to shake this mood as she knew it wasn't helpful. It had actually been proven that a pessimistic outlook when investigating cold cases hindered the progress and although she had nothing to go on, she had to start somewhere. Maxie decided that the local school they had both attended as girls might know Rebecca's surname and a conversation with her sister's best friend at the time was as good a place to start as any.

The school had changed as much as the town. Huge new buildings sat where the all-weather hockey pitch had been. She followed the signs to the school's main building and then asked to be pointed to the Head's office. She had no appointment booked but Maxie hoped that her history and relative local fame would grant her an audience, if even for a few moments. Happily, it did.

'Professor Reddick,' said the head teacher, shaking her hand enthusiastically. 'It's so good to meet you in person – I follow your podcast.'

The head, who insisted she call him Tom, was a large bearded man who wouldn't have looked out of place in a lumberjack shirt. Instead he wore the "smart casual" uniform of cords with a V-neck jumper and checked shirt.

Maxie explained what she was doing without revealing the information about the fingerprint. 'It's a bit of a personal crusade,' she said. 'I've reached the point where I simply have to know what happened.'

'I can understand that,' he said, stroking his beard as he thought. 'But I'm not sure what information we still have here or what I can legally or ethically give you.'

Maxie asked if she could simply look at the school photographs and registers from the years her sister attended. She explained she was simply trying to find out Rebecca's surname. Tom expressed doubt that they even still had them but called his secretary Fiona in and asked her to lend Maxie a hand.

'I hope you find something useful,' he said as they parted ways. 'I'll be here for the rest of the day so just ask if there's anything else we can do.'

Maxie thanked him and followed Fiona to a small office where walls were lined with cupboards and a desk bore the weight of a large desktop. Maxie walked towards the computer but the secretary shook her head and led her to a cupboard, opening it to reveal shelves and shelves of dusty boxes.

'We digitised the past twenty-five years of records but if there's anything from around nearer thirty years ago then I'm afraid it'll be somewhere in the paper files,' explained Fiona. 'I'm so sorry but we've just had no need for them and it's a hugely time-consuming task anyway.'

Maxie felt her whole body drop but put on a grateful smile and said she completely understood. The secretary replied she was off to a meeting but would bring Maxie a coffee before she went and otherwise leave her to it.

Maxie turned back to a stack of boxes that looked as if they hadn't been touched for years. Despite the task ahead of her, and having arrived at the school with a degree of trepidation, it felt as if she'd been given a warm hug by these incredibly friendly, helpful people and Maxie took this as an omen that she'd find something useful here. Well if that was going to happen, she'd better get started.

Maxie knew it would save time in the long run to be thorough from the outset; there were no labels on the outside of the boxes but inside each box there was a slip of paper with the year it referred to. Maxie guessed that there was no guarantee that the contents would match the slip so decided to empty a cupboard then sit at the desk to go through each box and put it back if there was nothing helpful inside. After a couple of boxes, she found a rhythm, realising that the records that had been kept were fairly consistent – a register of pupils, awards and disciplinaries, plus a few newspaper cuttings. If the boxes had been in chronological order then this wouldn't be too onerous a task but they weren't and Maxie couldn't help but get distracted when she came across her own school year. Her childhood was recorded here on scraps of paper; she hadn't been part of any of the sporting triumphs but she had helped the school to a debating trophy in her time. Maxie smiled to herself – if only she'd known then that she'd be making a career out of arguing or "debating" with people for the rest of her life.

She ploughed on; at some point Fiona had brought in some coffee but it stood untouched and turned cold as Maxie finally found the box she'd been looking for – Susan's year in the upper sixth. There was her name on the register, and there were photographs of her being appointed Head Girl and captaining the winning netball team. Down in lower sixth, Maxie had often found her big sister's conformity very embarrassing but she remembered that day. Susan had been phenomenal on court and afterwards, their parents had taken them to the newly opened Tex-Mex restaurant. Maxie smiled fondly at the memory of that night – her dad hadn't been keen on the "overly sloppy foreign food" – as he described it – and would have much preferred to be at their usual carvery.

Maxie put the photos to one side, planning to ask for copies and continued to search through the box. There were a couple of Rebecca's on the register and neither name rang a bell but within the next raft of dog-eared papers, Maxie found that one of them – Rebecca Henderson was there, listed as a prefect when Susan was Head Girl. Maxie thought she could recall the girls with their badges proudly displayed on their blazers although she was also aware that she could be making up this memory. None of the other names rang any bells – although it was only one year above, she simply didn't know those in her sister's year at school. Like most teenagers, Maxie had been more concerned with her own social life and the gossip taking place in her own year. As a rebellious teenager, Maxie found her perfect big sister old and boring.

She stood up from the desk, stumbled as she took her first step and cursed out loud. Her stiff ankle was reminding Maxie of the other part of the deal – that she would start doing the exercises she'd been given. She perched herself on the edge of the desk, slipped off her shoe and started doing one of them – tracing the letters of the alphabet with her toe. She was brandishing her foot in an elaborate "Z" when the head walked in.

'Ankle exercises,' explained Maxie.

'Oh I know,' said Tom. 'I recognise them from a stupid fall I had getting the Christmas decorations out of the loft. How did you do yours?'

'Rescuing a kidnap victim.' Maxie's tone acknowledged she recognised the incredulity of her words.

'You win that one,' he said, laughing. 'Anyway, I was just wondering if you found anything useful.'

Maxie shook her head. 'I found Rebecca Henderson who was one of Susan's friends and a prefect when my sister was Head Girl. I don't suppose you know what happened to her?'

He shook his head but then his furrowed brow turned to a smile. 'Sorry – but I do recognise that chap,' he said pointing at one of the photos Maxie had put to one side. 'He was Head Boy in the same year – Mike Priestly.'

'Really? That's brilliant.' Maxie vaguely remembered the name. She was genuinely shocked to be getting a positive response. 'Any idea where I can find him?'

'Here, in about seventy-two hours,' said Tom. 'He became a chemistry teacher at the school and left just before Christmas to head the department at the new academy. We didn't have time to say goodbye then so are hosting a small party for him at the end of the week – you should come, I'll introduce you.'

The delight she'd felt turned to frustration at the thought of having to wait any longer to talk to the man. 'Do you have his address? Or could you call him and ask if he'll talk to me before then?' she asked.

'Sorry,' he said, ushering her out of the room and towards the exit. 'His new job doesn't start till next week so he and his wife have been enjoying a sunny climate over winter and we're on strict instructions not to make contact. She wants him to have a complete break and arrive at his party tanned and refreshed – can't say I blame her.'

Maxie shrugged her acceptance, got a photocopy of the photos and thanked him for his help. She took the details for Friday and promised to be there.

Back in the town centre, Maxie made straight for the pub that had always stood at the end of the main street, the one she'd been at that night. While the others in town had changed name over the years, The White Horse had remained the same. Maxie walked in and inhaled the beer on carpets, polish-on-tables aroma that seemed so familiar. This place had been a regular haunt of hers from her mid-teens as it turned a blind eye to the underage drinkers most of the time. How grown up she'd felt in her black eyeliner, drinking snakebite and yet those two very things were most definitely the signs of a teenager.

Maxie ordered a tonic water and found a booth that enabled her to watch the world go by without being seen. The last time she'd been in this pub was the night of Susan's death … Maxie remembered that she'd been having a wild time, snogging the face off some guy she'd just met and cadging drinks when she ran out of money. She had no idea what lay in store for her when she got home, no idea of the tragedy her late night out would cause … She was suddenly very relieved that she'd had a son rather than a daughter. She wasn't at all sure how she'd have coped with parenting her teenage self.

The old-fashioned jukebox that hung on the wall struck up and Maxie smiled. That was another reason this place was so popular – it always had the best jukebox in town. She recognised the song as Guns N' Roses and out of curiosity looked up to see who had put it on. Her jaw dropped; it couldn't be … could it?

A woman who looked slightly older than she actually was, stood holding a beer and gently moving to the music. The face was worn but the eyes which now bore the creases of time were still lined black, and the teased blonde hair was not too different – even if the colour had been helped along by L'Oreal.

Maxie stood up and walked towards the woman. 'Rebecca? Is that you?'

Chapter Eight

Rebecca swung round and faced Maxie, looking her up and down but judging from her puzzled frown Maxie could see that this woman had no clue who she was.

'Do I know you?' she asked with a voice that spoke of many years spent smoking.

Maxie turned on her most charming and friendly smile then held out her hand in a welcoming handshake. Maxie caught a whiff of perfume that seemed familiar. 'I thought it was you,' she said, shaking Rebecca's limp hand with more enthusiasm than it had been proffered. The effort of still smiling so much was making her cheeks ache. 'I know you won't remember me but I recognised you straight away – you haven't changed a bit.'

It was an obvious piece of flattery but as Maxie watched Rebecca stand a little taller and smooth her hair down, she knew it had worked.

'I'm Maxine Reddick,' she continued. 'You were friends with my big sister Susan back in the day – I'm her annoying little sister.' She gave a little laugh to soften the situation as on the mention of Susan's name, Maxie noted a shift in Rebecca's expression but couldn't quite work out what it was.

'I think I remember you,' said Rebecca. 'Always getting into trouble.'

'That was me,' replied Maxie. 'Completely different to Susan.'

Rebecca snorted.

'I was just visiting the school,' continued Maxie. 'So I thought I'd check out some of the old haunts too. This place hasn't changed much has it?'

They both looked around the bar in silence and then Rebecca returned to her drink.

'I remember the jukebox,' said Maxie trying to draw this woman into a conversation. 'You always liked rock music didn't you?'

'Still do,' said Rebecca nodding. 'Rock songs always start off being mocked by the music pundits but a few years later they're classics and everyone claims to have always liked them.'

'True,' Maxie said. 'I imagine it was like that with the Rolling Stones too – they were the long-haired louts compared to The Beatles and yet something like "Sympathy For The Devil" has to be one of the best songs ever written.'

'I loved "Paint It Black",' said Rebecca. 'They have both of them on here.'

She moved back to the jukebox and selected the Stones songs they had discussed. Maxie could see that Rebecca was far more comfortable discussing music and as the woman appeared to be alone in the bar, she ordered them both a beer and sat down on a bar stool as Rebecca swayed along to Mick Jagger's voice.

'I'm surprised to see the jukebox is still here,' said Maxie as the songs came to an end. 'I'd have thought the bar would have some streaming service.'

'They do but they kept the jukebox in good nick and it's switched on during weekdays.' Rebecca picked up the drink that Maxie had bought her and raised it in thanks before taking a sip. 'Jake, who runs this place now is about the same age as us and remembers what it used to be like. He wanted to keep the best bits when he refurbished it.'

'So he kept the jukebox but hopefully sorted out the plumbing,' said Maxie. 'Do you remember the loos were always blocked and overflowing?'

Rebecca grimaced and nodded. 'Oh God, yes. But we were probably trying to flush all sorts down there back then.'

'True – our kids would be horrified by our teenage eco-credentials.'

'Or lack of them,' Rebecca said, finishing her drink. 'What you having?'

Maxie was barely halfway through her beer but didn't want to rattle the rapport that seemed to be building. She held out her foot. 'I would love to but I had a skinful with a friend last night and I've twisted my ankle.' She let it sound as if the two events were related. 'I just can't risk going over on it again.'

Rebecca shrugged and got herself a refill. She sat down beside Maxie. 'So you went up to the old school?' she said. 'Now there's a place that's changed a lot – what made you want to do that?'

'I don't know really.' Maxie was trying to sound casual and keep her drinking partner on board. 'I moved house recently and found some old photos – that's how I recognised you so quickly. They just took me back and I had this urge to see the place again.'

Maxie bent down and took the photos out of her bag, handing over the first – of Susan and Rebecca. The woman laughed. 'Oh my God, what did we look like? We were so young – and skinny. You never think you're thin enough when you're a teenager do you? And yet there we are and we're tiny.'

Maxie moved closer to her and held one corner of the picture. Rebecca's reflection was something she'd said so many times herself – youth is so beautiful and yet when we're young we worry about the tiniest pimple or ounce of weight and despite all the body-positive messages, she knew it wasn't that different for her own students nowadays.

'You were both gorgeous,' said Maxie. 'I was so jealous of you – you were so cool back then. A real rebel, not like my sister.'

'I was Bodie and she was Doyle,' replied Rebecca referring to an old TV series – *The Professionals* where one detective was a headstrong rebel and the other did things more methodically and by the book.

'I can just imagine that,' said Maxie laughing. 'My sister would never have crossed any lines.'

'Yeah, right.' Rebecca almost choked on her drink. Maxie looked at her but she said no more and handed the picture back. It felt as if the conversation was about to be halted so Maxie pushed some of the other pictures towards Rebecca.

'I had these too,' she said. 'More of your old school friends – I could get you copies if you like.'

Rebecca looked through them all and smiled softly at the images.

'I understand this guy has been teaching at the school.' Maxie pointed at Mike Priestly. 'Do you still have contact with him?'

Rebecca shook her head.

'Shame,' said Maxie. 'There's a party for him up at the school on Friday. I'm going if you want to come along.'

'No thanks, I don't tend to dwell on the past and you shouldn't either,' she said. 'It wasn't all good.'

Maxie reached into her purse and pulled out a business card, handing it over. 'If you change your mind give me a call.' She was trying to sound as casual as possible. 'It would be good to have someone to go with.'

Rebecca read the card and her eyebrows raised. 'You're a professor? Bloody hell.' She gave an appreciative nod. 'Never saw that coming. And still Reddick … you never married?'

'I did but kept my name. I was the only one who could carry on the name so felt as if I should. What about you? Are you married? Any kids?'

'No and no,' replied Rebecca. She looked directly at Maxie as she gave an ironic shrug. 'A call centre isn't exactly a hotbed of romantic opportunity – who'd have thought?'

Maxie nodded knowingly then excused herself and told her companion that she had to go to the ladies' room. Staring into the mirror, washing her hands, Maxie pondered the woman outside. Granted, teenage memories were rarely accurate but she remembered Rebecca being loud and lively; if she'd ever tried to imagine how Rebecca's life would be, she'd have guessed at her having found an athletic-looking husband and having at least two kids, both of whom were as rowdy as her in her teenage years. The woman sitting in the bar seemed to have had the life sucked out of her. She seemed sad.

Maxie bypassed the hand-dryers that were never effective and wiped her hands on a tissue before going back out into the bar. Rebecca was sitting waiting for her to come out; her stance had changed as she held a phone aloft.

'I've googled you – you work with the police,' she said as Maxie sat down again. It was a statement that sounded like an accusation.

'I have done,' Maxie said. 'I run the Applied Criminology Unit up at the university. We do research to help the police in their day-to-day jobs – just last month one of my students developed a new search function for their databases.'

She tried to make it sound as boring as possible but Rebecca wasn't convinced. 'It says in this article that you helped solve a crime – I remember now that you kicked up all that fuss when Susan died.'

'I think I was just really angry,' Maxie said. 'And I blamed myself.'

'That's right,' said Rebecca. 'Weren't you the one who left the door open for the burglars? That must still sting.'

Maxie resisted the urge to correct her.

'It was a horrible time,' continued Rebecca. 'I couldn't believe I'd lost my best friend overnight. When you're young, death isn't something that happens to you – it happens to old people and you generally know it's coming.'

The women sat in silence for a moment and Maxie heard Rebecca sniff a couple of times before pulling out a tissue and blowing her nose. Rebecca raised her glass and said, 'To Susan,' then finished the final mouthful.

Maxie had barely touched her own beer but made a show of repeating the toast and clicking her glass against Rebecca's.

'So where else are you going on this trip down memory lane?' asked Rebecca.

'I don't really know,' Maxie said. 'Probably back to our old house and maybe the hall where the youth club was held.'

'That's long gone,' said Rebecca. 'And I'm not sure the house will hold many memories either. It's changed hands so many times. It's not worth you bothering.'

'Possibly,' murmured Maxie.

'On TV shows,' continued Rebecca, 'people go back to the scene of the crime years later and they find a tiny thing in the corner of the garden, a toy car or yo-yo or something. And for some reason, they're always painted red. Is that what you're hoping for?'

'Detective shows always make it look easy but it's never like that,' said Maxie. 'You said "scene of the crime" – do you remember anything about Susan's death?'

Rebecca shuffled in her seat and Maxie noted her discomfort. 'Just an expression. It was a burglary wasn't it, and whoever did it left no evidence,' said Rebecca. 'I wouldn't go poking your nose in now, you won't find anything. Not even if you are the university's Miss Marple – as they called you in that article.'

Maxie shook her head in despair. 'I hate that name. Journalists can be so lazy – honestly, you're a woman who teaches crime so you must be like an interfering old spinster in tweed. I'd much rather be called Sherlock if anything.'

Rebecca frowned at her but looked deep in thought. 'Interfering is the right word,' she muttered, gazing into her empty glass.

'Can I get you another drink?' asked Maxie wondering what was going on in this girl's head.

Rebecca paused, evidently weighing up the question. The pull was too strong though and she nodded so Maxie called over to Jake, the landlord and asked if they could have a refill. He shouted grumpily that it wasn't table service but then brought over their drinks and Maxie gave him a generous tip for his trouble. His expression changed to a broad smile immediately. 'Just shout when you're ready for the next,' he said, giving Maxie a salute as he left.

'I'll have to try that on a Saturday night,' said Rebecca, raising her glass to her lips. 'It would save me hours standing at the bar.'

'Do you still hang out with any of Susan's old friends?' asked Maxie. 'I can imagine you all coming here.'

Rebecca put down the glass and folded her arms on the table. 'Why the sudden interest?' she asked. 'I can't remember you coming back here before. And it's not her birthday or anything – hers was just before mine. So what's going on?'

'Nothing.' Maxie raised opened palms. 'I just found those photos as I said and thought I'd take a trip down memory lane.'

'And you just happened to get an invitation to a party for Mike Priestly?'

Maxie nodded. 'I didn't know who he was until I went to the school.'

'So you're just going to turn up uninvited?' said Rebecca. 'He won't be too happy about that.'

'I have been invited,' Maxie said. 'By the Head – he doesn't think it'll be a problem.'

'Well he wouldn't would he?' said Rebecca turning back to her glass and taking a large swig.

'I don't understand,' said Maxie. 'Is there something I should know?'

Rebecca downed the last dregs of her drink and stood up to leave. She wiped the back of her hand across her mouth and looking Maxie straight in the eye said, 'Trust me there are just some things that should stay in the past.'

And with that she turned and walked out.

Chapter Nine

The visit to Barwick yesterday had left a bad taste in her mouth. As Maxie brushed her teeth extra hard that morning, she wondered why she felt so unclean. The school visit had gone almost as well as it could – they had no real answers but were helpful and had at least provided her with a potential lead and as long as channels weren't closing down, there was always hope. No, it was the time spent with Rebecca that had sullied her and Maxie had struggled to sleep just thinking about the woman she'd become. It was a bit like that old adage of never meeting your heroes; Susan's friend had never been a hero as such but she was an older girl and a pretty popular one at that. When you're young you imagine that the cool kids will grow up to be famous or at least wealthy and still cool. That was rarely the case.

Maxie mentally went through a list of her own former classmates trying to remember where they'd all ended up and had to conclude that it was the ones who'd worked hard who'd come out the other end successful. She was as much of an example as anyone else; she'd been the rebel until Susan's death. After she'd worked through some of her grief travelling around Asia, Maxie came back and knuckled down, determined to make the most of the brains she had. She ploughed through university acing all her exams and gaining a reputation in her chosen field of Criminology. The more she learned, the more she understood why Susan's case had not been solved. The police had to work within too many rules and constraints. That's why setting up the Applied Criminology Unit was so important to her; Maxie could help the police and that had to some degree enabled her to scratch the itch.

Maxie couldn't face driving so called a taxi. She felt drained as she made her way to the university; she really needed to talk things through with someone. Normally, she'd be working on a case with Andrew and they could bounce ideas off each other but in this instance, he was investigating the death at the care home and she couldn't even discuss that with him.

She dialled Craig's number after she'd got out of the cab, having arranged for it to come back for her at the end of the day; her co-host was always happy to discuss cases but it went straight to voicemail so she left a message asking what he thought of her proposal for the podcast.

Walking down the corridor to her office, Maxie realised she was getting several strange looks from people and it wasn't until she bumped into the Dean who told her he was "sorry for her loss" that she remembered the reason she'd given for her absence yesterday. Maxie nodded her thanks but felt such guilt over the lie that she knew she'd have to come clean as soon as possible.

She reached the lecture hall and plonked herself on her chair with a huge sigh of relief that no-one asked who had died. The throb of her ankle seemed to be pulsing up her leg and through her body like the tell-tale heart in Edgar Allan Poe's story.

The hall filled up and she began her lecture but she knew she was delivering it without her usual gusto and before long, the students noticed it too. She'd asked them a question about how media was shaping criminal activity and how, given the speed of change within media channels, the justice system could ever keep up. It was a question that her students could debate enthusiastically and at any other time, their responses would enthral her as the students had a much better grip on media channels than she did. Where Maxie read about cyber-crime, they tended to live it. She hadn't noticed but the room had gone quiet as evidently one of the students had asked her a question.

'Professor?' asked a girl in the front row. 'Are you okay?'

Maxie shook herself out of her daze and rubbed her face. As she lowered her hands she saw a roomful of eyes staring back at her. For a millisecond, she thought of bluffing her way through but then announced, 'No actually, I'm not.'

She allowed the low murmur and uncomfortable shifting to subside and then stood up. 'Complicated traumatic grief,' she said. 'It is associated with survivors in sudden death experiences. Put simply, you're not expecting it and therefore you have difficulty processing your feelings. The murder of someone close would cause this but can anyone tell me when it's most prevalent?'

'When there is no resolution, when the crime isn't solved,' answered a student.

Maxie nodded. 'That's right and I'm afraid that I've been distracted this morning by that very condition.'

The room went quiet as she explained what had happened to her sister and the intense feelings of guilt she'd experienced. As she couldn't divulge the information about the fingerprint, Maxie told them that she'd been invited back to her old school and this had reignited her compulsion to find out once and for all what had happened to Susan.

'You mean like a cold case?' asked a student.

'That's exactly what it is,' Maxie said. 'But I'm beginning to realise cold means positively freezing. I might not be able to keep up with your technology but you lot would be completely stumped by what I had in the nineties. There was this stuff called paper – lots of it.'

The room laughed and Maxie felt cheered by having shared what she was feeling. A student towards the middle of the room raised a hand and she pointed at him to go ahead with his question.

'Would there be a credit in helping you out?' he asked.

'In what way?' asked Maxie.

'Like, a paper on understanding historical investigation methods or something,' came the reply.

The students suddenly became animated.

'We could definitely help find out what happened.'

'Please Professor let us work on this with you.'

'What have you got to lose?'

Maxie listened to their pleas and concluded that she really did have nothing to lose. A group of the brightest heads were certainly better than her one – especially one wearing rose-tinted spectacles. She held up her palms to calm the furore.

'Okay,' she said. 'Thank you for your offer. For those of you who want to do this, I will think very carefully about how this can be incorporated into the curriculum. However – I need to say that I truly do not expect everyone to get involved and I accept that we may not get a resolution. So leave this with me for a day or two and I'll get back to you all with a proposal.'

Maxie went back to the original subject they'd started, with a lot more enthusiasm. At the end of the lecture, a few students approached her to say they'd like to be involved. While they may have been doing it purely for the course credit, Maxie left the hall feeling bolstered and certainly more optimistic.

When she finally got a moment in her office, Maxie sat back in her desk chair and took a breath. The sun was low in the sky outside her window and dappled the clouds with a pale peach glow. The effect was serene, as if nature was telling her to take it slowly. Although she'd never been happy with the verdict on Susan's death, she had to accept that it may have to stay that way and she might not find any new leads. The case was old and even those people close to Susan at the time had probably forgotten all about that night – certainly the details. Maxie was very well aware that her need to find an alternative answer was borne out of survivor guilt. She had been desperate for someone to blame, to know that it wasn't all down to Susan having left the door open for her that night.

But what if that was the conclusion they came to? Could she draw a line under it? Could she cope with having it confirmed that she had caused it? Maxie took another very deep breath and closed her eyes; there was no point going down this path if she couldn't. What had she always said to victims who blame circumstances – people who said *"I shouldn't have been out at night"* or *"I shouldn't have taken a short cut through the park"*? She'd told them that the only person responsible for the crime was the one who inflicted it. She had to listen to her own advice – she hadn't burgled her parents' home. No matter how much she tried to convince herself of her innocence, it wasn't working yet. Truly knowing what had happened was the only solution.

Getting the students involved was a good idea – they would challenge her and keep her on the straight and narrow. If they came across any paths which felt uncomfortable for her, they'd force her to investigate them as objectively as possible. If their support was to contribute to their grading then it was more likely that they'd stay the course and there were several ways of building this into the curriculum.

Every student had to develop a piece of original research which consisted of both a literature review and an applied criminology study. Rather than attempt to prescribe the research field, the professor decided to draft an email to her class thanking them for their interest and inviting them to submit a proposal to show how involvement in a cold case could contribute to their learning. Maxie figured that by doing it this way she'd only get offers to help from students who really were interested. She pressed send and got back to her work.

It was Valentine's Day over the weekend so for the final day of the week she'd promised the students a day of lectures about crimes of passion – although now as she pulled up her notes on the subject it seemed like a strange way to celebrate the third century Roman saint who, she discovered, was also the saint of beekeeping and epilepsy. 'Hmmm, murder by bee sting,' said Maxie to herself as she typed into her search engine. 'That would be a very apt conclusion to the day.'

The sky was dark and clear as she got back into her taxi for the journey home. Already she could see Orion's Belt against the blackness – there were others and she had tried to learn a few but had never been able to remember any except the three in a row. She mentioned this to the taxi driver just to start a conversation.

'Now I know that one up there on the left,' he said nodding his head towards his window. 'See it, the big W? That's Cassiopeia – she was one of the most beautiful goddesses in Greek mythology. I always remember it because my first wife was called Wendy and she was the most beautiful woman I'd ever set eyes on – a stunner she was.'

From the tone of his voice, Maxie could tell that death rather than divorce was the cause of the past tense in his sentence. She wondered just how many people were living with a loss that still affected them but lay hidden most of the time.

He dropped her at the door and although it was still only early evening, waited until she had safely unlocked it before giving her a wave and heading off. Maxie pushed the front door open against the pile of post on the other side. She'd often thought of leaving her recycling bin outside the front door so the postman could put all the leaflets and junk mail straight in to save her the effort.

After dumping her briefcase down she sorted through the flotsam that had landed on her doormat, quickly spotting a large envelope that obviously wasn't junk. It was hand-written and although the handwriting looked familiar, she couldn't place it – as most communication was via text and email these days, handwriting wasn't something one often saw. She flexed the envelope; it contained something cardboard and stiff. For a tiny second, her heart did a little skip as she thought it might actually be an early valentine's card – although who it might be from was anyone's guess. In the past, her worst fear had been that she'd get something like this from a student but one of the advantages of aging was being beyond even Mrs Robinson fantasies.

Still, she would defy anyone not to get just a little bit excited by the idea of a secret admirer. Maxie opened all the rest of her post, leaving the envelope until last. When she finally opened it, she burst out laughing at her own idiocy as she pulled out a cardboard file from Andrew and her brain made the link to the handwriting which she'd rarely seen. He'd sent copies of the cold case files she'd been granted access to and on the front he'd stuck a post-it note which read, "*Will pop round Saturday to discuss – with food!*"

Well at least she had a date on Valentine's Day.

Chapter Ten

Maxie sat on the edge of the bed doing her rehab exercises – she'd discovered that tracing the alphabet with the tip of her toes was actually far more entertaining if she spelled out some profanities instead. She could exercise her ankle and exorcise her demons without getting dressed and that was a winning start to the day in her book. Today she'd added a little mental challenge to use swear words with the highest scrabble scores – should they ever be allowed on a board.

Having entertained herself, Maxie got on with her morning routine, arriving at the university at her usual hour and facing her students with her usual high level of enthusiasm. The lecture on crimes of passion went well and as expected, resulted in a good level of debate and banter. Over a lunch at her desk, she noted that a couple of students had come back with outline proposals for involvement in the cold case and others had posed some questions. She dealt with them without emotion, not wanting to impose her own biases on their ideas and suggestions. The students who eventually got involved had to be able to challenge her and that had to start with a robust academic case. In truth, it wasn't really the professional in her that was guiding this objectiveness – her mind was simply now focussed on other things – specifically the evening ahead.

Maxie glanced at her phone and saw she had less than six hours to wait until the leaving do at the school. Just one tutorial and a faculty meeting to go and then she would be free to get back to her sister's case.

The excitement while getting dressed that evening was not just down to the anticipation of finding out some new information. Maxie secretly hoped that she might meet some of her own contemporaries; that she'd find out what happened to people she'd both loved and loathed.

Maxie dressed simply in a mid-length button through dress with opaque tights and boots – it was still winter after all. She made extra effort with her make-up, putting on lash-lengthening mascara to make her eyes pop and a smoky rose lipstick which complemented her olive skin beautifully. She wanted to look friendly and approachable so added some large turquoise drop earrings that didn't quite go with the outfit but were rather dramatic and a gift from her son Karl so would be an ideal subject for small talk if needed.

Maxie looked at herself in the mirror one last time as the taxi driver texted that he'd arrived. She touched the earrings and smiled broadly, practising conversation with her reflection, 'Oh these – they're my lucky earrings. I put them on whenever I'm going to have to mingle with people; it's often quite scary isn't it?'

She knew from the experience of hundreds of conferences that being the first to admit fear of mingling was a sure-fire way of engendering trust. Once in her taxi she mentally rehearsed more opening lines until the driver called out, 'Are you talking to yourself?'

Maxie was shaken from her thoughts and then burst out laughing. 'Was I doing it out loud?' she asked.

'Not quite,' replied the driver smiling at her. 'But you were doing all the nodding and shaking your head – and your lips were moving.'

'Don't worry, I haven't gone mad,' said Maxie. 'It's an old school reunion and I haven't a clue what I'm going to say to these people.'

'Best thing is just to ask them about themselves – people love talking.'

Maxie nodded, she'd certainly found that worked in the past. Although on this occasion she would have to be wary of diving in with the only question she wanted to ask – *"Do you know how my sister really died?"*

'Anyhow,' continued the driver. 'You might not recognise them now. No offence love, but it would have been a good ten years ago.'

Maxie guffawed at his tongue-in-cheek comment. 'Oh at least ten,' she replied. 'But I've been studying old photos and trying to keep their images in mind. I've given them little nicknames to try and remember them by – like "rugby nose" and "mop top".'

'Charming,' the driver said, laughing out loud. 'I wouldn't want you to be giving me a nickname – probably be something like fatso. Anyway, this mop top might be bald now.'

Her nervous excitement had calmed significantly by the time they arrived at the school.

'Just call me when you're ready to leave and I'll be right here,' said the driver as he parked up. 'Don't get too drunk now – I know how these reunion things can go.'

'Oh I won't be drinking tonight,' she said. 'Just don't like driving on this ankle.'

In truth, she'd developed a slight wariness of getting back into her Jeep, fearing that her ankle wouldn't be strong enough to stop it in an emergency. And it wasn't just that; the Jeep had been her gift to herself but nowadays when she got into it, she thought of her divorce and of the last case – the car seemed linked to the past. Whether she liked it or not, Orlando – the man responsible for her ankle injury – had given more than her foot a real bruising.

The leaving party was taking place in the school assembly hall. Now bedecked with balloon arches and bunting, it reminded her of every school disco she'd ever ridiculed as being "just for kids". The room wasn't full, and people seemed to be milling around without purpose but she'd arrived bang on time and seen as her cab pulled away, a minibus arriving so there'd be a large group filing in soon.

Sure enough, as she picked up a glass of wine from the table, a cheer went around the room as eight people walked through the door, the main man leading the way. The atmosphere changed and suddenly the party seemed to start. Maxie whipped out her phone and took both video and photos of the room as it started to liven up. The DJ cranked up some Ace of Base which Maxie remembered from her school days and the room began to sway awkwardly.

Maxie smiled watching them and someone beside her said into her ear, 'Did we ever think we'd start dancing like our dads?'

Laughing, she turned to see who had spoken – it was Tom. It amused Maxie to note that his party gear wasn't too dissimilar to his work attire – a different checked shirt and no jumper but he was most definitely still rocking the woodsman look.

'If you need an introduction to anyone, just let me know,' he said.

Maxie nodded her thanks and as she looked over the room full of smiling faces, replied, 'I can just see Susan here – she'd have absolutely loved catching up with everyone.'

Tom shrugged in the way people do when they don't know what to say. Then he gave Maxie a little squeeze of the shoulder and said he had to mingle but hoped to catch up later. She very much doubted the second part of that statement was true but replied it would be lovely.

Being at someone else's party wasn't proving much fun and Maxie started to wonder about those people who liked to crash weddings – why on earth would they want to spend their evenings making small talk with people they didn't know? The room was now very animated but she had a job to do. She made a quick trip to the ladies to freshen up her lipstick and take another look at the photos she'd been studying and then re-joined the throng on the dance floor. Holding two glasses of wine as if she was carrying one for a friend, Maxie began threading through the crowd, studying each face as she went. The driver had been right – the men in this room were grey or balding and the women sported bold and glossy hair colours that quite possibly bore very little relation to the colour they had as teenagers. She had made one full circuit of the room without recognising a soul when the only face she did know appeared. 'Rebecca, I thought you weren't coming!'

Maxie handed her one of the wine glasses she was holding and Rebecca took a large gulp. 'Wanted to see how they'd all turned out,' she said slurring heavily.

It was only then that Maxie realised her sister's old friend had evidently consumed a lot of Dutch courage judging by the way she was propped against the wall. She instantly regretted handing her that glass but to suggest water or some fresh air would be patronising. Maxie knew as well as any other woman that there were times when you just needed a little fortification to face your demons. If she kept her talking, she might at least slow the consumption of more alcohol.

'Do you recognise anyone here?' she asked. 'I've got Susan's old photos but can't spot anyone, except Mike of course.'

Rebecca waved an unsteady finger towards the dance floor. 'That lot there,' she said pointing at a group of middle-aged women excitedly dancing around Mike and screaming out the lyrics of "Relight my Fire" by Take That, 'have always been Mike's groupies.'

Maxie examined them from a distance, trying to find a facial feature that wouldn't have been altered by time. One of the women had a very distinctive smile – so broad it seemed to fill her whole face but with slightly wonky teeth. She could have had the teeth changed but not the smile. Maxie took out the photos she'd found among her sister's old things and switched her phone torch on to see them better. She looked only for that smile and although the quality of the snapshots was appalling back then, she found someone who looked quite similar and this person was with a group of girls who could be the same people now on the dance floor.

'Is this them?' she asked Rebecca who nodded and took the photo from Maxie.

‘They haven’t aged well have they?’ said Rebecca. ‘You never think you’re going to end up looking like your mother do you?’

‘My God – Rebecca!’

Both women swung round to see Mike Priestly, his arms out in a welcome, approaching them. He gave Rebecca a peck on the cheek and then looked her up and down. ‘Wow, you haven’t changed a bit.’ Maxie imagined that he’d said these words so many times during the evening. ‘Are you still into your rock music? I can get the DJ to play some for you if you like.’

Without waiting for her answer, he turned to Maxie. She thrust out a hand and shook his robustly. ‘You don’t know me,’ she said. ‘Susan Reddick was my sister and I’m just here to take a trip down memory lane. I hope that’s okay – Tom kind of invited me.’

She noted that on hearing Susan’s name, Mike’s expression changed from curiosity to fake delight and stayed that way. His eyebrows were so high on his forehead, it looked as if they were trying to escape through his hairline.

‘Wow,’ he replied taking Maxie’s hands in both of his. ‘That’s a name I haven’t heard for ages. It was such an awful time for everyone – especially you. I’m so sorry for your loss – I don’t think I ever said that back in the day. Susan was great fun.’

‘I wanted to ask you about her if that’s okay,’ said Maxie.

Just then, the crowd of women described as Mike’s groupies descended upon him. Maxie stood at the edge of the group while they hugged and kissed the main man, taking photo after photo with him. Maxie discreetly took a few more of her own and as Mike explained who she was, the women invited her into the group and the photo session continued. The group dispersed as another Take That track started blaring from the speakers. As they danced, Maxie was accosted by Tom’s secretary, Fiona.

‘I’m so glad I’ve found you,’ she said. ‘I found something you might be interested in.’

As she recognised Mike and Rebecca, her smile broadened. ‘Actually you two might be interested in this as well,’ continued Fiona. ‘In the depths of my cupboard I found a lovely record of an away match you all went on.’

‘I don’t remember that at all,’ said Mike frowning. ‘Do you have it with you?’

‘It’s just in my office, I’ll go and fetch it,’ Fiona said. ‘Oh the hairstyles back then – I think you’ll have a bit of a laugh.’

Mike rolled his eyes towards Maxie. ‘I’m not looking forward to reliving my flock of seagulls look,’ he said. ‘I’ll catch you later.’

He left and Rebecca followed close behind, leaving Maxie once again standing at the edge of the action like the uninvited guest that she was. As the evening wore on, the guests were getting more animated and tipsy – there was very little chance of making any progress here and it didn’t look as if Rebecca was coming back. Maxie decided to find Fiona and check out the photo she’d mentioned; she was walking towards the exit when the smoke alarm started blaring. As smoke began appearing in the corridor outside it slowly dawned on the crowd that this wasn’t a drill.

‘Everyone out.’ Tom appeared red-faced and soot-covered as he herded the party towards the emergency exit.

‘What’s happened?’ asked Maxie as she tried to hold back and covered her mouth with her scarf.

‘Just get out now,’ shouted Tom, pushing her along. ‘All those paper records in the office have gone up in smoke. I tried to put it out but I couldn’t.’

‘What about Fiona?’

‘What do you mean?’

‘She was in there.’

Chapter Eleven

Maxie stood outside anxiously waiting as every emergency service blasted its way into the schoolyard. Both she and Tom had to be held back when he tried to lunge towards the smoking office. They both breathed huge sighs of relief when Fiona was eventually brought out of the building on the stretcher and not in a body bag.

Until then, Maxie had stood numb as she imagined Fiona lying in that room with its dusty cupboards, choked by the fumes. She was still instinctively clutching her own throat, remembering the fire her own husband – ex-husband now – started in their home. He hadn't been thinking straight but also hadn't known that their son Karl was upstairs.

Maxie felt tears forming as she relived the moment and the horror of what her husband had done. It was one of her recurring nightmares – that Karl was still in bed, suffocating and she couldn't get to him. She tried to climb the stairs but the flames would beat her back. Maxie had to drag herself back to the present and remind herself that they'd all survived; her family was safe. And although complications could always set in later, for now it seemed as if Fiona was too.

Fiona had been so perky when she'd spoken to her at the party, so delighted to have found something useful and yet her helpfulness had almost cost her her life.

Why hadn't she followed Fiona back to the office? Could she have helped her if she had? Could she have spotted how this fire started? Maxie felt completely useless but knew that she was a witness to this incident so wouldn't be invited to join Andrew.

The fire service declared the building safe for entry by the authorities and the crime investigation team were getting suited up while Andrew stood allocating tasks to his team.

It was bitterly cold and the temperature was well on its way to the forecast freezing point. Maxie hugged herself but the chill was coming from inside as well as out. She looked around at the others waiting – they weren't dressed to be standing out on a winter night and at least she could do something about that. She turned to Tom and asked whether they could commandeer the gym to wait for questioning as from her schooldays, she remembered it being far enough away from the crime scene.

'It's just that everyone is freezing out here and we don't know how long the police will want to keep us.'

'Good idea,' he said. 'Sorry I wasn't thinking straight what with Fiona …' He approached an officer and cleared it with them then led everyone across the yard and into the gym.

The building had been dramatically transformed since her days but one thing hadn't changed and as soon as Maxie walked in, that smell hit her – sweat, testosterone and failure. She'd never been sporty and had come to dread Wednesday afternoons at school – a whole two hours of humiliation. She'd been so pleased to be able to drop any sport whatsoever in sixth form.

'Brings back some memories doesn't it?'

The voice behind her belonged to Mike and as he spoke, Maxie realised she hadn't seen him since he'd left the party. 'I was a big basketball nut,' he continued. 'What about you?'

'Just a nut,' she said, shrugging while Mike snorted at her weak joke.

'Susan was brilliant at netball obviously but loved basketball too I seem to remember,' he said, stroking his chin. 'She came to all the games with Rebecca.'

'Where is Rebecca?' asked Maxie looking around the gym and not seeing her. 'She followed you out of the party.'

'Did she? I can't say I noticed. I went to the gents and she certainly didn't follow me in there.'

Maxie spotted Andrew coming into the gym so excused herself and walked towards him. 'Any news?' she asked. 'Is she going to be okay? Do you know if it was arson?'

Andrew pulled her to one side. 'You know I can't say anything officially but they think the fire was started on purpose. Fiona looks as if she'll be okay although problems can arise later with smoke inhalation.'

Maxie was aware of such complications but gave a silent thanks to that power she didn't believe in; she had steeled herself ready to hear that the friendly woman had already died and was now on her way to an autopsy so the relief was enormous.

'Did you see anything suspicious? Somewhere I could start the questioning?' asked Andrew.

Maxie pulled herself together and explained about Mike leaving with Rebecca just after Fiona, then together they walked over to the former head boy.

Mike went on the charm offensive and promised that he would answer any questions whatsoever to help understand what had happened to "poor

Fiona". 'I obviously know her quite well,' he said, 'she's a real asset to the school.'

After reiterating his whereabouts, he repeated his claim that he hadn't noticed Rebecca leaving at the same time. Mike explained that he'd known her at school but they hadn't been close and he hadn't seen her in decades. He'd been surprised to see her as she wasn't on the guest list.

'I'll need a copy of that guest list,' said Andrew.

'No problem at all,' replied Mike. 'My wife organised all of this so I'll email you a copy as soon as I get home.'

'Was there anyone else here not on the guest list as far as you know?' asked Andrew.

Mike looked directly at Maxie.

'Mea culpa,' she said. 'But Tom suggested I come along so he may have invited others.'

'I guess it did turn into a bit of a school reunion rather than a leaving do,' said Mike. 'Not that I minded, it made me look far more popular than I actually was.'

It was said with an air of false modesty and Maxie imagined that if any of his dance-floor entourage had been close, they would have protested that he'd been extremely popular. Maxie pinched herself hard on the arm to get out of this frame of mind. She didn't know Mike or his groupies and if she wasn't careful, her bias would colour her investigation. Keeping at eavesdropping distance, she followed Andrew around the room as he spoke to everyone else but his questioning provided equally few answers.

After taking statements he decided to call it a day and gave everyone permission to go home. The party crowd left details with his constable and filed out, leaving just the detective and Maxie. They stood silently for a few moments but even their quiet seemed to echo around the gym.

'Can I take a look at the scene of crime?' asked Maxie breaking the hush.

Andrew looked directly at her and raised his eyebrows. She knew she'd been given his "no way" look and shrugged. 'Can't blame a girl for trying. I was just hoping the photo Fiona was getting for me might have survived. Does she have family?'

'A husband and grown-up children,' he said. 'One of my team took him to the hospital and I imagine he's going to stay there all night.'

Maxie gave a heavy sigh, picturing that poor man praying to every god he could think of to look after his wife. They began walking towards the exit as Andrew's thoughts streamed out, 'I'm guessing this thing she went into the office for might have something to do with it. Perhaps someone was trying to stop her showing it to you?'

'Lord, I hope I'm not the reason this fire was started,' murmured Maxie.

'The arsonist was the reason it started,' asserted Andrew. 'Do you think Rebecca is capable of that?'

Maxie was about to say that she didn't think so but stopped herself. After all, what did she really know about any of these people?

'You have to ask why she was here,' continued Andrew. 'She might have been part of the crowd back in the day but hasn't seen these people for years and there doesn't seem to have been a bond of affection or friendship does there? She wasn't invited and only found out about it through you. Then when she gets here, from your account, she hides in the corner, speaks to no-one but you, then vanishes just before an arson attack and appears to have fled the scene.'

Andrew opened the door for Maxie and they walked back into the freezing night air. A frost was starting to form on the tips of the lawn and Andrew blew clouds of mist as he continued to talk. 'I want to pop back to the hospital but I'll get my team to find Rebecca and bring her in for questioning.'

He offered Maxie a lift but she could see her cab waiting and headed off, telling Andrew that if he had any other questions about Rebecca he could call her at any time.

Maxie hadn't actually consumed any of the wine that she'd carried around the room while trying to look like she belonged there, so having thrown off her party clothes and pulled on her slouchies when she got home, she headed straight for the fridge and poured herself a large glass. The first sip caused the reaction she'd hoped for – it calmed her slightly but then she put it down knowing she needed a clear head for both tonight and the weekend ahead.

She grabbed her laptop and phone then snuggled under a blanket on the sofa with both propped on her lap. On the coffee table, she spread out Susan's old photographs and the copies from the school then transferred the shots she'd taken over the evening onto the laptop so that she could view them on the larger screen. When she reached an image of Rebecca, Maxie felt her heart pick up a beat.

She had never really known the woman – in her teenage years and especially not now. She'd been Susan's friend and being the elder sister Susan hadn't hung around with Maxie and certainly hadn't shared her best buddy. Was Rebecca the kind of woman who could start a fire? Did she have something to hide? And if not, why had she vanished from the scene? If Rebecca had started this fire then it was Maxie who had invited her to the school in the first place. Maxie dropped her head into her hands and pressed her fingernails into her forehead wanting to feel the pain. Was it guilt that she somehow caused this? She knew that was ludicrous but the sensation wouldn't go away and there was only one thing she could do. 'I will find out who started that fire too, Fiona,' she vowed.

Maxie's first task was identifying all of Mike's groupies and fortunately that was fairly easy. She'd guessed that they'd be uploading everything onto social media and, because of their age, the platform of choice would be Facebook. Her students mocked that only middle-aged people used it nowadays but that's what they all were.

Maxie looked at Mike's page and found pictures that he'd been tagged in. From there she took the names of people she recognised from the party and searched those pages then cross-referenced them with LinkedIn to try and establish where each of them worked. It was a slow methodical process but incredibly helpful and by just past midnight, she had a factsheet on each of the groupies: Jane Meuhr, Trish Harrington, Liz Dixon, Cheryl Murray and Carole Hodgson. And Maxie also believed that she'd found the foundations of the group – two of them had been prefects in the same year and it wouldn't take much digging to establish whether all of them had been. Rather unkindly, Maxie pictured them ruling the school under their egotistical leader Mike. But if that were anywhere near the truth, how did Susan fit into it? And why wasn't Rebecca still part of the entourage?

Chapter Twelve

On Saturdays Maxie didn't set an alarm. Her only obligation was the podcast recording and as this took place late afternoon, she generally had a good lie-in. Nevertheless, when she opened her eyes and saw it was after ten, she was horrified. She made to get up but her body refused; she was absolutely shattered – mentally as well as physically. An evening in heels, the fire and then hours slumped over a laptop had given her the backache she was now attempting to stretch out while still lying in bed. Still, sore muscles were a small price to pay for the progress she'd made.

Maxie felt extremely satisfied with her evening's work and late last night she'd put the factsheets on Mike's entourage to one side, planning to look at them with fresh eyes in the morning. However, it didn't quite work out like that. Maxie simply couldn't get their names out of her head and so even in bed, she googled them, read more of their social feeds and even began to think of some questions she wanted to ask each person. Now in the cold light of day, she couldn't remember any of those questions as not wanting to turn on the light she hadn't written any of them down.

Arching her back in a final stretch, Maxie rubbed her face hard with the palms of her hands and reluctantly threw back the duvet whose weight had been both comforting and protective so she felt rather exposed without it. A quick round of ankle exercises and then she stood up, noting that her ankle was actually the part of her body in least pain this morning.

While grinding some beans for a strong morning coffee, Maxie messaged Andrew asking how it had gone at the hospital. Within moments her phone rang. 'Well we have some good news at last.' His voice sounded as weary as Maxie felt and she could imagine that he'd been up all night. 'Fiona is going to be okay – they'll keep her in for a couple of days as she inhaled a lot of smoke but she's out of danger.'

'Oh thank goodness for that! I don't really know her but she seems like a good person and I'd have hated her to have suffered real harm just because she wanted to help people. That never seems fair – how is her husband doing?'

'Relieved but exhausted,' continued Andrew. 'I sat with him for a little while last night and the hospital have persuaded him to go home and change but I imagine he'll be back there as soon as he possibly can. His daughter is arriving today so I hope that helps.'

Andrew sighed out loud and the effect was more of a wail of exhaustion. Maxie turned off the noisy electric grinder and asked the detective how he was holding up. 'I'm okay. I just need to get some sleep. I'm home now and I've assigned one of my team to the arson at the school. I'm just relieved I'm not looking at two suspicious deaths.'

'Me too,' Maxie said. 'Go get some rest and I'll see you later.'

Maxie inhaled the aroma of the coffee beans but her throat seemed to have tightened and she couldn't imagine swallowing even a cup. She let out a huge breath of relief; she hadn't realised just how anxious she'd been about Fiona as no matter what Andrew said, that lovely woman wouldn't have been attacked if she hadn't been trying to help with Susan's case.

Maxie needed to be out there doing something, finding out why all this was happening. She had to get to the studio and speak to Craig Johnston before the recording that afternoon. With the podcast she had an outlet and if Craig needed a new idea then how did solving a cold case sound?

Maxie rushed through washing and dressing, opting once again for a cab rather than driving. Outside the weather was starting to look spring-like with a pale blue sky and fleecy white clouds giving the sense of hopeful times ahead. She looked up and pursed her lips, not fooled. February was full of false promises. The bright crocuses that reached above the earth were often destroyed by a late month snowfall. No, February frequently brought dark days and she guessed that this year would be no different.

Maxie climbed into the back seat of the taxi and spotted a heart-shaped air freshener dangling from the rear-view mirror – her driver's nod to Valentine's Day.

'Nothing says romance like a pine freshener does it,' she remarked with a little laugh. The involuntary act of her muscles creating a smile across her face made her realise just how tense she felt so she forced her shoulders down and kept the smile going. 'Did you tell your wife you'd prefer a box of chocolates?'

'Shows how much you know.' The driver smiled along with her. 'That's what this smells of – chocolate.'

'Never,' said Maxie genuinely intrigued.

As they stopped at traffic lights, the driver took down the air freshener and passed it back to her. She sniffed the heavy vanilla aroma and grimaced. 'That does not smell like any chocolate I've ever had and believe me, I've had a lot.'

The amicable chat for the rest of the journey helped to relax Maxie. Without it she would have arrived at the studio like a swirling dervish demanding air time immediately. As it was, she sat down with Craig and explained the concept. He liked the idea and expanded on it, saying that it if were to work it would need a catchy title, visual content and interviews. It would be a full production piece going out across YouTube and the podcast channel.

'But all of that will take ages and I don't want to wait that long,' said Maxie.

'If we get the title, a logo and maybe a starting visual then we can announce it this evening but it is full-on, Maxie – can you manage it with your work commitments?'

She nodded. She had no idea whether she could or not, just that she had to do this. Having brainstormed some ideas, they settled on using a photo of Susan and some iconic images from the year she died. The graphic designer for the studio agreed to freelance for an hour on his weekend off and created a logo that they could use across social media and in any other promotional work, around the title *"My Sister's Killer"*.

Seeing those words alongside Susan's picture made Maxie's heart beat a little faster and she hoped she was doing the right thing. Her parents might hate this – especially her father. Maxie knew the chances of him listening to a podcast or viewing YouTube footage was pretty much zero but she'd have to warn her mother.

'Are you okay with this?' Craig had put an arm around her shoulder. She gave a small nod in response and told the designer to upload everything. It was time to go into the recording studio and set these wheels in motion.

They settled themselves in their usual positions across a small table with the microphones in the middle. Outside the sound booth the engineer gave them the thumbs up and the introductory music began.

'Hello,' said Craig with a more grave tone of voice than he normally adopted. 'You're listening to *Criminal Thoughts* with me Craig Johnston and my co-host Professor Maxie Reddick – head of the Applied Criminology Unit and renowned academic at Lonsdale University. Today's episode will be a little different to our usual format and we're announcing an extremely personal endeavour. Professor, why don't you explain?'

Maxie licked her lips a little as they'd dried so much she wondered whether they would actually open. She sat up straight and began.

'On Saturday the sixteenth of September 1995, my sister was killed,' she said, needing to get those words out straight away. 'No-one was ever convicted of the crime and I have never believed that a proper investigation was carried out at the time. I need your help to conduct one now.'

Craig gave her a thumbs up and she slumped back in her chair while he picked up the reins. 'That's right,' he said. 'We want your help. We know that if you listen to this then you love solving crimes; we know that you love cold cases and hate ambiguity. You're the type of people who wouldn't settle for a verdict you weren't happy with, you can bring clarity, you can see the clues that others often miss and we invite you to find *My Sister's Killer.*'

They explained that there would be extra content with photographs, witness statements and any updates shared online. They gave listeners Maxie's old street name and prompted them with things that had been happening that September – not only the details of the three children who'd gone missing at that time but simple things like the fact that Shaggy had been number one in the charts with "Boombastic", that John Major had been prime minister and that the weather had been awful that month.

'Go back in time,' said Maxie. 'If you lived in the area and were around that street, did you see anything? Did you go to school or hang out with Susan? Did you know any of her friends? Let's build a picture of what was happening in and around Barwick back then.'

'And for the ninety-nine point nine per cent of our audience who live nowhere near,' added Craig, 'listen to what you hear and tell us what we're not seeing – maybe what we don't really want to see.'

He'd lowered his voice dramatically for the last part and then the music played for the end of the episode. Despite feeling that she'd probably sold her soul with this, Maxie looked across at Craig with optimism.

'I've a feeling this might work,' she told him.

The episode would be edited and uploaded early evening but the promotion of it began immediately. Social media adverts and posts showcased the initiative to the extent that local media picked up very quickly and as they all had digital feeds which needed constant content, news spread fast.

As Maxie waited in the foyer of the studio for her lift home, she scrolled through an online edition of the local paper which had Susan's picture right at the top. They had also inserted some of their own old front pages to prompt memories – Maxie was delighted with that as it was bound to help.

However the paper had also named the officer in charge of the original investigation and Maxie wasn't as happy about that – nevertheless, it was bound to come out and she would have to tread carefully. She had a very good relationship with the police and couldn't stomp in there, accusing them of failing her nearly thirty years ago. She'd walk that tightrope later.

Right now Maxie was relieved to see that their idea to create a public cold case had captured imaginations and was spiralling. She knew that the listening figures for their show wouldn't be the problem now; the problem would be keeping everything under control and sorting the wheat from the chaff when it came to information. Soon there would be more leads and opinions than she would ever have time to cope with. She really needed to get her team of students in place first thing Monday.

Chapter Thirteen

As Maxie was leaving the studio for her cab, she got the call she was waiting for from DCI Heather McAlister. Thanks to her relationship with the force through the Applied Criminology Unit and in particular the personal trust that she'd built with the Chief Inspector, copies of the original case notes were going to be released to her and she was going to be assigned a cold case investigator.

'She's obviously a civilian now but can provide you with the link to the force that you're going to need,' the DCI said during the call.

Although Maxie was delighted to have the resource she hoped that wouldn't hamper things. After all, she'd openly criticised the police investigation of Susan's death and didn't want anyone else deciding how she should proceed now. She wanted to be able to look at any lead for as long as it took without budget restraints or other cases clouding the horizon and had already secured a room at the university which would act as the cold case office.

'Home m'lady?' asked the cabbie when Maxie was comfortably settled into the back seat.

'Actually I need to shop first,' she said. 'I have to cook for someone tonight.'

'Hot date eh?'

'Not quite,' Maxie said, smiling. 'But he needs feeding – I've promised. Although I have no idea what on earth I'm going to make.'

Her driver told her he had the perfect solution and drove her to an upmarket grocery store and accompanied her inside. 'See?' he said. 'Valentine's meals for two – not much cooking and even the wine's thrown in on the deal. It's what I'm doing for the missus tonight.'

Maxie gave him an appreciative nod as they each loaded baskets with steak, salad, triple-cooked chips, dessert and wine for the very reasonable fixed price. As they took them through the checkout Maxie couldn't help but find it amusing that her driver would be lighting candles or putting on soft music with his steak whereas she'd be studying old police reports over the same meal. Job done, they reached Maxie's flat and she gave him an extra tip for saving her a huge amount of time and mental angst with the food. The driver returned her thanks with a "no problem" salute.

Maxie had a hot shower and changed into comfortable clothes for the evening ahead. Alone in her flat she felt strong, emboldened. Things had fallen into place today and although they might not be big things it was enough to believe that the universe might just be on her side.

She took a quick glimpse at her work emails on her phone and saw that she had three considered proposals from students who wanted to work on the cold case. Maxie had to force herself not to read them now – they were for Monday. She distracted herself and used up some of the nervous energy she felt by scrubbing the flat then setting out her factsheets on each of Susan's old friends in neat piles across the dining table. They could eat at the breakfast bar as they needed this bigger space to spread things out and try to spot connections.

The doorbell rang and Andrew announced himself through the intercom. Maxie buzzed him in and bit her lip anxiously as she stood in the doorway waiting for him. Andrew turned the corner, carrying a box which Maxie recognised as coming from the archives. She stepped back to let him in and directed him to put the box by the table.

'Is there just the one?' asked Maxie more in hope than expectation.

Andrew looked directly at her and nodded slowly before opening the lid. Maxie took a step forward to look at the contents and her heart sank. The detective really hadn't needed a box to carry the meagre contents. Maxie picked out half a dozen foolscap files each of which was at most a couple of inches thick.

'I don't know what I was expecting,' she said trying to keep her voice more steady than it felt. 'I always thought the investigation was superficial. Susan's death wasn't important to them.'

'I don't know what to say,' he said, squeezing her arm. 'There doesn't seem to have been many leads but we might find something new now.'

Maxie swallowed back a flood of emotions that were threatening to take over. She put the files back in the box and told Andrew that he was right and that the evidence would be ten times that size by the time they'd finished.

'But first,' she said, speaking loudly and brightly in an attempt to conjure up the strength she'd felt earlier. 'I want to thank you for bringing the case notes round and as your reward I will now assemble the very best in Valentine's Day supermarket meal deals.'

Maxie busied herself putting together the food, refusing any offers of help from Andrew. 'Honestly,' she said. 'I can stretch to shaking a salad out of a bag.'

She put him in charge of wine as she crashed together baking trays and serving dishes in an attempt to busy herself so much that she could ignore the weight of disappointment that was in danger of settling on her and ruining the evening. She'd always believed that old expression "fake it till you make it" had a lot going for it. She noticed that Andrew was being almost conspicuously quiet; he was looking through the factsheets that she'd drafted and nodding to himself quietly. When she saw him read the same sheet for the third time, Maxie knew he was picking up on her mood and that she had to break the ice.

'The good thing,' she said more cheerfully than she felt, 'is that we have somewhere to start. Even the very slim case folders are more than I had a few days ago.'

'And these factsheets are pretty comprehensive for an internet search,' added Andrew. 'But then I don't know why that should surprise me.'

He got up and brought a glass of wine over to Maxie. 'To answers,' he said as they clinked their glasses together.

The food worked wonders and as she ate, Maxie imagined the endorphins firing off in her brain as the fats and sugar entered her body. A smaller meal certainly couldn't have coped with that evidence box. Rather than dive straight into what was or wasn't in it, Maxie told Andrew about the podcast and the student help.

'You've assembled a cast of thousands.' Andrew skewered a fat golden chip with his fork and closed his eyes in pleasure as he ate it. 'These are very good.'

'And other people's always taste better.' Maxie smiled and pinched a chip from his plate. She got a rap on the fingers with the back of his spoon but the mood had lightened.

'I felt that I needed to involve others,' explained Maxie. 'I'm too close and to be honest, beyond the prefect gang I'm not sure I know where to start.'

'Your cold case resource will be a great help,' said Andrew. 'Do you know who you're getting yet?'

'Not yet,' she said. 'Shall we have coffee and start looking over everything? I don't think more wine will help.'

Maxie could feel her heart starting to pound with anticipation as she stood clearing the dishes and making the coffee. She turned from the sink and watched as Andrew opened the case notes and started laying out the contents in neat piles on the dining table. Maxie swallowed hard as he pulled out the crime scene photos knowing that there'd be one of her sister lying at the bottom of the stairs. Maxie watched as Andrew put this pile of evidence furthest from the chairs they'd be sitting in and turned the top picture face down. She couldn't help but feel a surge of warmth towards him knowing he was doing all he could to protect her. It was a long time since a man had been so considerate. She walked over with the coffees and put them down on the table.

'Thank you,' she said. 'But I have to look at them some time.' Maxie reached out to turn the picture over. Andrew grabbed her wrist.

'Some time,' he said. 'But not necessarily now – it makes more sense to start with the statements anyway.'

Maxie nodded and sat down beside him. It was only a brief reprieve as there were very few statements. The incident had taken place in the middle of the night so the neighbours' statement "we were asleep and didn't hear anything" was as useful as the officer at scene report: "the body had been moved and scene of death disturbed". Maxie's mouth fell open as she read these words. This is why she'd always blamed herself for the crime not being investigated more thoroughly.

'Why does it say that?' asked Andrew.

'I walked into the house.' Maxie almost choked through a throat as dry as a chalk duster. 'And saw Susan on the floor. I remember being confused – her being dead wasn't the first thing that came to mind. I didn't know what she was doing lying there. I shook her but she just wouldn't get up ...'

Andrew got up and brought back a glass of water which Maxie sipped at.

'I still didn't realise she was dead. I thought she'd fainted so I lifted her head into my lap and kept telling her to wake up but she wouldn't. I remembered that smelling salts worked but didn't have any so got perfume out of my bag and sprayed so much around her nose. I was desperate. I was eighteen and just back from a night out. Things like this aren't supposed to happen.'

Maxie realised that tears were falling down her cheeks – she wiped her face with her hands and took another sip of water. 'I scrunched up my coat and lay her head on it then rang an ambulance. They sent a police car too and it was only when my house was surrounded by all the flashing blue lights that it sunk in.' Maxie fell silent for a moment remembering that night.

‘I’d watched so many detective shows that I thought I’d know how to react and how it would feel. People scream and wail when they find someone but I didn’t. It was like an out-of-body experience – I tried everything to wake her up but she’d already gone.’

Andrew reached out and squeezed her hand.

‘I jeopardised that crime scene,’ continued Maxie. ‘All these years I’ve been blaming the police but I know it was my fault. They couldn’t have done a proper investigation with the mess I’d made of the scene.’

Maxie dropped her head into her hands. A hideous cocktail of shame and anger tore at her heart and she felt her jaw set hard. How could she have been so stupid all those years ago?

‘Stop it right now,’ ordered Andrew. He tried to take a hand from her face but she pulled away. ‘You’ve said it yourself so many times. Cop shows aren’t real life, people don’t react according to some script. And sometimes investigation teams are sloppy. I don’t know if they were here but we’ll find out.’

His words pulled her back slightly from the emotional cliff edge.

‘You were still a kid really, high on life and cheap cider,’ said Andrew getting a small snort of laughter from Maxie. ‘Now you are Professor Reddick – you have much more expensive taste in alcohol and if anyone can solve this then it’s you. Are you ready?’

Maxie nodded at him and, pulling a handkerchief from her pocket, wiped her eyes and blew her nose loudly causing them both to laugh and come back to the moment.

‘Okay then,’ said Andrew. ‘We know that the witness statements weren’t a lot of help. Let’s take a look at the other evidence collected – we obviously know some prints were collected, most of which were never identified but let’s go over who was definitely there …’

‘No,’ said Maxie firmly but gently stopping the detective mid-sentence. ‘While you’re here I’d rather get the worst bit over with – I need to look at the photographs of her body now.’

Chapter Fourteen

The images were imprinted on her mind as she said goodbye to Andrew, as she tossed and turned in bed, as she sleep-walked through the rest of the weekend, as she'd been driven to the university and now as she sifted through the applications to join the cold case team. Maxie had to stop dwelling on them as they were only reinforcing her own memories of that night and she needed to see them with fresh eyes. The professor needed to gather her team.

She wanted to keep the numbers very small and to ensure the students weren't committing themselves to extra-curricular work, they'd had to develop a research proposal by which participation in the investigation would also satisfy the requirements of their end of year dissertation. There were a couple that really interested her – one student, Joseph, had developed an idea around pre-digital investigations and how so many cold cases might have been solved quickly with today's technology. The student who'd put his hand up during the lecture – Sonny, had taken up the strand of police resources and how budgetary constraints were at the heart of a number of unsolved crimes. He would look into tests that weren't ordered or leads that weren't followed up because of cost. Remembering that the whole force was consumed with the child-killer case, Maxie knew he'd find evidence of this but equally knew that there was little that could be done about that now. Her final selection – Belle, had proposed a theme that would be personally challenging to Maxie; familial bias and its impact on investigations. As a student, Belle frequently questioned assumptions made – although Maxie had often thought she just enjoyed being argumentative – and this would be useful to the team. Just talking to Andrew last night, she had realised how hazy her view of the past had been.

Maxie emailed each of them, congratulating them on their ideas and announcing that they'd been selected to join her. She suggested that they have a quick meeting later that day to agree on how they'd work together. She added that her ideal would be a regular Tuesday meet-up which would give her time to collate and check their findings in preparation for the podcast recording.

Maxie was buzzing with a nervous energy but couldn't forget that she also had a job to do and a duty to the other students. Consciously closing down everything to do with the cold case, she stretched her face wide and walked away from her desk ready to teach her first year students about the crime myths and realities. Maxie always opened this module with a series of provocative questions which would get the students thinking and fortunately for today, would keep her mind away from Susan. After a detour to the bathroom and a fresh application of lipstick, she was ready.

A hush followed her entry into the lecture hall as she walked to the front and asked, 'How does the media inform our perception of crime? And if it didn't exist what would our criminal justice system look like?'

The hour that followed was lively and a great distraction for Maxie. These first year students were extremely promising but equally very serious about their subject. She had often though that the increasing intensity of each fresher year seemed to correlate directly with the rising costs of study and wished she could do more to support them. She truly believed that encouraging the students to debate and think for themselves enabled them to learn collectively and was less pressurised than spending days with their heads stuck in online searches or academic journals – although this had to be done too. Nevertheless, watching her students leave the lecture hall still debating the topic was extremely satisfying. They'd probably still be debating this over a drink later and so it would stick in their heads for longer than a traditional lecture would.

Maxie pulled together her notes and was stuffing them into her bag when she heard the sound of steps approaching. She looked up and saw Joseph, Sonny and Belle – her three cold case students. The boys stood slightly awkwardly behind the confident figure of Belle who wore a big smile on her face. 'We just wanted to say that we're delighted that you chose us,' she said turning to the boys who grunted a "yeah".

'And we won't let you down,' added Joseph.

Maxie looked at the keen young faces and felt a warm glow of gratitude spread through her body. She was glad to have them on board but she had to keep this professional – if this came to nothing, they couldn't feel responsible and they had to use all they found for those dissertations.

'Thank you,' she replied in a business-like tone. 'I think you're going to find this a fascinating area of study. Shall we get started?'

The students were as outraged by the extent of the original investigation as she had been. Maxie explained the seriousness of the crime that had taken all police resources during that month but she was pleased to see that it didn't placate them either.

'I can see how everyone would be out searching for the children but it's like they didn't even try with your sister,' said Sonny. 'It was still a murder case but I'm guessing people didn't sue police forces way back then.'

Hearing the words "way back then" startled Maxie slightly; despite everything, she still didn't think of this as a historical case. It felt like yesterday to her but to her students it was rightly a step back in time – "the olden days". The words formed in her mind and she smiled slightly before responding simply, 'I don't think it was as prevalent.'

'I'd like to talk to your old neighbours,' said Joseph. 'I want to get a feel for how they saw your family and whether they thought the questioning was robust.'

'That would be a really good place to start,' added Belle. 'And now that so many years have passed, they may be more willing to dish any dirt.'

'I don't think there was any dirt,' Maxie said, too quickly and too defensively.

'Yes but that's because you currently filter memories of the incident and are therefore the source of familial bias in this cold case,' said Belle quoting some of her own lectures back at her.

Maxie held her palms up in surrender. 'You're right,' she said. 'I need to let you do the work. I'm not sure how much you'll get out of them but as I mentioned, they still live in the same house so finding them isn't an issue.'

'Let's all go,' said Joseph. 'We can see the house, check the access routes and compare them to historical records then interview the neighbours and be ready with a "setting the scene" report for the first podcast.'

'If they'll agree then we can record the interview and play it out so listeners can hear their words directly,' Belle said. 'It'll be straight from the horses' mouth, unfiltered and without interpretation.'

'I'll do some video for the social media channels,' said Sonny. 'Maybe use a sepia filter so it takes people back in time.'

'We did have colour TV back then you know.' Maxie laughed but was feeling rather like an ancient relic. 'Oh and we'd invented the internet too.'

The students either didn't get the sarcasm or were ignoring it. They busied themselves consulting their schedules and arranging a time to get on with this first task. Maxie could see that they were excited and enthused so knew in that moment that even if they found insight that she'd rather have left buried, this was the right thing to do.

However, their focus did make her feel like a bit of a spare part in her own investigation. The three young people would certainly get more from her old neighbours than she would so it was absolutely right to let them get on with it. She'd scoured the case notes so didn't need to study them again and had to wait until Andrew had finished with all the attendees of the leaving do before approaching them with her own questions. Who could she talk to that her students couldn't? Of course – the police force. She could find the original investigating officers and fudge permission to question them. After all, the review of the case had been sanctioned so surely that included the officers themselves. She'd just have to be on her very best behaviour to avoid calling into question any of their efforts.

Maxie didn't need to look up their names; DC Will Hardcastle – who had been the Senior Investigating Officer and new recruit WPC Jean Carruthers were etched on her brain. She couldn't remember much else about them but knew a woman who would – the DCI's secretary had been around the force for decades and had the best network in the county. Sure enough, with a phone call Maxie established that Will had emigrated and was now a politician in Canada while Jean had also left the force when she'd had a family but had returned to work on cold cases as a civilian.

'She's actually been assigned to you,' said the DCI's secretary. 'Hadn't you heard?'

Maxie felt a wave of dismay as she replied that she hadn't. Why would the DCI assign someone who'd failed the first time around?

She began to remember the DC in a little more detail. Her sister's case hadn't been closed because of some fuddy-duddy old copper close to retirement as is often portrayed on TV. No, Will Hardcastle was young and very ambitious – fresh from his policing degree, he wanted to make his mark and that certainly wasn't going to happen with a case that might turn out to be a domestic accident. He wanted to be the one to find that third child. And find her alive.

Memories are strange constructs and they can so often be fake so whether Maxie remembered this or was simply now inventing it, she didn't know but in her mind Hardcastle had turned to Carruthers and said,

'No offence, but we aren't going to make a difference here are we?' She could envisage the WPC scurrying out after her boss but this again, might just be her imagination. There was only one way to find out.

Jean Carruthers called shortly afterwards and they arranged to meet in the university break room. Jean looked slightly uncomfortable as Maxie approached with hand outstretched, but still she shook it then sat down opposite with her elbows on the table looking down at her hands. Maxie looked at her but the woman in front of her bore very little resemblance to the WPC she remembered.

'Thank you for doing this,' said Maxie, keeping her voice as steady as she was able. 'I'm really grateful for your help.'

Jean looked directly at her. 'I'm sorry,' she said. 'I'm sorry that we didn't get him the first time around and I'm sorry that we failed you. I will do everything I can to remedy that now.'

Maxie was taken aback by the gentleness and sincerity of the woman's words. 'It was a difficult time,' she replied. 'The force had a lot on and you had to follow orders.'

'Even so, we should have been there for you. I was never happy where things were left – you were both just teenagers and you were distraught, all alone in that house. We should have done more.'

'You remember us?' asked Maxie, surprised to hear someone else reliving the moment.

'Oh I'll never forget you and your poor sister – it was the first death I ever attended,' Jean said. 'I really won't fail you this time, so shall we get started?'

Chapter Fifteen

Jean got straight to work and the next day was questioned by the cold case team during their lunch hour.

'Why weren't more people fingerprinted and eliminated from the investigation?' asked Sonny almost as if he was acting for the prosecution. 'Nothing seems to have been followed up – it looks as if you just ignored a whole load of evidence sitting right in front of you. Was there a budget limit set for this case?'

Jean's eyes opened wide at the tone of this first question and Maxie had to remind everyone that she was part of their team – she could explain the investigation that took place at the time but should not be barraged with criticism. 'Until you have been in the same situations as Mrs Carruthers,' said Maxie, 'you cannot know how you would respond or what you might do differently. It was a different era and it's not like TV as I keep telling you all.'

The team seemed to take their rebuff and Maxie noted three sets of shoulders relax back. Jean cleared her throat and spoke. 'You're right in that we collected a lot of fingerprints at the house and there were probably more that we could have collected,' she said. 'The problem was that there were too many. Do you remember why Maxine?'

The professor found it strange to hear someone use the name Maxine rather than Maxie – her parents were the only people who did that nowadays. She nodded ruefully. 'We had a party.'

'So there we were with practically all of our forensic resource focussing on the murder and abduction of the three children – and trust me that case was absolutely horrific,' continued Jean. 'If I'd been in charge and had to make the choice to put all our resources into finding that final child, I'd do it and I'd do the same now. I'd like to bet that you all would too.'

The team went quiet and Jean continued. 'Then we get a call to say there'd been an accident at a house – a young woman is dead. We arrive to find the door open and initially it looks like a fall. The body has been moved, the house looks ransacked and then we begin to believe it's a burglary gone wrong. The crime scene examiners try to take prints but then we learn that two teenage girls had a party and we do our best but it would have taken an army to collect all the fingerprints around the place and getting a prosecution from a crime scene like that would have been near impossible.'

The student team give their professor an amused look and Maxie knew this was the first time they'd ever considered that she might have been their age at any point in her life.

'Maxine couldn't give us the names of all her sister's friends but my boss at the time said that as they would most likely have been college kids at the party, we probably wouldn't have had any matches on the database anyway. And that's how it worked out – we couldn't find matches to anything so logged the prints that we had as unidentified. Plus, there was a very narrow window for any crime to have taken place and no witnesses that saw anyone at the house on the actual night of Susan's death,' said Jean. 'The neighbours certainly didn't see anyone that night.'

'We're talking to them tomorrow,' said Joseph. 'I'll check that's still what they remember.'

'We know Professor Reddick moved her sister's body,' said Sonny. 'Can you tell us anything more about that?'

'An open question,' replied Jean. 'Good technique.'

Maxie noticed Sonny trying to suppress a slight smile of pride. Jean looked up at her, her eyebrows raised in question and Maxie nodded that she could continue.

'When we arrived,' said Jean, 'a teenage Maxine was sitting on the floor with her sister's head in her lap. She was frantically trying to revive her but of course, Susan had already gone.'

A moment of silence fell until Sonny spoke again. 'And because she was moved, you cannot tell how she fell?'

'We knew a little,' Jean said. 'The cause of death was a blunt force trauma conducive to having fallen and hitting the head on a step. The coroner said it was likely that she'd been pushed but not conclusive.'

Sonny considered these words and turned to Maxie asking, 'Professor, can you remember the moment you walked in on the scene?'

Maxie was startled at the question and replied that of course she could – she would never forget it.

'Then if Belle were to lie down on the floor,' continued Sonny, 'can you pose her body in the same position as your sister's was when you found her?'

The students had been taught to try and replicate or re-enact scenes to better understand an environment or motivation but Maxie had never had this technique turned back on herself. She didn't need to ask why she'd never thought to do it with regard to Susan as she knew the answer – she was afraid that she'd find something else that she was to blame for. Some other way in which she'd failed her sister. Her students wouldn't let this pass though and it was time to find out. She took a deep breath and on the exhale nodded.

Maxie needed a set of steps to be able to visualise it all properly so the group headed towards the main hall where a small flight of stairs led to a stage. Using chalk that they'd brought, the students marked off the shape of the hallway where Susan had been found.

'When I walked in,' said Jean, 'you were kneeling just here, adjacent to the bottom of the stairs and your sister's head was on your lap.'

Maxie closed her eyes and let the scene come flooding back. Then she got into the position and Belle lay on the floor with her head on Maxie's thigh – it all felt extremely uncomfortable so Maxie checked that the young student was okay to continue and she told her she was. With a few adjustments, they recreated the position as well as Jean could remember it.

'So how did you actually find your sister?' asked Sonny.

Maxie directed Belle to lie in the position that she'd visualised. Her sister was lying on her back with her head near the bottom step and her body was straight out in front of her with her arms by her side like a corpse.

'Are you sure this is it?' asked Joseph taking photographs from all angles.

'I am,' replied Maxie aware of what everyone could see quite clearly.

'There's no way a person could end up in this position from just falling down the stairs,' Joseph said. 'If Belle had tumbled down head first then she would probably be face down but her arms would be beneath her or stretched out in front as she'd automatically tried to break her fall.'

'Why was there any view that she'd simply fallen?' Sonny asked Jean.

'She was wearing a dressing gown with a long belt,' came the reply. 'The assumption was that she'd slipped on it and slid heavily on her back, banging her head against the stairs.'

'In that instance,' continued Sonny, 'she'd have reached out to grab the handrail or baluster. Her arm would be behind her and she might have broken a fingernail as she'd reached out and missed.'

There was a silence as the group considered what would have been very evident at the time if only the young Maxie had been asked these questions back then.

'Susan was moved before I even got home wasn't she?' said Maxie.

There was a quiet collective nod.

While the students became animated looking through the crime photos with fresh insight, Maxie stood to one side, lost in her own thoughts.

'What are you thinking?' asked Jean.

'I'm not even sure,' Maxie said after a pause. She pressed her hand to her stomach. 'I'm just churning inside – a melange of everything and nothing – fury, despair, self-hatred? And I feel utterly stupid. I blame everyone else for failing Susan and call myself an expert yet I didn't even see this?'

'You were eighteen years old,' said Jean placing a hand on Maxie's arm. 'That feels like adulthood when you're that age but it's really not. You'd been having the time of your life and came home to this. I should have been the one to ask you the very question that your student did.'

'But you were wet behind the ears and your boss wanted to get off this case as soon as he could,' murmured Maxie. 'We all let her down.'

'We won't this time.'

'Thank you,' said Maxie. 'That means a lot but I'm not sure we'll have much to work with.'

The students were packing up their notes when the two women went back to the group. They certainly didn't appear to have been struck with the sense of hopelessness that Maxie had. 'Where are you off to?' she asked.

'Well as Mrs Carruthers said, there's a very precise timeline here,' Joseph said. 'So we're going to try and get a few details about the hour in question – between you calling your sister and you returning home.'

'What sort of details?' asked Jean.

'The weather that night, the bus timetables, any news apart from the missing children, what was on TV as there was no streaming back then – anything that might prompt you to know what you were doing at that moment.'

Maxie had gone down that route when she'd made her own teenage investigations but they hadn't helped. However, she had to let the students run things as they felt appropriate and there was always the chance they'd hit on something else that she hadn't. They left with Jean as Maxie had to get back to work and attend a compulsory faculty meeting.

Maxie didn't hear a word of the debate in that meeting and was dragged from a blur of thoughts by the Dean checking she was happy with an action point she'd been assigned.

'Professor Reddick,' he said, 'I'm not sure where your head is but it doesn't seem to be with the rest of us. Can I leave the open day organisation to you?'

Maxie blinked herself awake and realised she'd been completely stitched up by the rest of the staff. Everyone hated organising the open day but as she'd been distracted during the conversation, she had no choice so simply nodded. With the meeting closed, she walked slowly back to her office, her ankle aching as she pressed down on it. Maxie actually felt glad to be feeling something because the rest of her was numb.

Back at her desk, she pulled up the schedule from the previous year's open day as it had gone smoothly and there was no point in reinventing the wheel. She changed the date at the top and updated the staff list then forwarded it to the Dean suggesting they keep it simple.

Her phone rang: it was Andrew. Maxie felt a surge of adrenaline as he was exactly the person she needed to talk to right now. Jean seemed very keen but Maxie needed someone who knew her well, someone who knew how she worked and thought. 'Am I glad to hear from you,' she said, stabbing at the "accept call" button.

'I'm not sure you will be when you've heard my news,' he said.

'Go on.'

'We've had confirmation that the fire was started on purpose. Fiona tripped over as she was trying to get out of the cupboard and knocked herself out – that's why she was still in there.'

'Oh no.' Maxie felt her heart sink to the pit of her stomach. 'Poor woman, she wouldn't have stood a chance if the fire hadn't been discovered quickly.'

'She wouldn't,' Andrew agreed. 'I don't suppose you've heard from Rebecca have you?'

Maxie said that she hadn't. 'I'm guessing she's under suspicion for this?'

‘We certainly need to talk to her,’ he said. ‘She leaves the room just before the fire and has been missing ever since. She hasn’t turned up at work this morning so I’m making finding her a priority.’

‘I just hope she’s okay.’

Maxie thought back to the moment that Fiona had left the party after telling everyone about the photo she’d found. Rebecca had followed her out but so had Mike Priestly. She reminded Andrew of this but he was already on the case.

‘I hope you haven’t prodded a hornet’s nest with your cold case,’ he said. ‘But just in case, promise me you’ll take care.’

Chapter Sixteen

'So they still haven't a clue where she is a week after Mike's leaving do?' asked Joseph.

'That puts the suspicion on Rebecca for the fire and Susan's death then,' continued Sonny. 'She was at the party in 1995 and it wouldn't have looked strange if she'd come back later on the Saturday to see Susan. Hers could be one of the unidentified prints and might be the one on the cricket bat. Did you ever think she could have killed your sister?'

The team were gathered in the studio waiting room ahead of recording that week's podcast. Maxie considered her student's question but in all honesty she didn't believe that Rebecca would hurt Susan. During the conversation in the bar, Rebecca hadn't been all that forthcoming and had almost warned her that some things should stay in the past. But she was sure that Rebecca had loved her sister, that their friendship had been genuine. She'd said they were Bodie and Doyle – maybe Rebecca was missing because she'd started her own investigation? Had she found the person who caused Susan's death and confronted him? While everyone else seemed to believe that Rebecca had fled the scene, Maxie was more and more concerned that something might have happened to her.

Andrew had said that the blow from the cricket bat hadn't killed George Fairview, it had been the subsequent fall when he'd hit his head. So it wouldn't have needed that much strength and could have been a woman. Had Rebecca lashed out at him making George swerve backwards to try and avoid the swing? But if so, how did she know him and what about the fire? Whatever the truth, Rebecca knew some of it and had to be found.

'I don't think she could have hurt Susan,' Maxie eventually replied to Sonny. 'But it's too big a coincidence and you know what Agatha Christie would have to say about that – *any coincidence is worth noticing. You can throw it away later if it is only a coincidence*.'

'So we need to know more about the man that died at the care home and find out if he knew Rebecca, ' said Belle. 'What was his name?'

'George Fairview,' replied Maxie. 'And yes, I think it is valid for our cold case to try and see if he had a connection with Susan's best friend.'

The doors to the studio swung open and Maxie's childhood neighbours walked in looking like slightly greyer versions of the people she used to know. Her parents primarily referred to them as “the young couple next door” as they’d been in their mid-twenties when they first bought the house.

‘Mr and Mrs Kennedy, thank you for coming.’ Belle stretched out a hand to greet them and walked them towards the recording studio. The studio would be overcrowded with everyone piled in so Maxie and the male members of the cold case team would be sitting outside with the producers, giving Craig, Belle and the Kennedys space to feel comfortable. Maxie had also been slightly wary of the boys blurting out questions that would sound accusatory as they had done with Jean.

As Maxie watched them getting ready through the studio window, she noticed how comfortable Belle looked in what would ordinarily have been her seat. Maxie smiled at the thought that her legacy might go on and the warmth of it slowly spreading through her body gave her a little boost of hope. The recording light went on; it was time to begin.

‘Welcome to the first podcast in our new cold case series – *My Sister’s Killer*,’ said Craig. ‘Throughout the series we will be shining a light on the death of Susan Reddick back in 1995. We’ll be presenting the evidence and asking – what actually happened? Do you know something? Because believe me, someone does know.

‘I’m joined today by Belle Bailey who is one of Professor Reddick’s most promising criminology students and by our first expert witnesses – Mr and Mrs Kennedy – who were the victim’s neighbours at the time of her death. I’d like to welcome you all.’

The three people nodded and got a prompt from Craig reminding them to speak. They quickly thanked him and said they were pleased to be able to help out. ‘Although I’m not sure how much help we can be,’ added Mrs Kennedy. ‘It was so long ago.’

‘Let’s begin with you moving in,’ said Craig. ‘What year did you arrive and what were your first impressions of the Reddicks?’

‘We moved in late 1992 – the November and they seemed very nice,’ replied Mr Kennedy. ‘The husband had a new car – a gorgeous Peugeot which was a fabulous car at the time and he was always out there cleaning it.’

Maxie gave a little laugh remembering her father’s pride and joy. They weren’t allowed to eat anything in it and the one time she’d snuck a Malteser chocolate had been the time that she’d dropped it and it had melted on the seat.

‘And I remember thinking – “oh good, two teenage girls – that’ll come in handy for babysitting” – our Daniel was just coming up to his fifth birthday,’ added Mrs Kennedy.

‘And did either girl babysit for you?’ asked Belle.

‘Yes – when the oldest one was sixteen, Mrs Reddick suggested it. She told us Susan was very sensible and that as she was only next door, she could look in every now and then.’

‘It was a godsend,’ added Mr Kennedy. ‘Susan was totally reliable and if we ever wanted to stay out a bit later, we’d just call up and she’d been fine with it. We always slipped her a little more money those times.’

‘Oh she was very enterprising,’ continued Mrs Kennedy. ‘She was very keen on making her own money – I think she was saving to get a place of her own when she’d finished her studies. She had a few irons in the fire. She said she wanted to be a teacher but I always thought she’d turn out to be a famous business woman – the female equivalent of Richard Branson.’

Maxie listened as they spoke and remembered the babysitting but hadn’t ever thought of her sister as some entrepreneur. Then she remembered a detail and muttered the words almost simultaneously with Mrs Kennedy, ‘She had an Avon round.’

‘Well it wasn’t exactly hers,’ added Maxie’s old neighbour. ‘I think her friend’s mum had the official round and gave them some of the commission for anything they sold to their college friends.’

‘Sounds like a lot of work for not a lot,’ said Belle.

‘Well you have to remember that we couldn’t just go on that TikTok or sell our old stuff on eBay back then – we had to work,’ replied Mr Kennedy rather aggressively making Belle look rather uncomfortable. ‘Lots of teenagers had a few jobs – shop work, babysitting and waitressing.’

‘Plus helping out with the Avon round, Susan got a lot of free make-up samples,’ said Mrs Kennedy smiling at Belle and getting a small smile back from her.

‘What about the younger sister?’ asked Craig giving Maxie a sneaky wink through the studio window.

‘Oh she was almost the complete opposite,’ said Mr Kennedy. ‘A bit of a wild child – they say the youngest is always the one who gets the most freedom don’t they? Well Maxine as we knew her then was certainly the one who gave her parents the run around.’

‘It’s quite amazing that she turned out to be a professor isn’t it?’ Mrs Kennedy was talking to her husband but he gave her a nudge and nodded at the window where Maxie simply shrugged.

‘Oh, I’m sorry, I didn’t mean …’ Mrs Kennedy looked embarrassed but Craig just laughed and told them not to worry and that they would edit that out.

‘Can we move on to the night in question?’ asked Belle. ‘Do you have any memories of that night?’

Mr Kennedy cleared his throat and then his wife reached into her bag and pulled out a notebook. He explained that when they knew the case was being reopened and they were coming onto the show, they spent some time trying to remember what had happened all those years ago.

‘Although you never know just how important any day of your life is going to be until it’s too late do you?’ said Mrs Kennedy.

Those words softly spoken hit Maxie hard. She dipped her head and closed her eyes as she listened to their recollection of that Saturday night.

‘The parents had gone away for a long weekend and on the Friday night the girls had decided to have a party,’ began Mr Kennedy. ‘Susan had come round earlier to say that they were having a few friends around and that there might be some noise.’

‘We weren’t that old back then and still remembered having our own parties so we were okay with it weren’t we?’ said Mrs Kennedy. ‘And we trusted Susan.’

‘But it got out of hand pretty quickly,’ continued her husband. ‘Bikers started roaring up the street and people they didn’t know were at the door demanding to come in. We were looking out of the window and could see that Susan was struggling to get rid of them.’

‘So what did you do?’ asked Craig.

‘Well I’m not Mr Universe,’ said Mr Kennedy pulling his shoulders back and looking pretty pleased with himself. ‘But brains can beat brawn. I pretended I was her dad and went out there saying “Cooee, I’m back. Shall I put some tea on for your friends?” I turned down the pop music and put on some classical then they all seemed to get the message – that the party was over.’

‘He got the classical music idea from a news article,’ added Mrs Kennedy.

‘Brilliant,’ replied Craig. ‘And everyone just left peacefully?’

‘Well there was one chap who seemed very angry wasn’t there?’ said the husband. ‘I remember him telling me my daughter – he obviously meant Susan – owed him. To be honest I didn’t take much notice, I was glad to see the back of them all. I avoid confrontation if I can.’

‘Susan owed him?’ Belle jumped on the snippet immediately and Maxie opened her eyes. ‘Do you think she owed him money?’

‘I honestly don’t know. It could have been that she owed him a night out – she’d promised a party and he didn’t get one.’

Maxie watched her old neighbours’ facial expressions and it was clear that they hadn’t really seen these words as either a threat or important.

‘Did you mention any of this to the police in the original investigation?’ asked Craig.

‘Of course,’ Mrs Kennedy said. ‘We told them there had been a party and some uninvited guests turned up but we saw them off pretty quickly.’

‘They were all just kids really,’ added Mr Kennedy. ‘You must remember turning up at someone’s house because you’d been told there was a party when you were younger – I certainly do.’

‘And they might have been acting all tough, but you could tell they were just local teenagers,’ said Mrs Kennedy. ‘Although I think a couple of them were from Brookfield.’

Maxie held back a little snort. She remembered their old Neighbourhood Watch had their entire village terrified of the council estate that bordered the back of the high street. That’s where the criminals lived, not in respectable Barwick. It was laughable but nothing had changed. She knew you could look at any community Facebook page and see residents reporting that they’d seen a youth from “across the way” wherever that invisible line was. Pure snobbery dressed up as neighbourly concern. Now Maxie had to wonder whether a fact had remained unreported for all these years simply because her neighbours had decided that “one of their own” couldn’t possibly have done anything wrong.

‘I’m guessing your neighbours don’t know that Ted Bundy went to Washington University,’ mocked Joseph after the Kennedys had left the studio. ‘Or that Lord Lucan didn’t live in social housing.’

Maxie signalled him to be quiet although she completely empathised with what he was saying – working-class injustice was as prevalent as racial bias in many areas. Nevertheless, her neighbours were no different from many and they’d taken time to come here and help. They had certainly added to her personal memories of that weekend; she’d been in her bedroom on her own during the latter stages of the party so hadn't known why it ended. She'd remembered her and Susan buying the Kennedys a box of chocolates as an apology for the noise but she hadn't known about this boy. If Mrs Kennedy hadn't thought he was from Brookfield then he might have gone to their school and Maxie might even have a photo of him. They might be able to ID him, but that was for tomorrow. Right now, Maxie would go home and wait for the podcast to air. She'd listen to everything they'd recorded objectively and see if anything else leapt out at her. She'd ask her students to do the same.

The mobile phone rang with a "number unknown".

'Hello?' The reply for the sales call or a very distant relative, was cautious.

'Have you heard what she's doing?' The caller didn't announce themselves but the voice was familiar. It took a moment but then the memory returned.

'Oh it's you; you must have a new number. Is something up?' The light tone of voice was entirely faked but conflict was to be avoided at all costs.

'Listen to her podcast,' came the reply. It was an order not a suggestion. 'She's stirring it up and is asking everyone who remembers that night to speak up.'

'Who's stirring it up?'

'The sister of course.' The scream at the other end of the line was angry and impatient. 'Professor Bloody Reddick – or Maxine as she was called back then. She's going to cause trouble – I know it.'

'But it's just a podcast – does anyone really listen to them? I certainly haven't.'

The voice at the other end blew out a loud exasperated sigh. 'Get with the programme, thousands listen to them. Then there's social media and all that crap – and watch what you say on your accounts or at the very least make them private.'

'I'm sure it'll blow over – and I had absolutely nothing to do with that night.'

'Woah – don't give me that, you were every bit as involved and if I need to I will make sure everyone knows. Now what are you going to do about this?'

'Okay, okay – I'll take a listen and see what I can do.'

‘Good – because I’m telling you, you need to sort her out.’

Chapter Seventeen

The following morning Maxie visited Rebecca's parents. The police had already been and from what Jean had told her, Maxie could imagine the couple were now terrified that their daughter had done something terrible. Mr Henderson was still a very robust-looking man but Rebecca's mother looked as if she'd been made frail by the very thought of whatever their daughter might be involved in. She wanted to talk to Maxie and make her see that Rebecca couldn't have been part of all these crimes.

Mrs Henderson held Maxie's hand tightly as she reminisced about the girls as teenagers as if not wanting to let go of more innocent times. Although the father looked reticent, the mother eagerly handed Maxie the keys to Rebecca's flat and pleaded simply that Maxie help find Rebecca and ask her to come home.

'I'll do my very best,' she promised as she was leaving their home. 'And please call me if you hear from her or need any support whatsoever.'

Leaving the distressingly stale air of the Henderson house she walked the length of their garden and onto the street. Maxie watched an old man posting letters and a dog walker struggling to get her pooch to sit at the end of the kerb. She couldn't help but contemplate how the world just kept turning even when a little corner of it had stopped completely.

Maxie had taken her usual cab to the Hendersons' but for the rest of the journey Sonny was picking her up. Having given him a quick call to say she was ready, Maxie walked to a small parade of shops where it would be easy for him to pull in. Her ankle was feeling much better after only a week of the exercises so Maxie knew it was probably time to get back to swimming and trying to regain her fitness. But standing here having witnessed so many deaths in her time, getting fit for a long life seemed utterly futile. You simply never knew when your time was up. The blast of a car horn shook her from her thoughts and Sonny waved at her from the window as he parked.

'This is very nice,' she said, looking at the neat electric car that Sonny was proudly showing off. 'I don't know why I was expecting some beaten-up wreck – that's what we used to have at university.'

'It's a present from my parents obviously,' her student replied. 'They said it would be cheaper in the end – no petrol, tax or breakdown bills.'

'That's probably very true. When I was an undergraduate I was always having my old car towed to a dodgy garage and getting the minimum possible fixed. It was probably a complete death trap – always had smoke of one colour or the other streaming out of the exhaust pipe.'

She got into the passenger seat and was pleasantly surprised by how comfortable it was. Sonny used voice control to set the directions while the vehicle glided out of the parking space silently and Maxie felt as if she was in driving heaven. She could see it was an automatic and could imagine her poor ankle crying with joy in this car rather than her fabulous but cumbersome Jeep. Yes, Sonny's life looked so light and carefree whereas hers seemed heavy and gained baggage by the minute.

'Should we be doing this?' asked Sonny as they arrived outside Rebecca's flat. 'I mean have the police actually finished with the place?'

Maxie shrugged but recognised that she shouldn't be getting one of her students into trouble. 'We're here at the request of her parents and I'll be wearing protective clothing but why don't you stay out here and buzz me if anyone approaches.'

Sonny nodded and got back into his car while Maxie put on protective overshoes and gloves. Rebecca lived in an old Victorian semi-detached that had been converted into two flats. Maxie pushed the main door open cautiously and noticed that whoever lived in the top-floor flat had piled all the mail addressed to Rebecca on the hallway table but after a quick flick through, Maxie could see there was nothing in it that aroused any interest in her. She opened the door to Rebecca's home and stepped inside.

Maxie wasn't sure what she'd been expecting but it was incredibly pretty. High Victorian walls, austere fireplaces and ceiling roses were softened with spring-like colours and plump soft furnishings. This was a place to come home to, to feel welcomed. Because of this, the sight of surfaces that had been dusted for prints looked like an intrusion. Obviously the police had removed anything they thought might be useful – there were no electronic devices anywhere – no laptop, tablet, phones or desktop.

Maxie entered Rebecca's bedroom where the aroma of Obsession filled the air – that's what she'd recognised back in her first meeting with Rebecca at the pub. Almost instantly, she was transported back in time. She never needed to hear their voices or their music; that perfume had followed Rebecca everywhere. Maxie's olfactory system had fired up and was doing its job and the neurons in her brain were triggering her limbic system structures – the area that processed emotional information and helped consolidate memories. The heavy scent evoked pictures of being thrown out of her sister's room as the two girls lay on the bed scribbling their future plans.

The flat was tidy and seemed to have no secret hiding spaces or unused cupboards. The police had been through the place thoroughly but Maxie doubted they had found anything. Rebecca didn't look to be a hoarder. She was looking at the few photographs on the mantel piece when her phone buzzed.

Police here. Get out qck

She grabbed one of the pictures showing Rebecca against a cornflower-blue sky, holding a tropical cocktail and smiling as if the world were a wonderful place. Then Maxie ran bang smack into Andrew as she left the flat.

'What on earth are you doing here?' he asked. 'We're still processing the place – not that I need to tell you that.'

'It's not as if I disturbed a crime scene and anyway, I just wanted to pick up this.' Maxie showed the photo she'd grabbed. 'I went to visit Rebecca's parents and they asked for it.'

Andrew shook his head. 'Is that the best you can come up with?'

'In the time I had – yes.' Maxie shrugged.

The detective insisted on accompanying her and Sonny back to the Hendersons' house and once there he stressed with them the importance of not allowing anyone into Rebecca's flat while the enquiry was ongoing. Andrew took the spare set of keys and left the four adults sheepishly glancing at one another.

'I feel like a naughty schoolgirl,' said Rebecca's mum. 'Although it shouldn't surprise me with you involved Maxine – Rebecca was always telling me about the trouble you got yourself into.'

'You should have told us she could get into trouble for giving you those keys,' added Mr Henderson gruffly. 'I don't want any more of our family being a suspect just because of you.'

The old man grabbed a coat from a rack in the hall and stormed out. Maxie couldn't have felt worse. She looked across at Sonny who was staring awkwardly at the floor. Maxie hadn't only acted contrary to protocol herself – but she'd involved one of her students. Logically she knew she hadn't jeopardised anything or disturbed any evidence in that flat but she'd misled these worried parents and that was unforgiveable. She took hold of Mrs Henderson's hands and looked directly at her.

‘I’m so sorry, I shouldn’t have gone there. I want to find Rebecca and my instincts are telling me that what happened at the school is linked to Susan.’

‘All those years ago?’ Mrs Henderson’s eyes were wet with sadness.

‘I think so,’ Maxie said. ‘But I couldn’t find anything at the flat – your daughter wasn’t a hoarder was she?’

A wrinkled smile broke through Mrs Henderson’s tired face. ‘She wasn’t,’ she said. ‘But I am. Now what do you need?’

Maxie and Sonny were taken upstairs and then Rebecca’s mother pointed upwards towards the ceiling. There was a large square cover directly above them.

‘Rebecca has no space in that flat so I kept everything here,’ explained Mrs Henderson getting a metal lever from the airing cupboard. ‘Not that she would have wanted it anyway – she thought I was silly, keeping all the school reports and little stories she used to write.’

Maxie knew exactly how she felt, even though she’d moved out from their large family home into her flat after the divorce, Maxie had kept a suitcase of her son Karl’s childhood drawings and scribbles. He’d thought her mad and would often tell her that she could throw them out. ‘I’m not going to be famous one day you know,’ he’d say. ‘You won’t make your millions from one of my verses about a cat on a mat.’

Sonny took the lever from Mrs Henderson and reaching up, loosened the cover so that it flopped down. Maxie felt a frisson of excitement at the black hole it revealed. Sonny pulled down the ladder and went up first, finding the light switch and telling her that it was safe, ‘No huge spiders that I can see,’ he said.

Maxie took each step of the ladder cautiously and accepted Sonny’s hand to drag her into the loft. It was a big space and she could stand easily in the centre of it.

‘Rebecca’s things are at the far end – you’ll see her old computer there,’ shouted Mrs Henderson from the landing.

Sonny and Maxie turned in the direction they’d been given and both uttered, ‘Wow,’ simultaneously.

‘She wasn’t kidding when she said she hoarded was she?’ whispered Sonny.

‘Have you found it?’ Mrs Henderson called out to them.

Maxie replied that they had and it was fabulous but would take them a little while to sort through. Rebecca's mum yelled back that they should take their time and went off to make tea for them.

Maxie could see that Sonny was in danger of being distracted by the retro technology as he pulled out a box of floppy disks.

'Woah, I've heard of these – didn't they have eight inch versions too?'

Maxie rolled her eyes at him and snatched the box off him. 'Very funny,' she said looking around. 'But there's so much old tech here, we need to see what can be recovered.'

'I can get onto that,' he said. 'I got all my parents' old videos and stuff converted but we can't take everything so have to try and sort out what is actually useful.'

Maxie nodded her agreement and told him to focus on the years 1990-1995. She continued to dig through this junk yard of memories until it happened; a tingle ran down her body and the hairs on the back of her neck stood up. She'd spotted a flash of red that instantly took her back to Susan's room on that fateful Saturday. Her sister and Rebecca were as ever sitting on the bed and on the floor was the red satchel that Rebecca always brought. Maxie remembered wondering what was in it and reaching out for it only for the bag to be snapped up and for her to be pushed violently away by her sister.

'That's none of your business,' Susan had said. 'Get out of my room.'

Maxie could still recall that sting of being excluded and instinctively reached up to put her hand on her heart. That rejection had been one of the reasons she'd decided to stay out late and make Susan suffer. Maxie remembered responding that she wasn't interested in their stupid secrets anyway and yet now here she was, about to open one of them. The satchel was partially buried under old text books but Maxie braced herself and pulled it out, coughing as the dust rose in the air.

It was made of canvas and had stiffened in the damp air of the loft. Maxie's fingers were clumsy with anticipation as she tugged at the buckles. Then it was open and she emptied everything it contained onto the floor.

'Retro Avon catalogues.' Sonny laughed, appearing behind her and picking one up and flicking through it. 'Excellent – Belle will have a real laugh at these.'

Chapter Eighteen

The following Friday at the end of the work day, Maxie went in to check on Jean Carruthers and the cold case team. They were all still absorbed in the investigation and Maxie could see that the former WPC had a glow about her as she took Maxie through the potential evidence that they'd unearthed.

When Maxie eventually told the team that she had to leave, they barely acknowledged her but Belle said they were going to continue although Maxie had already guessed that from their engrossed expressions. She knew her students were completely absorbed in the task but still asked Jean if she was sure she didn't want to get off home.

'Of course not,' she replied. 'I really think we're going to get a breakthrough soon. I wish my team had been like this back in the day.'

Maxie resisted the urge to remark that she also wished the team had been like this back in the day as then they might have actually discovered what really happened to Susan. She knew it wouldn't have been a fair comment so bit her lip and headed to her waiting taxi.

It had been a relentless week and she was relieved that the weekend had finally come around. Her university work had kept her in the faculty all day, every day and then her cold case students had ensured she stayed there for the night shift. Maxie looked out of the cab window as it drove off the campus and realised she hadn't actually seen daylight for some time.

'Penny for them?' said her driver.

'Oh, nothing interesting at all,' she said. 'Just thinking of all the admin I have to finish when I get back tonight.'

'Rather you than me.'

That was another thing bugging her right now; the level of admin she was required to submit seemed to be increasing by the day but the most recent request – a justification of involving her students in the cold case – niggled the most. As professor and a senior member of the faculty, she had the authority to sign off research studies knowing that they would be randomly verified by an independent body. The dean had never asked her to explain her decisions before. It was probably the profile of the podcast making the university nervous. Still, it was a piece of work that she could really do without right now.

'Here we are,' called out the driver as they pulled up outside a café bar. 'Supposed to be nice this place – bring me a doggy bag if you can't finish it all.'

'Since when have I not finished a meal?' Maxie said with a laugh.

The restaurant did have a good reputation and Maxie had chosen it as a peace offering. She hadn't seen or spoken to Andrew since Rebecca's house and needed to know she'd not completely burnt her bridges with him. Maxie was directed towards a booth and hadn't been seated for long when she noticed Andrew walking into the bar. It surprised her to see that as he strode towards her, a number of women gave him a quick glance. She'd never really thought of him as an attractive man but of course he was and it did look as if he'd dressed up for the occasion. Maxie looked down at the workmanlike wrap dress she was wearing and wished that she'd at least popped to the loo to freshen up her make-up. It was too late now. She stood as he reached the table and they gave each other a friendly peck on the cheek. Inwardly Maxie relaxed a little having dreaded that they might have retreated back to the handshake stage.

'You look very smart,' she said as they both flicked napkins onto their laps.

'I thought it would be worth making an effort,' he replied. 'I know lots of eligible ladies come here for cocktail hour.'

Did he know that in one sentence he'd made her heart rise then fall? Maxie gave him the benefit of the doubt. 'Well they certainly clocked you coming in,' she said.

They ordered then waited until the wine had been poured before starting any real conversation. 'I'm sorry,' said Maxie. 'I overstepped.'

Andrew nodded but said nothing.

'It just feels as if it's now or never,' she continued. 'The wind is blowing in the right direction and if I don't ride this wave I'll never know what happened to Susan.'

'I do understand,' he said. 'I'm just worried that you'll create some tsunami in your wake that buries the rest of us. Sorry – that was the only wind-based analogy I could come up with.'

'It was pretty good,' said Maxie laughing. A broad smile had broken out across her face as she realised they were okay. She raised her glass and clinked it against his. 'To only gentle breezes hereon in,' she said.

'I very much doubt that but I'll drink to it.'

They passed an amicable meal discussing their mutual dating failures, the latest Netflix crime series and family – in fact everything except work but as the plates were cleared and the bottle of wine was emptied into their glasses, Maxie couldn't help herself. 'So how are the cases going? I mean the care home and the arson.'

'I didn't think you meant the robbery at the pet store,' Andrew said. 'And you know I can't talk about them.'

'It's just that they're undoubtedly related to my cold case,' Maxie said. 'And it's common sense that finding out a little more about George Fairview would be a valid line of enquiry if the DNA on the bat was in my house. Was any found at the fire? One of the former pupils would link all three events.'

'I'm not saying anything, Maxie,' he said. 'Barwick is a small place and it's entirely likely that a former pupil at that school might have been at your sister's party and might now have a parent at a care home.'

'So you *have* found something?' Maxie leapt at Andrew's comment.

'You don't give up do you?' Andrew shook his head at her. 'Even if we had found something, it doesn't mean that George Fairview is in any way related to Susan and I'm just afraid that you're going to tie yourself in knots looking for an explanation that wasn't a burglary gone horribly wrong. I know that sounds harsh but it could be the reality.'

'We're pretty sure that isn't what happened.' Maxie now gazed directly at the detective. 'We firmly believe that her body was moved before I got home.'

She explained what she'd remembered through the cold case team re-enactment.

'Hmm – that relies on your memory which may be telling you what you want to believe. You know that isn't firm evidence and besides, there is a very tight window between you calling home and actually getting there. It was probably little more than an hour at most.'

'But you don't hang around to move someone if they fall during an attempted break-in,' continued Maxie delighted to be able to discuss this with her usual partner. 'You leg it quickly.'

'Unless she fell and blocked the exit,' said Andrew. 'Is that possible?'

Maxie shrugged. 'Even if you were just pushing someone out of the way, you wouldn't position them in the way that Susan was left. What about George's death – do you still think that might have been an accident?' she said – fishing and knowing that Andrew could tell what she was doing.

'I bet you're still asking questions in your sleep,' he said. 'It'll soon be a matter of public record so I can tell you that we do think that the cause of death was the fall and hitting his head on the rock. He wouldn't have fallen if he hadn't been hit by the cricket bat but that wasn't hard enough. Our first instinct – that he probably swerved to avoid it and toppled over is the most likely scenario.'

'So it may not have been an attack at all,' said Maxie. 'One of the residents could have been brandishing the bat playfully and caught him on the head.'

'Not likely given that we found him first thing in the morning before they were all out and about, besides which we've questioned everyone there now including the postman and there isn't a viable suspect among them.'

Maxie drummed her fingertips on the table as she thought. 'I suppose we could have predicted that,' she said thinking aloud. 'Well perhaps George was up to no good. Could he have gone there to rob or hurt one of the residents and maybe one of the staff ran after him but hasn't confessed because they didn't actually mean to kill him – just scare him off?'

'I'd thought of that but during all the questioning, haven't found anything to suggest that's what actually happened,' he replied. 'And as we haven't released anything other than an outline description of the man found, no-one has come forward yet so we don't know if he had any enemies or if there was a reason to kill him. No-one of that description has been reported missing so apart from his place on the quiz team, we don't know who George actually is or why he was there and we're still slogging away to find the garage that fits the key fob, and the mythical partner. But there were fabric samples under his finger nails that fit a coat so we think he grabbed someone and they lashed out at him.'

'That's a lot of evidence to leave behind,' said Maxie. 'We're not talking about a master criminal here are we?'

'And yet they're managing to stay out of sight right now,' Andrew said with his hands stretched out in an expression of disbelief. 'We need to speak to Rebecca urgently.'

'Listen,' said Maxie. 'I know I can't be involved in either cases but could I please, please be kept updated on George's real identity? I might be able to shed light on him from the old cold case files. And obviously

I'm worried about Rebecca so any news on her whereabouts would just let me sleep at night – you may have noticed that I've aged ten years in the past few weeks.'

Andrew sighed and picked up the bill that had just been placed on the table. He reached into his jacket, took out a credit card and tapped it on the machine. When the waiter had left Andrew reached across and took hold of both of Maxie's hands which took her completely by surprise.

'I don't want us to fall out over this,' he said not taking his eyes off her. 'I know you, and I'm genuinely concerned you'll do something stupid over your sister so I'll make you a deal. We'll have meals like this and talk – I'll share what I can and you tell me how it's going. If at any point I think you're doing yourself more harm than good, I will ask you to stop and I want you to take that seriously.'

Maxie didn't know what to say – this concern seemed truly over the top. She knew she got emotionally involved in cases but had she ever gone too far? She shifted awkwardly in her seat and as she did so got a flash of pain up her leg. It made her snort with laughter as she pictured that her body was answering the question for her.

'I mean it, Maxie,' continued Andrew. He'd taken her snort of laughter as a dismissal.

'I'm sorry,' she replied. 'I was about to say that I never get too involved and then the ankle that I twisted pursuing a criminal into a tunnel started playing up. It was perfect timing.'

'Don't forget that you'd also dated the criminal you were pursuing,' he said, smiling at her.

'How could I forget?' she said. 'Look, I can only promise that I'll try to stick to the deal but whatever happens, I do not want to jeopardise our friendship.'

'I'll take that,' he said.

They stood up, Maxie leaving a cash tip and they walked out of the café bar. The night was cold with a frosty fog threatening but nevertheless the fresh air was welcome as they walked slowly towards the spot the taxi would shortly pick her up.

'How is the ankle?' asked Andrew after a moment of silence.

'Healing slowly,' Maxie said. 'I've been doing some exercises and I've decided to take the plunge.'

'With what?'

'What we were discussing – I need a lighter car – an automatic and I think it should be an electric one. So can I take you up on the offer to come to some dealerships with me and help me decide?'

'I'd be delighted,' Andrew said. 'In fact, I'll take a look through some articles and let you know what they're saying might suit you.'

Maxie thanked him as the cab arrived and as she settled in the back seat watching Andrew wave her away, she at least knew their friendship had been restored.

Switching her phone back on in the cab, Maxie checked her emails and saw a reminder that the justification of using the cold case with her students had been due by close of play today. Even this was irksome after the lovely few hours she'd just spent. The dean rarely bothered with reminders; he knew she would get the work done. Her driver switched on Smooth radio and the gentle songs soothed Maxie as she thought back over the past three weeks and tried to look at them objectively. Had she inadvertently neglected any of her university work? She genuinely didn't think that she had. True, she was exhausted and had spent every hour outside of work on this case but she'd put on her best professor face every morning as she'd entered the university. Yes – she'd deserved Andrew's reprimand but surely the dean had nothing to complain about? The only course of action was to play the game. She'd get that justification finished tonight and get it in before the clock struck midnight – that would show him.

As soon as she got home, Maxie changed into comfy clothes and set up her laptop ready to complete the paperwork requested. It was a tiresome piece to do justice to as it involved reviewing the students' proposals and showing that the area of research they'd suggested was both valid and forward-thinking. She had decided to argue that successful completion of these theses would more than likely be featured in several academic journals and create interest amongst prospective students. Recruitment was a fiercely competitive game nowadays and anything innovative made those relentless open days just a tad easier.

She was thinking about going back to her open day proposal and pondered adding this to the agenda when her phone rang.

'Sorry it's late,' said Joseph unable to hide the excitement in his voice. 'We're all still here and we thought you'd want to know this straight away.'

Maxie quickly checked the time at the bottom left-hand corner of her laptop – it was past nine and she realised they'd been working all evening. However, curiosity overcame the twinge of guilt. 'What is it?' she asked.

'We had a response to the podcast,' Sonny called out and Maxie realised she was on speaker phone with all three.

'Someone saw something,' added Belle.

'They saw someone at your house,' continued Joseph. 'At the precise time we're looking at.'

Chapter Nineteen

The next day, the team went to visit the house of David Crawford – the man who had contacted them saying he'd seen something. The boys were setting up the portable microphone in the centre of the man's coffee table while Belle went over the approach she would take with their new information source. David's information was interesting but not enough to warrant a whole episode of the podcast so the students had come up with the idea of creating a series of news-bites – small clues that together might form a bigger picture.

'Some people might think it's not worth messaging us because all they saw was a car stopping or a dog-walker loitering but we could join the dots that they lay,' Joseph had explained. 'In fact maybe that's what we call this episode – Joining the Dots.'

Maxie had liked the idea so the team had immediately launched the idea on the social media channels and were collating the responses that had started coming in. Rather than take each interesting caller into the studio, they'd got hold of the portable podcast mikes and were taking them out onto the road and that's why they were in David's house this morning. The interviews collected would be edited together in the studio later.

Joseph signalled that they were ready to start so Belle and David sat down alongside each other on his sofa with the mike in the centre of the table. Maxie watched as they both took a deep breath and nodded towards one another to say they were ready.

'David, can you tell us why you remember that night in particular?' asked Belle. 'I mean it was thirty years ago.'

'It was my wedding day,' David said with a big smile on his face. 'When you played all those songs that were top of the charts back then, it brought everything flooding back. It was that one song – "Back For Good" by Take That.'

'So tell us what you remember,' prompted Belle.

'We were sitting in the back seat of the limo which was taking us from our wedding to our hotel for the night. I know lots of people drive themselves from the reception and have all that "just married" stuff on the car but we didn't want to do that,' David said. 'It was the biggest party of our lives and we both wanted to enjoy it.'

‘So had you had a lot to drink?’ Belle’s brow furrowed as she questioned him and David looked at her indignantly.

‘No!’ he replied. ‘I mean, a couple of glasses but let’s face it, I had to … well perform that night so wasn’t about to get plastered. And I was going to be driving the next day and alcohol stays in your system. I wouldn’t have driven my new bride anywhere with even one glass of champagne in me.’

‘That sounds really sensible. I wish more men were like you,’ said Maxie from the sidelines. David looked over at her and smiled, then nodded at Belle to continue.

‘So you were driving to the hotel – what happened next?’ Belle asked.

‘As I said, we were in the back and I had my head leaning against the window. I had my arm around my wife and her head was resting on my shoulder. *The Love Hour* was just finishing and the radio was playing that song – I was listening to the lyrics and thinking I’d never say anything I didn’t mean to my wife. I felt the happiest I had ever felt. You know when people describe love as something warm and fuzzy? Well that’s exactly how it was.’

David paused and Maxie could see from his beatific expression that he was reliving the moment. ‘We drove down Glenshiels Road and that’s when I saw them. The light was on in the hall and the front door was open.’

‘We’re talking about Susan’s house here aren’t we?’ prompted Belle. ‘How can you be sure of that?’

‘The pictures you posted and the fact that it’s beside a junction,’ David said. ‘We’d paused at that junction and I looked out the window. There was a man dragging a woman back down the path away from the house. He had hold of her by the arm and I remember being truly saddened by that and vowing never to let anyone treat my wife like that.’

‘So a man was dragging a woman against her will and you never thought to report it?’

‘I know, I know,’ said David dropping his head into his hands. Belle signalled for him to remove them so the sound wouldn’t be muffled and he did. He folded them across his chest but the sadness remained in his eyes. ‘We left for our honeymoon the day after so we were away for two weeks in Barbados and I never heard anything about the young girl’s death. It wasn’t big news at the time. Besides which, it kind of looked like a lovers’ tiff and I wouldn’t have interfered in that anyway.’

Maxie held back a shake of the head and wondered where people thought the line between a lovers' tiff and domestic abuse actually was? She knew the listeners would completely empathise with what David was saying and statistics showed that suspicions over domestic violence were the least likely to be reported. Neighbours didn't like to seem nosy or risk getting involved in someone else's business. Whenever she read these stats – which never seemed to improve – she often thought that in most areas you could pretty much beat your spouse up in public without any fear of reprisal.

'So you saw a man and a woman,' Belle was continuing the interview. 'Do you remember any further details about either?'

David's eyes glanced upwards and left – showing that he was recalling an image. 'I know it was a woman because she was shorter and had long hair although I can't be certain about the colour,' he said. 'I remember the outline of the strands against the hall light. I think she also broke free of him at the end of the path but to be honest, any more than that and I could just be making it up.'

'And the light in the hallway, you said the door was open? Was anyone standing there?' asked Belle.

'Yes,' he said. 'I only saw a silhouette but I'm sure it was another woman.'

A tiny fist clenched at her heart as Maxie realised that this man was probably talking about Susan and might have been the last person to see her sister alive.

'Did she seem okay?'

Both Belle and David turned to face her as Maxie croaked the question, unable to disguise the anguish she felt.

'Had the man hurt her? Did she try to help this woman?'

To her embarrassment, David stood, stepped towards her and put his hand on her shoulder. He looked at her with soft brown eyes bearing the lines of both laughter and tears which in that moment reminded her of her dad as he had been when he comforted her at Susan's funeral. 'She did seem okay and I am so sorry that I didn't come forward earlier,' he said softly. 'I hope my failure hasn't been the cause of all your years of sorrow.'

This stranger had put words to a feeling that seemed locked inside her. Maxie couldn't cope with it so took a deep breath and stood tall. She wiped away the tear that lay on her cheek and thanked him for coming forward now. David sat back down and Belle completed the final questions of the interview.

Maxie was mightily relieved when they had put some distance between themselves and David's house. They were now heading back to the university to go through other snippets of information that had arrived in order to sort out which of them might be useful for the podcast.

'I think it might be useful to recreate the scene outside the house that night,' said Joseph as he and Belle crammed into the back of Sonny's car while Maxie took the front passenger seat. 'Have a girl with long hair walking away from a guy outside the house to promote the episode and ask for more witnesses.'

'Yeah, we can sort that later,' Sonny said looking at his fellow students via the rear view mirror. 'You okay to be the girl, Belle? We could get the pic on social media by tonight.'

Belle nodded and Maxie relaxed her head against the car window. She realised that her team had almost taken over the investigation without her. While she felt very proud of them, she also felt negligent with regard to directing and tutoring them. 'It sounds like a fabulous idea,' she said turning to face them and forcing as upbeat a tone as she could muster. 'But I really don't want you guys neglecting the rest of your studies or social lives for this.'

'Too late for that.' Joseph laughed as his fellow students joined in.

Maxie sighed inwardly knowing she could hardly criticise her students for becoming obsessed with the case when she was thinking about it twenty-four hours a day. Still, she thought, at least they'd be getting their dissertations out of this.

Damn. In that second she realised that she hadn't finished those justifications. She was sure Dean wouldn't have read them on Friday anyway and he'd understand why they were late. Nevertheless, it was important for her students and really had to be her first priority – after reviewing all the information that was being considered for the podcast.

'I think we can disregard the clairvoyant,' Joseph was saying as Maxie tuned back into the conversation. He had his phone out and was showing Belle the photo of a man who claimed to have contacted Susan. He'd said that she had told him what had happened but that he would only reveal her words on the show.

'Oh I don't know,' replied Belle. 'Maybe we should invite him on and if it turns out that he's a fraud we can tear him to pieces asking why he'd want to cause distress with his false claims.'

'*If* he's a fraud?' Sonny raised his eyebrows at his fellow student in the mirror. 'You surely don't believe it could be real – these conmen take advantage of a person's grief. We should get him on the show and completely show him up.'

'Enough,' said Maxie raising her palms to restore peace. 'It's no to the clairvoyant. What else do we have?'

'I think we should look more closely at the week before Susan's death,' Joseph continued.

'Anything specific?' asked Maxie.

The young man hauled the bag that lay at his feet onto his lap then pulled out the old Avon catalogues and order forms that they'd found in Susan's loft. 'These forms have a layer underneath that duplicate the order,' explained Joseph. Maxie had to hold back a smile as carbon-copies were explained to her like they were a piece of ancient technology. She supposed they were to teenagers.

'The order on the top sheet is given to the customers and it has all their details on it,' he continued. 'So we know that in the days before that weekend, Susan and Rebecca had taken a number of orders but because of what happened, the orders weren't sent off or fulfilled. Perhaps the customers remember that – maybe they saw people hanging around the girls as they did their round.'

'Yeah – maybe someone knew that they carried cash around with them and thought they'd find it in the house,' added Sonny.

'Avon ladies collected the cash when they dropped off the orders,' Maxie said. 'But I suppose not everyone knew that.'

'The neighbour did say your sister liked to make money,' added Belle. 'Maybe she had a reputation for it, maybe she liked to flash the cash, talk about how much she was earning and someone got jealous.'

'Susan wasn't like that,' snapped Maxie. 'I can't vouch for Rebecca but my sister wasn't boastful. If that's the angle I think you'll be wasting valuable time if you pursue this.' She could feel her face colouring as she regretted her outburst. She sat looking straight ahead as an awkward silence settled in the car. Maxie inhaled deeply trying to calm herself down. Only when she felt the heat start to leave her cheeks did she dare to speak. 'I'm sorry. You have to investigate areas that you feel are valid. As you know, familial homicides are difficult on the remaining family members and because of survivor's guilt we tend to sanctify those we've lost.'

Belle cleared her throat and added, 'It's particularly hard for siblings as they experience intense guilt.'

'We certainly do,' replied Maxie. 'And you're seeing that academic research in all its real-life glory here.' She comically messed up her hair and let out a yell to relieve the tension in the air. 'It's a good job I have you lot to keep me on the straight and narrow. Okay then – let's try and find the customers. They may know nothing but let's find out. Now is there anything else we should cover?'

Peace was restored with conversation about small pieces of information that had come in; one of the bikers who'd been there that night had been in touch to say that as far as he remembered they were just checking out the scene and when they realised it was a teenage party, had left.

'I want to feature people who were in class with Susan,' said Belle. 'They're not related to the actual day of her death but maybe get one of the people who went to that reunion to come forward for an interview and tell us what she was like. I'm kind of surprised none of them have volunteered.'

Chapter Twenty

It was an order rather than a request. The dean wanted to see Maxie in his office at close of play. Thanking the heavens for their pitifully small mercies, Maxie had time to get those blasted justifications perfected and could also pull together what they had on the cold case to share. The Applied Criminology Unit was her baby and along with the regional DCI, Maxie decided which cases they would support so Dean had little say in that but the resources she tapped in to were the university's and therefore his to allocate.

Had they actually got anywhere with Susan's death? The facts seemed sparse and she could hardly present an underlying feeling that all was not well and they would find the key that unlocked everything soon. It certainly wasn't going to be found by going over the old case notes. Jean had eventually got through to Will Hardcastle over in Canada but he'd had nothing to add to his original scant investigation and had made it very clear he did not want to be contacted again. The past was not giving up its secrets easily.

Maxie began scribbling her notes; facts – Susan's body had multiple bruises consistent with a fall down stairs and hitting her head on the way. A young Maxie had always felt blamed for grabbing hold of Susan and disturbing the crime scene but now they knew the body had been moved before she arrived home and they also knew there had been two people at her house during that key hour. A man had dragged a woman down the path of their home while Susan watched from the doorway. Had that woman been Rebecca? She had long hair and that was the only description they had. And why would Susan just stand there when another woman was being threatened? Maxie hated to admit it to herself but growing like a tapeworm inside her gut was a wriggling sensation that her sister was not the saint she remembered.

She looked at her notes – they really were pathetic and even the facts were based on thirty-year-old memories. How could she be sure that the couple had actually witnessed the events at her house and not somewhere else? Yes they'd checked the route and as many of the details as possible but it was still just a memory, not a photograph. It wouldn't have been enough to convict anyone even "back in the day".

So what about the suspicions? Rebecca's sad, lonely life; the attack on George Fairview; the belief that he wasn't who he said he was and then the arson at the school. As Andrew had said, they might all be completely unrelated to an incident thirty years ago but Maxie's instincts were having none of that. Her students were still collating any responses for their "Joining the Dots" episode but she couldn't just wait to hear what had come in; she had to do something.

In putting together the justifications for her students, Maxie had incorporated some academic research which showed that the very words "cold case" hampered any investigation. She dug the paper out and reread it now; it had found that those investigating cold cases tended to rely more on emotional responses rather than rational thinking and that spoke directly to her current frame of mind. She was sitting there wallowing in her feelings rather than getting out there and digging up some more facts.

Maxie checked the time and her schedule; she had a couple of hours before she was due in lectures and then she'd be straight in to see the dean. She took out the list of Avon customer names and skimmed it quickly. There was one name on that list that she knew she could visit easily but one was enough. Maxie grabbed her bag and rang for her cabbie.

Carole Hodgson was a florist and at this time of year – post Valentine's Day and pre-Mother's Day – the shop was fairly quiet. Maxie watched her flicking through a magazine and sipping at a coffee but as soon as she saw Maxie, she leapt up busying herself with blooms that didn't need tidying and buckets that didn't need filling. 'You've caught me at a busy time,' said Carole getting a raised eyebrow from Maxie.

Maxie leaned over the gossip magazine and replied, 'I can see that, but I don't think these celebs are going anywhere soon.'

'What do you want?' asked Carole folding her arms indignantly. 'I don't know anything about where Rebecca is and didn't see anything at Mike's party – the police have my statement.'

Maxie plonked herself down on a wooden stool and rubbed at her ankle. 'Sorry,' she said. 'I twisted my ankle and it's playing up. I hope it's okay to sit down?' She sighed as if exhausted and gave Carole an Oscar-worthy look of weariness.

'I've given my statement too,' said Maxie hoping to seem on the same side as Carole. 'It was awful though wasn't it? I'd only just met Fiona and I would have hated it if she'd come to any real harm.'

The florist didn't totally let her guard down but she did unfold her arms and shove her hands in her pockets. 'Why are you here?' she asked.

'I just want to find out what happened to Susan,' Maxie said. 'I've always blamed myself and I need to know.' She rubbed her eyes and hoped her performance hadn't lapsed into theatrical.

'She disturbed burglars and fell down the stairs,' said Carole with a hard edge to her voice. 'It was tragic but sometimes it's best to accept that.'

'Maybe. And perhaps I'll have to because I can't find any other explanation. Although I am finding out more about Susan's life and that's been quite interesting – things I didn't know about my big sister.'

'Like what?' Carole had refolded her arms even tighter like a barrier between them.

'Like her Avon round,' replied Maxie. 'I'd forgotten she had one and you were one of her customers.'

'Big deal,' said Carole. 'So what of it?'

'Oh nothing,' Maxie said, pulling out the carbon copy sheets. 'I just like to picture you all going through the catalogues, choosing make-up and wearing it out. Although it looks as if you only ever bought lip salve.'

She held up several sheets that had Carole's name and only one product on each. Carole shrugged and glanced quickly at Maxie before opening her mouth to respond. The millisecond delay would have told anyone watching that the next words from her mouth would be lies. And Maxie was watching.

'I bought my make-up down the high street.' Carole was unable to stop a blush rising from her neck upwards and across her face. 'Avon was more expensive and I didn't have much money back then but I wanted to support her.'

Maxie nodded as if she accepted this answer because she realised that she didn't actually have any idea *why* Carole would lie. Maxie had seen that there were several other order forms with equally sparse orders so she couldn't help wondering whether the florist had wanted to support her sister or had been bullied into it. Maxie felt her pulse race a little as that tapeworm wriggled again.

Outside her cabbie sounded his horn causing Maxie to check her watch – she had to get back to the university. She thanked Carole for her time and noted that the woman's body dropped into a more relaxed posture as she left the shop. In the back of the taxi, Maxie revisited that reaction in her mind. There were a few ways a person could react at a visit from the sister of an old school friend; she could have been overwhelmingly sympathetic, wrap Maxie in a big hug and offer cups of tea. She could have told her what a good friend Susan had been and how she'd cried every day when she heard the news. Or Carole could have said that she didn't remember very much but that she was very sorry for Maxie's loss – even after all these years. Sympathy – whether real or fake – should at least have been on display but it hadn't been. Instead Carole was fearful and defensive; it could be that she had something to hide or simply that the florist didn't want to relive her school days at all. All Maxie wanted to do right now was question every other customer on Susan's list and that was the very thing she couldn't do.

Maxie tried to relax into her lecture but her mind wasn't on it and she snapped at a student who hadn't read the coursework before being pulled up herself by another as she drifted off into her own thoughts. All in all, it wasn't the best lecture Maxie had ever given and as the students piled out of the lecture theatre, she called out an apology for being in a world of her own and promised to be on form next time. She also cornered the student she'd shouted at and apologised to him but reiterated his need to do the reading before lectures if he wanted to pass the module. Having restored the equilibrium, Maxie headed to the ladies' to freshen up, and ensuring she had the cold case justifications in her briefcase, crossed the courtyard to Dean's office.

'Can I get you some coffee?'

'As it's too early for wine,' Maxie said in an attempt to lighten the mood.

Dean gave her a small smile which showed that he wasn't going to be distracted from whatever he had to say. He asked his secretary to fetch some coffee and as he sat down, the university's head of Personnel popped her head round the door and asked if she was needed.

'Not at this stage,' he replied. 'But thank you.'

Maxie caught the eye of the personnel head and looked from her to the dean – neither were giving anything away and he kept the mood awkward by saying nothing until the coffees had been delivered and the door to his office had clicked shut. Then he picked up his coffee cup and took a sip and Maxie wondered whether he was deliberately trying to get a rise out of her.

'Not at *this* stage?' she said wanting to get this meeting started and establish quickly whether those words referred to her.

He calmly put his cup down and intertwined his fingers on the desk in front of her. It was all very controlled. 'How are things going?' he asked softly.

'Fine – why?'

'I'm worried that you're taking too much on at the moment,' he continued. 'That perhaps you're stretching yourself too thinly.'

'Oh don't worry about me; I could have joined the circus with my juggling skills.' Maxie gave a little laugh. Dean's expression remained sombre.

'I need you to take this seriously, Professor,' he continued. 'I'm afraid we've had a complaint.'

'About me?' blurted Maxie instantly regretting her frantic tone – after all who else could it be about? She took a breath and then mirrored the dean's arm position, attempting to present as calm a presence.

'I'm afraid so,' he said after a pause. 'It's about the cold case you've taken on.'

'Ah, I have the paperwork here,' said Maxie reaching into her briefcase and putting the immaculately presented justifications on the desk. 'I apologise that they're slightly late but I wanted to give them to you personally and was hoping to talk you through them.'

It was a lame excuse and they both knew it. Dean pushed them to one side. 'Thank you but it's not directly related to the work,' he said. 'I'm worried about you. I fear you're dedicating more time to the education of the small cold case team and neglecting the rest of your students.'

'But that's ridiculous. We tend to do the cold case work out of university time.'

'And the exhaustion is showing, Professor,' he continued. 'I know this is not just a case for you, it's a personal pursuit and you will give everything you have to get to the bottom of it. Have you thought about how you will cope if you find that things were not as you remember them?'

Maxie said nothing; she couldn't face a scenario where Susan wasn't the innocent victim.

'Meanwhile the rest of your work is suffering. I have word that some of your recent lectures have been at best … lacklustre.'

Maxie didn't bother arguing with that; she thought back to the afternoon wondering if he'd heard about that and trying to recall who had been sitting in the lecture hall. Apart from the poor soul she'd shouted at, she honestly couldn't remember. And that was the nub of this complaint.

'I know the Applied Criminology Unit is your baby but, along with the DCI, it is *my* responsibility to assign the head of the unit according to the needs of both the police and the university,' he said. 'If I feel that the ACU and your role as a professor in this department is becoming too much, then I will have to act – for your sake as well as the students.'

His words sent a shockwave through Maxie and she felt her head spin. Her jaw fell open and no words formed. She had to speak, she knew that. She took a sip of cold coffee to lubricate her sandpaper dry throat and nodded. 'I'm sorry Dean … to have caused this,' she said croaking the first words and then pulling herself together for the rest of the sentence. 'I will apologise to my students and ensure that I restore an appropriate equilibrium. You know that I do not want to lose either my position in the university or my leadership of the ACU.'

Dean smiled his acceptance of her words and the end of the meeting. Maxie stood and walked towards the door, still in a bit of a daze. As she took hold of the door handle, she turned to face him but he was face down in paperwork already.

'Close the door on your way out,' he called, without even looking up.

Chapter Twenty-One

Maxie returned to her office dumbfounded. She slumped down at her desk and her whole body felt as if it were sliding bit by bit onto the floor. On the wall to her left were several framed photographs and certificates – her "Glory Wall" as she'd laughingly called it. She was delighted to have won all those prizes and accolades – not only for herself but for the faculty and her students who were usually part of the research. Maxie had worked hard to enter as many excellence awards as possible simply to keep the department in high esteem. The photos of her smiling while accepting various trophies were on the wall to impress anyone coming to check out the university and its reputation. People who might be deciding where to allocate grants or possibly where to study – and now one of these people had made a complaint.

As she'd listened to Dean's words, she couldn't help but feel it was all a bit petty – a student who wasn't part of the cold case team had complained to Mummy or Daddy and they'd snitched on her? Surely her academic work hadn't suffered that much? It didn't really matter what she thought, Dean had taken the report seriously – as he had to. And now she had to do the same. She had to fulfil her promise and focus on her students above the case.

Maxie fired up her PC and looked at the papers which still had to be graded; her heart wasn't in it and every time she read a student's name she wondered whether this was the one who'd made the complaint. Coming across a familiar surname made her sit up – Marcus Hodgson. It was a common enough name but also Carole the florist's, surname.

'Whoa,' she said to herself. 'What's this really about?'

Her mind was now racing down a new pathway – one where the complaint was simply a way of getting her to give up the cold case. She had to find out whether any of the people in Susan's old entourage now had children on her course. Maxie pulled up the student file for Marcus Hodgson and found his home address – it wasn't in Barwick but that meant nothing. Carole might live in one town and have her shop somewhere else. She checked the drive times between the two places and although she was desperate to make the connection, even she had to concede that a person who had to be up at 5 a.m. to get her flowers from the wholesale market wouldn't choose to live three hours away from the shop. Just to be sure, she checked Marcus's social media where he'd posted photos with his parents – neither of them Carole.

Just because her first attempt hadn't struck gold didn't mean this wasn't a valid line of thinking so Maxie typed Mike Priestley's name into Facebook. She'd reviewed his profile before but hadn't noted his children's names and now she couldn't – the profile had been deleted. She tried the names of his entourage but one by one was blocked out by privacy settings or a non-existent user. All of them gone? If that didn't say conspiracy, she didn't know what did. As she was sitting in front of Facebook not sure where to go next, she typed in Rebecca's name. The page hadn't been updated since the school reunion but just beforehand, she had changed her cover photo to one of herself and Susan smiling at what looked like an end-of-term party. Maxie reached out and touched the picture.

'All I want is to know what happened,' she said to the image with a sense of despair. 'I wish I could just ask you. Maybe I should go to that clairvoyant after all.'

Maxie closed Facebook and went back to LinkedIn, guessing that no-one would have closed their professional profiles. She was right but there was very little personal information here and certainly nothing about their children although Maxie knew that the women in particular would not want any hint of childcare distractions to appear on a site used to recruit. Nope, women had to look as if the only thing that mattered in their lives was their career.

Mike Priestly's CV was an immaculate record of achievement and progression from his first class honours degree to his recent appointment. Maxie let out a snort as she scrolled down Mike's profile to his list of other interests – this was the difference between the genders; they were allowed extra-curricular pursuits and this guy had dozens. The logo of one organisation caught her eye instantly – she'd seen it somewhere before. She clicked on the logo and it took her through to the website of the local cricket club where she got her answer. Holding a cup aloft and smiling for the camera was Mike and a little along the row was the dean – he'd had this picture on his wall. It didn't take a mathematician to solve this equation – the parent had spoken to Mike and he'd been the one to have a quiet word with her boss. Maxie could picture them shaking their heads and talking about her. Well one thing she knew for sure – she wasn't going to lose her job over some old boys' network.

Every ounce of her being wanted to charge over to Mike's house and throw the accusation at him to see his reaction. Or maybe she should wait until the next cricket match and turn up to let them both know she was onto them. She needed someone to talk her down and there was only one person who could do that.

'Howdy partner,' said Andrew cheerily and his voice instantly took her from the edge. 'What you up to?'

Maxie didn't stop talking until it was all out – the threat of losing her job or the ACU, her suspicions about Mike and her gnawing fear that something awful was hiding just over the hill.

'Okay, now I'm officially worried about you too,' Andrew replied gently. 'You need to press pause and get some perspective here.'

'I can't,' said Maxie. 'I just feel that if I stop, all the pieces will vanish. Their profiles have already been taken down – it's like sand slipping through my fingers.'

'Maxie – listen to me. If the facts are there you will find them but not like this. Not rushing from one crazy idea to the next. You need that step backwards or you'll run the risk of losing everything. Fortunately I have the very thing to distract you.'

'I doubt that.'

'I've got to be at the school on Saturday and by happy coincidence there's an electric car place on the way there,' he continued. 'So if we leave early, we can see a couple. I've narrowed down the ones you should look at and I think you should come out with me. I'll warn you now that I won't let you near the crime scene but you can talk to Tom if you like or we can discuss what's going on while you do some test drives and I promise, I'll get you back to the studio in time for recording and you'll go back to it all refreshed.'

Maxie liked the idea that she could talk things through and she did need her independence back. It felt like a distraction but one that kept her on track. She took a calming breath and agreed to Andrew picking her up first thing on Saturday.

A knock on her door roused her from thoughts about what she could ask Tom – it was her cold case students. Maxie glanced at the time and saw that they were all in the faculty far later than they should be. She looked at their tired but excited faces and knew she should be sending them straight home but could also see that they had something to tell her.

‘What is it?’ she asked pushing out chairs for them all to sit on. ‘You all look as if you’ve found out where your mum has hidden your Christmas presents.’

‘We’ve been listening to everything that has come in for the “Joining the Dots” episode,’ began Joseph as if letting each word sink in.

‘You really shouldn’t be working this late,’ Maxie said. ‘You all have other coursework which you can’t neglect.’

‘We wanted to get in every last piece,’ he continued. ‘To be honest, apart from the man dragging the woman down the path, there wasn’t much of interest. We were going to have to pad the episode with a reminder of the facts and the news of that day.’

‘Tell me what came in,’ said Maxie. She closed her eyes so she could focus on the words alone.

‘There was a party the day before that got out of hand and had to be broken up,’ said Sonny. ‘Bikers arrived but they left quickly seeing the party was pretty lame, one guy got pretty angry with Susan and said that she owed him.’

‘I know all of this,’ said Maxie. ‘I didn’t see much of it as I was banished upstairs but I heard the music and some shouting.’

‘On the next evening, you were out at the pub and you rang home. Susan was alive at that point, but by the time you got back she was dead.’ Joseph was rattling through the facts. ‘The body had been moved and it looked as if there had been an attempted burglary.’

‘Although nothing had been taken,’ added Maxie.

‘It was a very tight window of opportunity,’ said Belle causing Maxie to wince at the word – after all, it had been an opportunity to kill her sister. ‘And in that time, we know a man dragged a woman down your path watched by Susan.’

Maxie looked up at them. ‘I’m guessing you’re going to tell me something that I don’t already know sometime soon.’

‘Two things,’ said Sonny. ‘The first is that we’ve been contacted by someone else who was burgled that night. Not too far away and around the right time frame – they were just trying doors and if any were unlocked, they took a chance.’

‘What?’ exclaimed Maxie. ‘How come such an obvious connection wasn’t made at the time? Did you ask Jean what she thought of it?’

‘We did and she said that although it wasn’t far, these burglars tend to try a street at a time, going up and down before moving on,’ Sonny said. ‘It’s highly unlikely they got into a car and tried another street.’

Maxie knew that to be true and could see Jean’s point. ‘Did they ever catch that guy?’

‘Jean’s looking into it,’ he said.

‘Good and good work,’ Maxie said. ‘That’s a definite new lead and we should make sure that we ask our audience if they were burgled either before or after that night. It makes sense that someone tried our house and then ran when Susan fell, although I’m not sure they would have moved her body. What’s the other new information?’

The students glanced at each other and through silent agreement Belle was nominated to speak. ‘We’re not sure whether you’re going to want this to feature on the podcast,’ she said warily.

‘Go on.’

‘Do you remember a girl in the same year as Susan – one called Amy Barnes?’

Maxie thought about it; she’d been focussing on the prefects and Susan’s immediate entourage so the name didn’t ring any bells. ‘Not really but she may have been in one of the school photos. Why? Has she been in touch?’

‘Not directly,’ said Belle shaking her head slowly. ‘Her brother has. He contacted us because he believes that there were drugs circulating at the party.’

‘No, that’s not possible,’ Maxie declared. ‘Susan wouldn’t have tolerated it.’

‘Well,’ continued Belle pausing before adding, ‘he actually believes that Susan knew all about them. We want to interview him for the show and find out why he thinks this. Would you be okay with it?’

Maxie’s automatic reaction would have been to denounce this as nonsense not worthy of the show but something stopped her. Anyway, her jaw had fallen open so she couldn’t say a word. After a moment, she cleared her throat and nodded at the students.

‘Go ahead, we need to know everything.’

Chapter Twenty-Two

'You wouldn't have known her as well as you think,' Andrew was saying as they drove towards the car showroom. 'No nineteen-year-old is ever going to let their annoying younger sister into their inner circle.'

It wasn't what Maxie wanted to hear. She wanted her friend to tell her that Amy's brother was probably a phoney and just out for his fifteen minutes of fame. Maxie hadn't slept since that conversation with Belle; she'd been happy to hear about the potential burglary link but not the drugs – they didn't fit with her own personal narrative of her sister's life. 'Surely I would have spotted something.'

'Like what? You were a kid growing up in a small Lancashire town,' said Andrew. 'You might have thought yourself tough but I'd like to bet your experience of drugs was probably that character Zammo from *Grange Hill* and the "Just Say No" song.'

Despite her mood, Maxie couldn't help but smile remembering the old TV depictions of teenage drug addicts – greasy haired and sallow skinned. Healthy-looking recreational users weren't part of mainstream viewing – drugs had to be scary.

They turned off in the direction of the car showroom and Maxie began to feel twitchy. 'I shouldn't be wasting my time on this,' she said. 'I should be following up these two new leads.'

'You can't follow up on Amy's brother until later and Jean is the best person to tell you what happened with regard to that burglary,' Andrew said. 'You've put a good team in place – use them.'

Maxie pursed her lips and got out of the car, following Andrew towards a salesman. Over the next half-hour, she trotted behind the two men and nodded as often as she thought she should. Eventually Andrew reached a car he seemed very happy with and recommended that she take a short test drive. Not at all in the mood, but playing the game, Maxie agreed and got in, with Andrew taking the passenger seat. She'd come to feel really uncomfortable getting into the Jeep since Christmas but as the electric car glided silently away, she felt lifted.

The sensation astonished her, and she realised that for months now she'd felt somehow less than her usual self. Whether it was the burden of her ankle and the knowledge of how it had been caused or being forced to rely on her taxi driver, however friendly he was, she didn't know but right here and now, the baggage she'd been carrying was flying out of the open windows. She put her good foot down and the nippy little car whizzed through the streets bringing a smile to her face.

'How does it feel?' asked Andrew.

'Amazing! I feel like myself again.'

The simple vision of being able to go where she wanted whenever she wanted without having to wait around for someone else was enough to seal the deal. Andrew wanted to negotiate but Maxie insisted on paying the full price to take the car as soon as possible.

'I could have got a few hundred off for you,' he said.

'There was no need. And besides, now that salesman will feel as high as I do. He'll go home happy and maybe take his wife out for dinner. I'd rather be spreading joy right now – there's enough misery in the world.'

The salesman told her they'd even deliver the car after all its checks had been completed and Maxie beamed with delight, happy to have this little glimmer of joy just ahead of her. Andrew said he'd take the Jeep to a car supermarket and sell it for her so in one fell swoop something in her life was a little easier.

'Do you think I'm overcomplicating my sister's case?' she asked as they drove towards the school. With the car sorted out, her thoughts felt as if they were flowing a little easier.

He was quiet for a few moments before saying, 'Perhaps but I'm not sure I could live with not knowing what happened and you're even more of a dog with a bone than I am – you won't be happy until you know the truth.' After another pause he added, 'However, when the truth comes knocking on the door you have to recognise it and let it in. Then close this door and walk away.'

He gave her a sideways glance and Maxie raised three fingers in a "scouts honour" gesture. Although she'd never been in the scouts she couldn't bring herself to actually vocalise any promises.

Tom was waiting for them when they reached the main school entrance; he wasn't permitted to follow Andrew to the scene of the fire so showed Maxie to his office and made them both a coffee. 'How is everyone coping?' asked Maxie.

The head teacher beckoned with his finger then led her to a side office; he had to push the door against the weight of cuddly toys and Get Well Soon cards.

'From well-wishers,' he said. 'When Fiona is fully recovered we'll take the toys into the children's ward.'

‘I’m sure they’ll be delighted. And Fiona too – to see how much people care.’

‘I hope so,’ he said. ‘I’m so relieved she wasn’t badly hurt. She’ll do anything for anyone – always thinking of others first.’

Maxie looked at Tom to see whether this last comment was aimed at her. He hadn’t taken his eyes off the pile of toys so she decided it wasn’t; it was Maxie’s own guilt, making her feel that way. They walked back to Tom’s office and sat down with the lukewarm drinks.

‘How are you getting on with your cold case?’ he asked.

‘Slowly,’ she conceded. ‘I’m guessing the fire destroyed whatever it was that Fiona was going to show me?’

‘It took everything.’

‘I’m so sorry,’ she said. ‘This is all my fault, if Fiona hadn’t …’

Tom put his hand on her shoulder. ‘I know how you feel, but we can all blame ourselves somehow – if I’d given more budget for digitisation of records it wouldn’t have happened either. Do you have any leads?’

‘I’m beginning to think I’ve opened a can of worms,’ said Maxie. ‘Someone has suggested drugs might have been involved. I know it’s an issue you have to deal with now but I didn’t realise it was around back then.’

‘I moved here around then and it wasn’t huge but there was some stuff going on. Do you remember The Shamen? “Ebeneezer Goode”?’ said Tom. ‘Ecstasy was the thing but no-one really knew what they were buying. I remember one guy telling everyone about this fantastic trip he’d had only to discover he’d taken a parma violet.’

They both snorted with laughter.

‘Nowadays it’s very different,’ he said. ‘The subject is part of the lesson plans and I have to be constantly on the lookout. Did you know that around ten thousand children were excluded from school because of alcohol or drugs last year? And it’s not always the illegal stuff; there’s so much pressure, kids now take their parents’ prescription stuff to help with the pressures.’

‘My students are the same,’ said Maxie. ‘I’m so glad to have had my childhood when I did. A bottle of cider behind the bike shed and a sneaky cigarette – which I hated anyway.’

Andrew appeared at the doorway to announce he was finished and getting back to the station so offered to drop Maxie off at the recording studio.

She was nervous and that sensation surprised her as Maxie had recorded hundreds of these shows. As she walked in, Craig grabbed her by the arm and pulled her into the tiny studio kitchen. 'I need to warn you, he's very angry.'

'The brother?'

Craig nodded. 'Yes – his name's Paul by the way. He blames your sister and by association, you for everything that happened to his family,' he added. 'I don't think you should let your students interview him.'

'I wasn't going to,' she said. 'Thanks for the heads up.'

Craig left her to gather the students together while he went back into the studio to check that Amy's brother was comfortable and understood the layout of the mikes. Maxie peered through the doorway to get a feel for this man but he simply looked ordinary: brown hair, brown eyes, average build, stubble and checked shirt. Seeing everyone as their police description was her way of disconnecting so she didn't enter this interview brimming with emotions. From what Craig had just said, Paul would be bringing enough convictions for the both of them. Maxie told her students to focus on the social media feeds for the episode and then holding her shoulders back and her head tall, walked in to join Craig and Paul.

As Craig introduced them, Maxie held out her hand with a look that said she wasn't going to withdraw it until Paul had shaken it. After a moment, he did so but with very little enthusiasm. The podcast intro music was played and Craig began.

'Thank you all for listening to this episode of *Criminal Thoughts* which as regular listeners know is focussing on the cold case surrounding Susan Reddick's death in 1995. Tonight we're going to be looking at the day before, specifically the party that Susan held while her parents were away.'

The producer played some music from the year and then Craig asked Maxie to tell them what she remembered about that night. 'I was so excited that we were actually going to have a party,' she said. 'There were older boys and alcopops – what more could a teenage girl want?

'I'd helped Susan get the house ready that afternoon. We'd moved anything fragile up to our parents' room and rolled up their pale cream rug so that nothing could be spilled on it. Honestly, we thought we were being so ...'

'Sensible?' asked Craig.

'No it wasn't that,' said Maxie. 'We thought we were being clever – we were trying to make sure our parents wouldn't have a clue about the party or if they found out, then they'd be okay because the house was untouched. We even put crisps out but not Quavers because Susan said that if they got trod into the carpet they'd stain.' Maxie shook her head sadly as she remembered that silly detail.

'It sounds well thought out,' said Craig. 'Did it go well?'

'It started well,' said Maxie. 'But after a couple of hours, every room downstairs was filled with people and it was spilling upstairs. That wasn't in the plan and Susan was dragging people off our parents' bed and telling them upstairs was out of bounds. She made me stay in my room.'

'It sounds as if it was getting out of hand,' prompted Craig.

'Not at that stage but then some bikers turned up and our neighbours got involved. The party started to disintegrate after that. I think people took the booze and headed off to the park.'

'Paul,' said Craig turning to his other guest. 'Your sister Amy was at that party wasn't she? What do you remember about that night?'

Paul stretched each side of his neck as if getting ready for a fight and leaning into the mike replied, 'That's right, Amy was there and I'd say it was completely out of hand.'

Craig prompted him to continue.

'I dropped Amy off early on,' he said. 'Susan was in her garden surrounded by some other friends and she wasn't pleased to see me. She kind of jumped back as if she'd been caught doing something she shouldn't be and then she walked up to Amy all smiley and nice. She was fake – she thanked me for dropping her off and promised she'd have a good time.'

With every word, Paul's tone was getting more and more angry. 'It made me sick when everyone called her this ideal student after she'd died because believe me, she wasn't.'

'What makes you say that?' asked Maxie as calmly as she could. 'All I want is to know the truth.'

'Susan called me to pick her up and when I got there, Amy was drugged up to her eyeballs. She couldn't stand, couldn't form a sentence. I didn't have a clue what to do so I stayed up all night, giving her water and hoping she didn't fall asleep. I was terrified our parents would find out.'

'That sounds very frightening,' said Maxie. 'What makes you think Susan was responsible?'

‘Oh don’t patronize me.’ Paul spat out the words and the spittle landed on the table in front of Maxie. ‘I saw her – in the garden. She was handing out something to her little pals and she promised Amy a good time? What else could it be?’

Although Maxie had been dreading discovering that Susan was mixed up with drugs, she equally wanted some evidence that could lead somewhere and it didn’t sound as if this was going to. Amy may have been given drugs at the party but there was nothing to suggest that Susan knew about it. ‘Did Amy actually say that Susan had given her the drugs?’ she asked directly. ‘I hate to say this but your sister may have brought them with her.’

Before Paul had the chance to respond, Craig interrupted. ‘We’ve just had a tweet,’ he said. ‘From @ninetiesguy and it says *“Susan was selling more than Avon”*. Well ninetiesguy – if you know something, give us a call and we’ll get you on the next show.’

He closed the show as Maxie sat quietly and Paul flounced out triumphantly. Around her the producer and engineers closed everything up, her students said their goodbyes and the studio went dark. Eventually Craig told Maxie that he needed to lock up and they walked to the door.

‘How are you feeling?’ he asked her as the night air hit them both.

Maxie sighed and looked directly at him. ‘That somewhere deep down, I knew this all along.’

Chapter Twenty-Three

Maxie knew her mother didn't listen to the podcast but needed to warn her about the interview just in case any of her friends did. She waited until after nine to call her as any earlier on a Sunday morning would have caused concern.

'Thank goodness you didn't video call,' said her mother brightly. 'I've been treated to breakfast in bed this morning so I'm not dressed.'

Despite the years, Maxie still couldn't get used to the idea of either parent being a vibrant individual with a happy love life.

'Me neither,' she replied, looking down at herself in a big old dressing gown. 'Although no-one has spoiled me like that for years.'

'That's because you work too hard,' came the reprimand. 'How are you getting on?'

Maxie checked first of all that her mother definitely hadn't listened to the podcast. 'I'm not sure I'd want to or know how to,' came the reply. 'Where do they broadcast?'

Maxie avoided answering that question, deciding not to encourage her and explained that she was looking into memories other people had of Susan. She told her mum that people remembered her as an entrepreneur, someone who babysat and ran an Avon round to make money.

'Yes, Susan did all those things but I'd hardly label her an entrepreneur for babysitting,' her mother said. 'Although she used to tell me that Richard Branson began with a student magazine so I suppose it might have been the start of her story. We'll never know.'

Hearing the tinge of sadness in her voice as she spoke, Maxie felt yet another spike of guilt. It seemed to be constantly prodding at her even when she was trying to exorcise it by actually finding out what had happened. An image of the old-fashioned scales held by Lady Justice came to mind and she couldn't help but wonder if in tipping the balance to satisfy her need for the truth she might be sacrificing her parents' peace of mind. After all, they had managed to move on and build new lives – or at least her mum had.

'Did she have a lot of money?' asked Maxie. 'I mean when you were sorting out her things did you find anything?'

'She wasn't the sort to hide money under the mattress was she? And besides, I have no doubt that you would have found that if she had – on one of your searches to find her diary.' Her mother had lowered her voice using the tone she always used whenever Maxie misbehaved. Maxie laughed at the memory of all those times she'd been rumbled hunting through her sister's room.

'She put everything into a savings account,' continued her mother. 'Going into the building society to deal with that was even harder than giving away all her books and clothes. There was so much unnecessary paperwork. It was hideous.'

'I'm sorry,' Maxie said on hearing her mum's voice falter at the end. 'I didn't know.'

'You wouldn't have done, we kept all that from you.'

'Can you remember how much money there was in it?'

'Oh goodness,' she said with a sigh. 'Not really, I was in a bit of a daze. We gave it all to the local dog's home. I think it was a couple of thousand though. Not insignificant.'

Not wanting to put her mum through any more, Maxie changed the subject and told her all about the electric car she'd chosen.

'That sounds fabulous. Promise me when you get it, you'll come to visit us. It's been too long Maxine and we'd both love to see you.'

If guilt were a heavy coat then Maxie would be sweltering under all that she'd been swathed in recently. She promised that she would and said her goodbyes.

Maxie went straight from the call, to the Avon website and discovered that agents received around twenty-five percent commission. As Susan wasn't the representative but did some work for a friend's mother, then Maxie guessed that at most Susan would get fifteen percent on what she sold but probably less? The cogs whirred as she estimated that her sister would have had to babysit every week for most of the year and sell £9000 worth of Avon to earn anywhere near the couple of thousand that was in the savings account. Their parents hadn't been the sort to give money as birthday gifts and pocket money was fairly miserly. Maxie and her sister had been brought up to believe in earning their living and it looked as if Susan was certainly doing that.

'How on earth did you make that money selling lip salve?' asked Maxie with her eyes skyward. 'I'm not sure I want to know but I'm going to have to find out, Sis.'

She dug out the order forms that they'd found and looked through them. It was only a couple of months' worth of orders but the pattern was quite similar – small value items requested by each person. It would have taken a long time to make money on this lot. Maxie was trying to think of a scam that might work rather than face the prospect of her sister as a drug dealer. She knew that Avon ladies got free samples and wondered whether Susan could be selling these without putting them through the books but that really wouldn't be enough money. Her sister had to be selling her customers something on the side and Maxie needed an honest conversation with a florist to discover just what it was. A quick google told her the florist was open on a Sunday so Maxie called her cabbie and set off.

To say that Carole was not pleased to see her would be the understatement of the year. Before entering the shop, Maxie had watched her through the window as she put together a bouquet while singing along to the radio. Maxie had smiled seeing a woman so completely lost in her work and loving it. It was a shame to disturb her day but she needed answers so pushed open the door and as the little bell rang to announce her arrival, Carole turned and the smile immediately left her face.

'Oh, it's you again.' She turned her back on Maxie and continued to work. 'I'm genuinely quite busy today.'

'No hurry, I can wait.' Maxie strolled around the shop picking up blooms and smelling them then perusing the cards that Carole also sold. She picked a couple of them up and took them to the counter. 'I may as well get ahead on birthday cards while I'm here,' she said trying to keep a cheery tone. 'They always creep up on you don't they?'

Carole said nothing but as she reached out to ring up the sale, Maxie grabbed her wrist. 'I need to ask you more questions,' she said. 'I need to know what else Susan was selling.'

Carole pulled her hand free then put the cards into a little paper bag and took Maxie's money. 'I don't know what you're talking about.'

Another customer walked in and bought a large houseplant. Maxie stepped to one side as she did so and waited until the customer had left before saying in a resolute tone, 'I really need to know. So I can wait here all day and believe me, I will.'

Carole sighed and her shoulders dropped. She beckoned Maxie into her office in the back room and stood behind her desk with her arms wrapped tightly around herself. 'I heard your podcast and it's not what you think,' said Carole. 'Susan did have a sideline but it was in herbal stuff or at least that's what we all thought at the time – slimming and sleeping pills, study aids – things that teenagers need. I bought the slimming pills from her – it was almost a sin to be fat back then.'

'I think it always has been for women,' Maxie said sympathetically. 'But if it was all just herbal then why the secrecy?'

'We thought it was herbal – the packaging said it was all natural,' Carole said. 'Then it became clear that some of it wasn't.'

'Because of Amy?'

'Before that,' she continued. 'Susan wouldn't have been the one giving Amy drugs at the party because she suspected there was something dodgy in them and she stopped selling them before then. Amy must have got them from someone else there.'

'But Amy's brother saw Susan handing out something at that party,' said Maxie.

'I don't know what that could have been,' replied Carole. 'Sweets? Gum? Who knows?'

Maxie slumped down into a chair as relief washed over her body.

Hooray – my sister wasn't a drug dealer! Well only an unwitting one.

The thought of potentially having to reveal that discovery on the podcast and tell her parents had been unbearable but the narrative now seemed to be simultaneously both more palatable and yet more sinister.

'Whoever supplied Susan with these "remedies" wouldn't have been happy when she decided to stop selling them – do you know who that was? Did she ever say? Could it have been someone at the teacher training college?'

'I don't think so.' She shook her head. 'I'd been buying them since sixth form and so had the rest of the gang. When Susan quit, I didn't ask any details. I wasn't really that bothered because the pills had been giving me awful stomach pains. I moved on to those meal replacement shakes and thought nothing of it.'

'What about the official Avon rep?' asked Maxie. 'I've been told that Susan was working for one of her friends' mothers – do you have any idea who that might be?'

'I'm sorry, I really don't know any more and it was *so* long ago.'

Maxie nodded thoughtfully and thanked her. She was about to leave the shop when a final question came to mind. 'You said that you'd been taking these supplements since school, can you remember who else was buying them?'

'Honestly, I didn't ask,' replied Carole. 'But I think a lot of us were turbo-charged with something in upper sixth.'

'And Susan was the only one selling?'

Carole shrugged. The bell rang as a mother and daughter walked in to discuss bridal arrangements so Maxie took that as her sign to leave the florist to her work.

Jean Carruthers answered her phone quickly and brushed aside Maxie's apology for disturbing her on a Sunday. 'I was just thinking about you,' she said. 'I found out about that burglary.'

Maxie had been so embroiled in the prospect of her sister dealing drugs that she'd forgotten about the other lead they'd asked Jean to look into.

'I'm sorry but it looks like a dead end,' continued Jean. 'He was caught later that night so was in custody in the timeframe we're looking at. And he hadn't been doing houses anywhere near yours. Sorry.'

It would have been too obvious an avenue at the time so Maxie wasn't surprised by Jean's words. She told her what she'd found. 'Could you see if there were dealers known to be working near schools or supplying children at the time?' asked Maxie.

'They'll all supply anyone,' came the reply, 'but I'll take a look to see if anything stands out.'

Maxie only realised that she'd fallen silent when Jean called out to ask her if she was still on the line. 'I am. I was just wondering how many more twists and turns this is going to take.'

'Are you sure you want to keep going?'

'I have to,' Maxie said. 'I've started digging this tunnel and can't stop until I see light at the other end.'

They discussed next steps as Jean also agreed to look into any sports clubs, events or coaches that had been linked with drugs. Maxie would keep going with the personal connections; Carole might not know who else was "turbo-charged" but surely the former head boy would.

'I can't just hand out the numbers of my former staff members.'

Maxie was not surprised by Tom's reaction to her request for Mike's mobile number. She protested that it would just be a friendly conversation but the response was the same and in the end Maxie settled for the head teacher agreeing to give Mike her number and asking if he would call at his convenience. It was the most she was going to get.

Maxie had strolled into the local park to make her call and now she sat on the bench watching children laugh and scream with delight as their parents pushed them higher and higher on the swings. She could remember that feeling as if it were yesterday – flying high and free. Maxie wondered why no-one had invented an adults' play park; a few minutes back on the swings or twirling round on the witches hat would probably relieve more stress than a colouring book.

Her phone rang and she excitedly rummaged in her bag to get it, thinking perhaps Tom had already passed on her message. She calmed down on seeing it was only Andrew.

'You don't seem very happy to hear from me,' he said to her lacklustre greeting.

'I always am,' said Maxie. 'I was just hoping on this one occasion it might be someone else.'

He asked where she was and then told her that he was coming over to collect her.

'Where are we going?' she asked.

'To a lock-up just outside of Preston.'

'The key fob,' said Maxie reinvigorated by the anticipation of some progress. 'Have you found the door it opens?'

'We certainly have. And I think you're going to be very interested in its contents.'

Chapter Twenty-Four

'So how did you find this place?' asked Maxie as they flew along the motorway.

'Oh you know, pointed the fob to the sky, pinged the infrared signal off a passing satellite beam and used real-time location software to see which garage door actually opened.'

Maxie laughed out loud. 'You'll be auditioning for *Mission Impossible* next. So boots on the ground then?'

'Yep,' Andrew replied. 'Which is why it took so long but we got there.'

He signalled left and they took the next exit.

'And his real identity is in this place?' she continued.

'Yes – or at least we think the identity we've found is his – we're checking it out. I know we promised that we'd keep you up to date with who this guy really is. I've just caught up with Jean and given recent developments, but I think you should see this place before we take all the contents in.'

Maxie swallowed hard. 'I'm guessing that means you've found drugs in this place.'

Andrew nodded. 'A real smorgasbord of them but wait and see – it's only five minutes now.'

They pulled into a small industrial estate that was a hotbed of activity with police officers keeping mobile-phone bearing crowds out of the way as the forensic team swarmed around an ordinary-looking unit in a quiet corner.

Maxie and Andrew crossed the cordon and she peered into the unit from a couple of metres away. She didn't know what she was expecting but it certainly wasn't this.

'I was expecting some scene from *Breaking Bad*,' she said to Andrew. 'Some kind of meth lab with cooking paraphernalia and chemicals but this looks highly organised.'

In neat rows along each wall and down the centre, the unit was lined with racks of shelving and on those shelves were labelled boxes with barcodes facing outward.

'Nope, this is more of a mini-Amazon warehouse,' he said. 'We've definitely got the retail end of the operation not the manufacturing.'

'So what is he selling?'

Andrew beckoned with his finger and Maxie followed him to a table set up just outside of the garage. Having put on gloves and obtained permission from the crime scene team, Andrew picked up a small container and handed it over, telling Maxie to read the label – her heart sank as she did so.

'"Weight Loss Aid – Natural Formula",' she read out loud. She looked up and peered into the garage. 'Is it all slimming pills?'

'No – this man can help you with any ailment you can think of: sleeping problems, erectile dysfunction, memory loss – you name it, he can cure it.'

'As long as it's one of those middle-age things,' said a junior member of the forensics team in jest as they passed by.

'Does your diversity training not stretch as far as ageism then?' said Maxie giving the young guy a stern look. He apologised and scurried off into the safety of his team.

'You told him.' Andrew gave a little grunt of laughter. 'Anyway – you can see why I brought you here. It may be a thirty-year gap but it's so similar – someone was selling them then and doing the same now. It's a more sophisticated operation with an online store, in place of kids and Avon catalogues but it seems to be the same market.'

'It's not actually illegal is it?'

'If what's in the bottles is actually what's on the label then probably not. But if he owned a legitimate business why not just say that. I guess technically he is in sales but why give a fake name?'

Maxie nodded – he'd voiced her immediate reaction. She remained silent as they walked towards the door of an office built into the corner of the lock-up.

'What are you thinking?' asked Andrew as he opened the door for her.

'Having just called your colleague ageist,' she began as she walked up the stairs. 'I'm about to be size-ist. I was just wondering what he was doing at the care home and I was thinking about the nurse we met. She was probably a little bit overweight by society norms – wouldn't you say? And she knew him from the pub; do you think she might have been a customer? I can imagine her talking about wanting to lose weight for the summer – as we all tend to – and him overhearing and saying he had something that might help.'

‘It’s a possibility,’ Andrew said with a nod. ‘We can go back later. He might also have been selling those Viagra lookalikes to some of the residents. It’s one man to five women in those places.’

‘You should get yourself in there,’ said Maxie smiling at him. ‘You might actually find a girlfriend.’

The office was a simple affair with two desks set up at right angles to each other. One desk was stacked with three large computer screens and surrounded in clutter while the other was neat, bearing only a cable for a laptop, which was missing. There was minimal paperwork on either desk or anywhere else in the room. It also housed a tiny worktop which was set up for photography shoots – as well as the camera there were fake plants and fruits obviously designed to create that natural backdrop for the products.

‘So that is obviously the desk where the website is built,’ said Andrew pointing to the one with three screens. ‘And where the business is done – accounts, stock – that kind of thing. The question is, was George working alone and just liked to keep the two sides of the job separate or did he have a partner?’

Maxie glanced from one desk to the other and knew immediately that they weren’t used by the same person. She said as much to Andrew. ‘You’ve got the openness of a creative mind there and a near OCD level of secrecy on the other side. They could never work in the other person’s domain – it would be their idea of hell.’

‘Fingerprints will confirm which one he was but given it’s taken this long to find him I’m guessing he’s the latter,’ said Andrew as the crime scene team walked in and asked them to leave. ‘Come on – let’s see if your theory about Nurse Crystal is correct.’

The care home was extremely quiet when they arrived and Maxie almost felt the need to tiptoe around the reception as they waited for someone to greet them. After a few minutes, they heard a door opening and Jacqueline Morton emerged from her office. Maxie noted the spectacles pushed up into that sleek black crop and guessed that they’d disturbed her; the lack of any pleasantries as the care home manager asked how she could help them confirmed that. This was a busy woman who really wanted to get back to work.

‘I’m afraid Crystal isn’t here at the moment,’ she told them. ‘The early afternoon tends to be a quiet time so I give my staff their time off during it. She’ll be back for dinners and the evening routine.’

DS Dawson asked whether she thought Crystal or any other members of staff might take slimming pills.

‘I’ve no idea,’ Jacqueline replied with an exasperated sigh. ‘I really have no time for gossip or idle conversation. Why do you ask?’

‘We think the man who was found dead may have been selling them,’ said Andrew. ‘So that could be a reason why he was anywhere near the residence.’

Jacqueline’s eyebrows raised but she simply responded with, ‘I see.’ Maxie watched her face but she managed to remain expressionless and she knew they would get nothing more out of her.

‘Crystal is back on duty at 5.30 p.m. but she’ll be busy until around ten and then she’s usually keen to get off and catch her bus. I can’t give you her home address so if you really want to speak to her here, I suggest that you come back tomorrow morning at around 6.15 a.m. when she’ll be getting into her uniform and not technically on the clock. Does that suit you?’

The question was delivered in a way to make it more of an instruction – both Maxie and Andrew nodded like schoolchildren being told they could play out for an hour but no more. With the timing agreed, Jacqueline bid them goodbye and marched back to her office leaving them standing alone. Maxie couldn’t help herself; she started to laugh. ‘She certainly put us in our place.’

‘I think even the DCI would have been terrified of Jacqueline,’ Andrew said as they walked back out into the daylight.

‘She runs one heck of a tight ship there,’ Maxie said, thinking aloud. ‘I can’t imagine my mother being told when she had to nap.’

‘I doubt she’d have a choice. I have to get back to the station to see if we have his identity and whether the flat has given us any answers, what about you?’

‘I think Jean’s at the station this morning and I need to find out whether any of Susan’s old friends knew this guy so the station is good for me too,’ said Maxie, glad to still have the detective by her side.

Once at the station, they parted ways and Maxie headed to Jean's desk. The cold case investigator looked extremely pleased to see her as she walked through the door.

'Good news,' she said. 'Andrew's team have a confirmed name for the care home victim – David Wallace. No convictions or history with us but the archives show him getting a warning when he was sixteen.'

'What for?'

'Taking cannabis,' Jean said. 'There's only one incident and no sign that he was dealing.'

'Did you find anything related to Susan?'

'Very possibly,' she said with a triumphant look on her face. 'David Wallace lived in Brookfield.'

Maxie slumped down into a chair, open-mouthed. Her old neighbour's words echoed around her head: *'I think a couple of them were from Brookfield.'*

'So we have a number of links,' continued Jean. 'Wallace had some connection with drugs during his childhood – we know that from the warning. Your neighbour thinks someone from his housing estate was causing trouble at the house; he was killed – whether intentionally or not by someone who definitely was there and he now sells the type of lifestyle drugs that Susan seems to have been involved with – however unwittingly.'

Maxie acknowledged Jean's sensitivity with a nod.

'I've put in a request for the unidentified fingerprints collected at your house to be checked against any found in his office. It shouldn't take long.'

Maxie said nothing but her mind was sorting through the facts as Jean's email notification pinged. She watched Jean's expression move from one of excited anticipation to disappointment.

'We can't place him or his associate inside your house,' she said. 'But the other links still stand.'

'I just can't see him running an Avon round,' said Maxie eventually, getting a deep frown from Jean in response.

'He was eighteen or nineteen,' Maxie said. 'He took a bit of cannabis and went to parties – just like any other teenager. My sister was supplied with healthy-looking tablets to sell to other young people and we believe that she didn't know what was in them. You can say there's a drugs link but they're very different and Susan had to get those pills from someone – we still haven't found them.'

'Just because we didn't catch him dealing doesn't mean to say he wasn't,' said Jean. 'He may have been the person she owed or was trying to persuade Susan to start selling again. If we can get a photo of him as a teenager, we can ask your old neighbours if he's the one they saw.'

'He might have supplied Susan with stock that she then refused to sell,' added Maxie.

She wrapped her arms around herself as a shiver ran through her; she suddenly felt incredibly sad. Andrew had told her that when the truth came knocking she had to let it in, but not this truth. This couldn't be the reason for Susan's death – a teenage battle over drugs. For years she'd pictured Susan heroically fighting off an intruder and that's what she'd always hoped to find. How could she tell her parents this? How could she destroy their memory of their eldest daughter? Why on earth had she ever started this crusade?

Chapter Twenty-Five

The early morning start on Monday resulted in nothing useful. Andrew broached the question sensitively asking Crystal if she or anyone she knew ever bought the types of aids and supplements that Wallace was selling but she said she didn't. The DS also questioned the other staff while he was there but again, nothing. Jacqueline appeared from her office and pointedly looked at her watch as the time approached six-thirty so Andrew took the hint. He thanked her for her co-operation and together with Maxie they left the care home to its well-run routine.

They found a cafe and ordered two full English breakfasts as neither of them had had time to eat before setting off and they both felt that as it had been in vain, they deserved a treat.

'I'm heading out to meet Wallace's parents after this,' said Andrew. 'One of my officers has told them that the body has been identified as his so we'll be releasing his name but I need to find out how much they know about his lifestyle. I'll ask them a bit more about his childhood while I'm there.'

'Thank you,' Maxie said. 'And can you get a photo of him from 1995? Jean's going to ask the Kennedy's if they saw him at the party.'

Andrew nodded and then sat back slightly to give the waitress room to put the enormous breakfast down in front of him.

'You look like one of those cartoon characters with the huge long tongue lopping down and salivating,' Maxie said with a laugh.

'Well this certainly beats the canteen toast I normally have,' he said as he started on the rashers of bacon.

'Did your officer say why his parents hadn't reported him missing?' asked Maxie. 'I know he was nearly fifty but he won't have been in touch with them for weeks.'

She waited as Andrew finished his mouthful. 'All he said was that they don't seem to have been in close contact over the years and apparently David went on a lot of business trips. The team didn't ask too much on the first visit so I need to get to the bottom of it when I meet them. Are you back at the university today?'

'Yes and to be honest, I'm looking forward to having something other than the cold case to think about for a while,' said Maxie. 'It's starting to get me down.'

Andrew reached across the table and gave her hand a quick squeeze which startled her so much she pulled it back sharply and then regretted it as she knew he was only being kind. To hide her awkwardness, Maxie put on a broad smile and added, 'However – on the bright side, the car gets delivered this afternoon so I'll finally be an independent woman.'

Andrew raised his mug of coffee and clinked it against hers, 'To independent women.'

Maxie walked straight into the lecture theatre when she reached work. For the next hour she had first year students discussing criminal psychology and as it was her speciality, she had no need to prepare for this session. Besides which, it was a student-led lecture where they would get into groups, present a psychological profile and the other students would work out what crime they were most likely to have committed. It was a bit like that guessing game "Who Am I?" and Maxie always found it a fun way of getting the message across – that criminals were in the main, just like the rest of us. She threw her coat on a chair at the front of the theatre and settled down asking who would like to go first. She selected one of the people with hands raised and waited for them to choose a spokesperson. The group seemed keen to be first and yet no-one wanted to present their profile.

'Do you want me to pick another group to start?' asked Maxie but the students shook their heads and eventually pushed one person to the front. The young man cleared his throat and began. 'I'm usually male, although women do this too,' he said.

The students always began this way – trying to give away as little as possible and Maxie's mind began to drift.

'I'm often quite charming, intelligent and well-connected,' said the student pausing to wait for a reaction.

One of the audience shouted out "Tinder Swindler" and the rest of the room laughed.

'No,' continued the student now warming up to his role. 'Because I'm not like the stereotype you often see on TV. I start in my chosen field quite young – usually around nineteen but I also get out early.'

Maxie's ears pricked – she knew where this was going. She looked at the young man and he seemed to stare right back at her before continuing. 'I'm motivated by money,' he said. 'So you could call me an *entrepreneur* – I have similar characteristics.'

He continued with the psychological profile and every word he said seemed to describe Susan. Was he goading her? All the students knew about the podcast and the cold case so picking this profile, using that particular word and asking to present first seemed like a deliberate provocation or perhaps she was just being too sensitive.

'I have little concern for my clients who come from all walks of life and although I love the money I get from my crimes, I live with the fear of being caught although I rarely serve any time at all.

'I often regret my time as a criminal, not because of the effect on my victims but because of the disappointment I might cause my family if they ever found out.'

'You're a drug dealer,' shouted one of the audience and the young man took a theatrical bow before returning to his seat.

'Thank you,' said Maxie relieved to draw this profile to a close. 'Who'd like to go next?'

As another team began, Maxie looked over at the student who'd just spoken. He was having a quiet laugh with his team-mates so Maxie called for silence from everyone and again he looked at her and smiled mischievously. She could not take the bait; she could not make this lecture about the cold case or connect it in any way to the podcast. For all she knew, the parent who'd complained might have a son or daughter in this room right now. Still, the profile had started her thinking again and in a more constructive way. She'd become bogged down with the surrounding events but needed to go right back to 1995 and think it through – drug dealers were inevitably recruited by someone they knew so who had recruited her sister?

The interview with their old neighbour Mr Kennedy echoed around her head as she walked back along the busy corridor to her office. He had seen an entrepreneurial streak in Susan – had he exploited it? It would have been very easy for him to get in and out of their house and if his fingerprints or DNA had been detected, he could easily have explained that away – after all he'd been in their home so many times. And he was the right age – just old enough to influence a teenage girl yet young enough to have some kind of connection. Had her sister's killer been hiding in plain sight all these years? He'd willingly come on the podcast but that may have been Mrs Kennedy's doing and if she were an innocent party in all this, he could hardly refuse without raising suspicion.

Maxie knew she was speculating wildly and in danger of jumping the gun. One minute she suspected David Wallace and now her old neighbour. She couldn't go rushing in with an accusation – she had to do some investigating before taking either theory any further. After her lectures were finished, she marched straight to her office, closed the door firmly and sat down before picking up the phone to call Andrew. 'Did Wallace have any drugs in his system?' she asked and was told that he hadn't.

Andrew went on to say that he now had a photo of the care home victim as a teenager and that one of his team was emailing it to her. The brief but courteous call ended with them both saying they had to dash.

The next call was to Jean Carruthers. 'Did you search the Kennedy house at the time?'

'No. Why would we? We had nothing to look for – no weapon and they co-operated completely. What do you think we should have been looking for?'

Maxie explained her theory that it was Mr Kennedy who had supplied Susan with the pills to sell so may have some evidence of that at home.

'Bit of a stretch unless his wife was in on it too,' said Jean.

'The pills themselves might not have been in the house, just something to suggest it was him.'

'Honestly,' said Jean with a low regretful tone, 'we weren't looking for anything like that back then.'

Maxie ended the call resisting the urge to say the trouble was that they weren't looking for anything except evidence to find her guilty of having pushed her own sister down the stairs.

She knew that academic studies had shown that small-time drug dealers who weren't addicted to anything themselves often went on to bigger enterprises and effectively moved up the chain. If Wallace had been dealing at the same time as Susan then perhaps he took over her round when she stopped – perhaps he was at the party to get her contacts list. Or if the main customers were students of her sister's age, then there was a possibility that some of Susan's friends were approached to continue the trade. Maxie had a vision of a teenage network being exploited by a seemingly benevolent overlord. Someone who promised they could make a bit of money to see them through university; someone who told them that the goods they were selling were completely natural and harmless; someone who killed them when they wanted to stop. She had to speak to Mike Priestly and his entourage; if this business needed well-connected charming teenagers then he was the head of that tribe.

Her thoughts were interrupted by Sonny and Joseph hammering on her office door. 'Prof, are you in?' yelled Joseph.

'Your car's here,' added Sonny.

Maxie walked out with them both to see her means to freedom being offloaded. She still found it a very bizarre concept that a tow truck would come to her workplace delivering a car and if she decided she didn't like it then she could send it back. The delivery driver handed her the keys, told her it was fully charged and headed off. Everything was so simple. She was about to say that of all the things that had definitely changed for the better over the years then not having to haggle with a salesman when buying had to be right up there alongside Netflix. She opened her mouth then promptly closed it knowing that she'd sound like the old woman she felt she was becoming. Instead she joined her students trying out all the gadgets in the new car and then giving them a spin around the car park.

'I love it,' declared Maxie as they parked up and sat enjoying the smell of new car. 'Why didn't I get one of these years ago?'

'Boomers seem to like their overly big cars,' Sonny said without a hint of irony or animosity – and Maxie could tell it was just a statement of fact from his perspective.

'Hey,' she replied. 'I'm nowhere near Boomer age – Gen X at the most so we're almost next to each other in the alphabet.'

The students smiled at her, then Joseph pulled up a YouTube video for first-time electric car users on his phone and handed it to her. Maxie watched all ten minutes of someone telling her to remember to charge it and handed back the phone.

'Well, given that I never read car manuals in the past, that's the most instruction I've had on any vehicle,' said Maxie. 'Right you two – out. I have some investigating to do.'

'Do you want us to come with you?' asked Sonny grabbing the seat belt and getting ready to lock it in.

Maxie thought back to Mike Priestly's rather self-confident manner at the party and would have loved to hear the students question him with their trademark bluntness but she knew that would be the wrong move – particularly in the eyes of the dean. She looked at them both and shook her head. 'This is someone I have to handle alone.'

Chapter Twenty-Six

Maxie found the number of the academy Mike now worked at and called it on the way. Pretending to be arranging an open day she asked to be put through to the chemistry main office. Her plan was to drive there anyway just to get a feel for the place that had employed Mike and perhaps hope to catch him. Like university lecturers, teachers spent a great deal of time outside the classes doing preparation work but she didn't know his schedule so had no idea whether he would actually be there or be available at this hour of the afternoon. So it rather caught her napping when the call was answered promptly and the man on the other end announced himself as none other than Mike Priestly.

'Oh, hello – this is a nice surprise. You were just the person I wanted to talk to although I wasn't actually sure you'd be in or answering the faculty phone,' said Maxie stumbling over her first few words.

'Who is this?' asked Mike in a low serious voice.

Maxie matched the tone and replied, 'This is Professor Maxine Reddick – we were introduced at your party.'

She heard the slightly exasperated sigh and hesitation before Mike responded asking how he could help. Maxie told him that she just needed ten minutes of his time and was already making her way over to the academy. He started to reply that he was far too busy right now but Maxie had already shouted 'See you shortly' and cut him off.

The campus was huge but fortunately had a map of the buildings beside the car park. Maxie slid into one of the bays marked for electric vehicles, still feeling rather pleased with herself. She walked towards the science building and called Mike to say that she'd arrived. Within a few moments he was at the other side of the glass door, using his pass to let her in.

'I really do only have ten minutes. I'm still getting used to the way the academy works and need all the prep time I can get,' he said as they marched through the corridors to a chemistry lab.

'Wow,' said Maxie sniffing the air. 'This smell takes me back – although I have to confess I wasn't great at chemistry.'

'That seems unfortunate given the developments in forensic science over the years,' replied Mike as if she had in some way maligned his specialist subject. 'I imagine it's a real disadvantage so if you ever need a refresher lesson, let me know.'

Maxie could see that the overly-friendly person she had met at the leaving do was certainly not the Mike that stood in front of her now. He looked at his watch as if setting a timer and then leant back against one of the benches with his arms folded.

'Have you by any chance been listening to my podcast?' asked Maxie still determined that she would take this at her own pace.

'Sorry, I don't really have time with the pressures of the new job. Is it interesting?'

'I like to think so. I have a cold case team reviewing Susan's death now and we reach out for new evidence and witness statements.'

Mike's face remained expressionless – he simply checked his watch again and waited for Maxie to continue. She took a moment and then, looking directly at him, told Mike that they'd heard that drugs were circulating around the school while he was head boy.

'But I imagine someone in your position at the time knew all about that,' she said. 'I've been told Susan was selling something and in fact had an established customer base under the disguise of an Avon round. The thing is, I know she stopped selling before she died and I can't imagine those customers going empty-handed so someone must have taken over their supply and I hoped you'd tell me who that was. Did you have any inkling of someone doing that?'

Maxie hadn't given him the chance to deny knowledge of any part of the story and indeed he didn't flinch throughout. When she'd finished speaking he simply gave a wry smile and walked towards his desk, turning his back on her. He sat down like a king on a throne with his hands behind his head.

'If one of my friends had been foolish back then but had now turned their life around, I wouldn't snitch on them. Thirty years is enough penance don't you think?'

'Not if they got away with murder,' snapped Maxie, instantly regretting losing her cool.

Mike picked up a pile of notes and made a show of looking through them. 'I'm sorry for your loss but the past is the past in my opinion.' He didn't look up. 'I can't help you and your time is up. You don't need the pass to get out, just press the button at the side of the door.'

Maxie stood where she was for a moment but Mike took absolutely no notice of her.

'I'll come back when you have more time,' she said simply to make a point that in her mind, the conversation wasn't finished. As she reached the door of the lab, she turned to face him and asked, 'Just one more thing – did you know a David Wallace?'

And it was there, just before Mike settled back into ignoring her – the tiny twitch that despite the denial which came next, told her he most definitely did know that name.

Maxie got back into her car feeling completely dissatisfied with that session. She replayed it back in her mind, believing that if she'd handled it differently, she might have got more out of Mike. Now the likelihood was that he would call anyone remotely involved in the happenings of their teenage years and warn them who she was asking about.

Maxie thumped the steering wheel and the horn blasted out into the empty car park of late afternoon. It sounded the way she felt – a raging scream into a vacuum – so she blasted it again and this time let out a roar of frustration along with the car. She certainly felt better after it.

'Do you think we can have Mike Priestly arrested or at least brought in for questioning?' she asked Jean Carruthers after dialling her number.

'Why, what has he done?' she asked.

'Suspicion of withholding information and definitely guilty of smugness,' said Maxie lightening up on hearing Jean's laughter.

'Half of my bosses would have been brought in if smugness were a crime,' said Jean. 'Although I really wish it were sometimes.'

Maxie explained why she'd visited him and asked for the details of his entourage at the party.

'We obviously took some details and prints after the fire at the school but everyone had a right to be there,' said Jean. 'And I know that DS Dawson checked those against the prints found at the care home crime scene. There was no match so we can't connect him or his groupies as you like to call them.'

'They would have been at the party,' said Maxie. 'And there was nothing to connect the arson to the care home?'

'Nothing,' Jean confirmed. 'And nothing to connect the arson to your sister's death – none of the prints or DNA matched the unknown samples found at your house.'

'Although I don't think your DC Will Hardcastle was that thorough – basically if a person said they weren't there on the Saturday night he didn't process them,' retorted Maxie. 'It's like asking everyone if they were innocent and if they said yes – then letting them go.'

'You know it wasn't quite like that,' said Jean softly. 'But yes, we could have been more thorough.'

'I'm sorry, I didn't mean to imply anything about you,' said Maxie. 'I know you were following orders. Do you think this means we're looking for at least two people?'

'I don't know,' Jean said. 'But we do know someone supplied Susan with the slimming pills she was selling and I think we have to focus on that.'

'Do you think we could start right now?' asked Maxie. 'Can you call some of Mike's friends and ask if they'll see us tonight? They'll all be at work during the day and I just can't wait until the weekend.'

Jean said she'd make some calls immediately and within half an hour was back on the phone giving Maxie an address to meet her at.

Jane Meuhr's house was like something from *Homes & Gardens* magazine – immaculate with every soft furnishing, ornament and painting somehow coming together to create an ambience of peace and tranquillity. Even the woman's cashmere clothing was colour and fabric co-ordinated. In her own long dark coat and boots, Maxie felt completely out of place. She offered to take off the boots before stepping onto the cream carpet but Jane looked down at her guests' feet and sensibly suggested that they talk in the kitchen. A pot of coffee and some buttery biscuits were placed in front of them before the conversation could begin. Maxie took a biscuit – they were melt in the mouth gorgeous and almost made her forget why she was in this woman's fabulous home. Fortunately Jean was on the ball.

'I am the cold case investigator supporting this case,' she said. 'To be honest, we're starting to hit a brick wall. We know there were drugs circulating and we know Susan was selling some but we need to find out who was supplying her. I promise that anything you tell us will not reach your old school friends but I made a mess of this case the first time around and I don't want to let Maxine or her family down again. We really need someone to give us a new lead on this – will you?'

Maxie looked at Jean in surprise and admiration – she'd gone for a direct plea for help. She took a quick glance at Jane's reaction and she too seemed taken aback. The cold case investigator had put Jane in the position of helper rather than suspect and their host nodded her response.

As Jean and Maxie sat at the kitchen table, Jane paced around – her tiny heels clicking on the natural stone flooring.

'Okay – as long as this doesn't come back on me, I'll do what I can,' she eventually said. 'You're right, Susan was selling slimming pills and other things – study aids, sports performance pills – the kind of thing you can buy from the internet now, both legally and cheaply.

'She would visit our houses with her Avon catalogue and a separate order form for the pills. We'd buy something cheap from Avon and also order our "extras".' Jane gestured the inverted commas as she said the word extras.

'Why the secrecy?' asked Maxie. 'If you all thought these were natural, why the cloak and dagger approach?'

'That may have been what Susan was telling us but I for one didn't want anyone knowing I was popping pills to hit my four-hundred-metre time. And I can't imagine anyone else did.'

'Did you ever establish what was actually in these pills?' asked Jean. 'Were they safe?'

'Clearly not,' Jane said. 'Amy was taking them as well but I think she developed too much of a liking for them.'

'So when Susan stopped, did someone else start supplying you?' asked Maxie. 'Who took over the Avon round?'

Jane plonked herself down beside the two women and rubbed her hands over her face as she gazed upwards, thinking back. 'Susan wasn't selling either the pills or Avon for a while before the party,' she said. 'To be honest, we were all starting to drift apart, being at different colleges and things. That party was probably the last time we were all together. It wasn't a great night because Susan was freaking out that your house was going to get wrecked and your parents would be furious. It ended quite early and to be honest, none of us would have remembered it if Susan hadn't died the following night. Having to make statements kind of kept it in our minds.'

'But what happened afterwards?' prompted Maxie, getting impatient.

'I guess we all just got on with things,' Jane said. 'That third kid was found – you know the one who'd been missing? And that was the big news that distracted everyone. I really hate to say this but we didn't really think about what had happened to Susan much after that.'

Maxie remembered feeling that everyone seemed to be getting on with their lives as her family could never do. With Jane's words she realised that was true.

'And did anyone take over the Avon round or the drugs supply?' asked Jean.

'Tried to, but none of us wanted any of that ever again.'

'Who tried to?' persisted Maxie.

'Rebecca of course,' said Jane.

Chapter Twenty-Seven

Maxie couldn't get out of the immaculate house quick enough. As soon as Jane had mentioned Rebecca's name, she was ready to move. She felt a gentle steady hand on her arm and looked over at Jean who politely thanked their host for her help and promised that everything said would be kept confidential.

Once the front door had closed, Maxie practically jogged to her car, all pains ignored just to get to their next destination at a reasonable hour.

'I presume we're going to talk to Rebecca's parents?' asked Jean as she ran along behind her and jumped into her own car.

'Yep,' replied Maxie. 'Just follow me.'

Maxie told her Satnav where she was heading and managed to get there three minutes earlier than the half-hour it had predicted.

'It's a good job I'm not a serving officer,' said Jean as they got out of their cars. 'I'd have had to book you for speeding on at least one occasion.'

'Only slightly. And I was making up time for all those traffic lights – I think we hit every red in the county.'

'I was relieved that you actually stopped for them – I didn't think you were going to. Which house is it?'

Maxie pointed to the respectable semi-detached with its tidy lawn and low-maintenance shrubs, imagining that her own parents would have had a garden like this if they'd stayed together. She quickly checked her watch – it was bordering on late – the hour at which a knock on the door would worry elderly parents. That couldn't be helped. Maxie knocked on the front door and heard movement in the living room. As the internal door opened, the TV blared out into the hallway – the couple were watching a cosy crime and like her dad, had the volume turned up extremely loud. Mr Henderson opened the door dressed in his pyjamas with a dressing gown over the top.

'Maxine,' he said with an annoyed look on his face. 'What on earth are you doing here at this hour?'

Mrs Henderson rushed out behind him in her nightclothes too. 'Is it Rebecca? Have you found her? Don't tell me it's bad news, please not that.'

Her husband wrapped an arm around his wife as Maxie apologised and promised she didn't have bad news but equally she hadn't found

Rebecca. 'I'm guessing this means that you haven't heard from her either?' Maxie asked getting a shake of the head from both parents. Maxie introduced Jean but the Hendersons didn't invite them in; Maxie could see that this was not due to any impoliteness, it was simply that they'd been shocked by seeing her and dreading the worst.

'I didn't mean to upset you,' she said. 'But we've been working late and I guess we didn't realise the time. I've just heard that Rebecca took over an Avon round from my sister after she stopped selling it – and I wondered whether you remembered that?'

Mr Henderson looked at his wife but she shook her head and said that she didn't although she knew Rebecca was always into her make-up. 'Black eyeliner mainly,' she said.

'You didn't have an Avon round did you Mrs Henderson?' asked Jean.

'I'd have said if I did,' came the sharp reply, followed by a sad shake of the head.

Mr Henderson led his wife back down the hallway and into the living room then came back to the front door. 'I think you need to go now,' he said. 'You're upsetting my wife.'

This time Jean apologised on behalf of them both and handed Mr Henderson her card. As they were heading back down the pathway, Maxie turned and asked, 'Rebecca was always a pretty girl, do you remember whether she had a particular boyfriend back when her and Susan were friends?'

The old man shook his head and said that if she did, she probably wouldn't confide in him and he wasn't about to ask his wife any more questions. Jean took Maxie by the arm and thanked Mr Henderson for his time.

Back at the cars, Maxie stood for a moment looking up at the stars, blowing clouds of breath into the cold night air. 'That didn't go well did it?' she said.

'Well at least we know Mrs Henderson isn't the friend's mother who got Susan into Avon,' said Jean.

'If she's telling the truth.'

'You can't think everyone is lying to you,' said Jean.

'Someone is.'

Both their notifications beeped to tell them that a message had arrived; it was Andrew. The women opened the messages simultaneously to see an apology from the detective:

Sry – last email didn't go through – photo of David Wallace in 1995

Maxie's mouth dropped open when she looked at the smiling youth. Like all the pictures from that era, it was grainy but clear enough to show the Guns & Roses T-shirt a teenage David Wallace was wearing. And also clear enough to show a young Rebecca drinking from a cider bottle in the background.

'They had to have known him,' said Maxie spinning back round to the house.

Jean lurched after Maxie but wasn't fast enough. Maxie ran up the path she'd just left and hammered on the door. Mr Henderson looked furious to see her on his doorstep again and refused to look at the photo telling her to come back in the morning. Jean tried to pull Maxie away but she wasn't budging and shouted behind Rebecca's father asking Mrs Henderson to just look at the picture and see if she recognised the young man. The weary older woman appeared and told everyone to calm down. She took the phone from Maxie and put on her glasses to study it.

'That's Rebecca,' she said pointing at her daughter. 'I'm sorry I don't know any of the other names.' She tried to hand the phone back but Maxie held it close to her face and forced her to keep looking. 'Please, look again,' said Maxie. 'You must know someone.'

'No I really don't,' insisted Rebecca's mother trying to pull back from Maxie. 'You must have known them too they were near your age – why don't you remember? Please, leave me alone, I don't know any more.'

With that Mr Henderson reached out, grabbed the phone and threw it out on to the lawn. 'Keep away from my family and stop pestering us,' he yelled as he slammed the door on them.

Maxie scooped down to pick up her phone and was heading back to the Henderson's front door when Jean grabbed her arm tightly and didn't let go until they were at their cars.

'Now promise me you'll go home and get some rest,' Jean said as she took hold of Maxie's car key, opened the door and pushed her inside. 'It's too late to question anyone now and we're more likely to make headway if we're refreshed and thinking straight.'

Maxie nodded but couldn't bring herself to voice a promise that she had no intention of keeping. She started the car and drove away, just far enough for Jean to have to turn off in the opposite direction. As soon as she knew she wasn't being followed, she stopped in a supermarket car park and called Joseph.

'Woah, Professor,' said her student sounding either surprised to hear from her, drunk or perhaps both. 'What's up?'

'I want you to chase up that request we made to Avon for details of the agent in 1994 or 1995. And if you still can't get a response then go back through those carbon copies and check again that the appointed agent isn't listed somewhere on them. Also get onto the births, deaths and marriages database and be sure that we have the maiden names of every single woman we're looking at – we've missed something somewhere, I just know it.'

Maxie didn't stop for a breath but when she did, the line was quiet. 'Are you still there Joseph?' she asked. 'Did you take all of that down? I'll be in early so you can brief me on what you find.'

'Whaaaa?' came the reply. 'Are you thinking I'll do all that now? It's late and I'm in the pub.'

'You've got a phone haven't you? The internet never sleeps and you're never off it,' said Maxie sharply.

'Sorry Prof but no can do,' he said. 'And I've got American Law tomorrow morning but I'll come and see you after that. See you.'

With that he rang off leaving Maxie feeling frustrated that no-one else seemed to be taking this as seriously as she was. She couldn't simply go home as Jean had suggested but couldn't think straight. She was wondering what to do next when her phone rang and her angst eased a little when she saw it was her son, Karl.

'I hear you've got some trendy new car,' he said dispensing with any greetings or asking how his mum was. 'Gran was telling me about it.'

Maxie brushed over the fact that he'd called his gran before his mother and gushed as she described her new wheels, running her hand over the leather seats and playing with the driver console as she spoke.

'Sounds great,' said Karl. 'So why don't you come down and see me in it? I'll cook you dinner.'

It was too good an invitation to turn down so Maxie arranged to visit later in the week. She was feeling uplifted by the conversation when Karl added, 'And we can talk about Aunt Susan's case if you like. Gran is really worried about you.'

Later that night as Maxie was getting ready for bed her son's words echoed in her head. Her mother was worried about her and now she'd shared that with her son; the dean was concerned as were Andrew and Jean but none of them could see that her diligence was simply a reflection of how important this case was to her. If anything, she should be the one to worry – worry that they weren't doing enough to find out what happened.

She lay on her bed looking at the picture of the teenage David Wallace and Rebecca. It looked like one of the youth club trips that used to take place when they were around fifteen or sixteen. Maxie hadn't been on as many as Susan but she remembered that those trips were accompanied by an adult volunteer. Maybe that volunteer was the supplier she was looking for but how would she find a name? The youth club had closed down at least two decades ago so they would have no records and teenagers took so little notice of adults that she doubted anyone else who attended these trips would remember. Memory was such a fickle tool and yet her whole case seemed to rely on it. Maxie sat up to put her phone on the charger and then lay back on her bed. She wasn't expecting to sleep but soon found her eyes closing and her head sinking into the pillow.

It was pitch black but the air was damp and from the faint light of her torch she could see that she was in a long tunnel where the miles and miles of walls were dripping wet. Maxie shivered as she waded through ankle-high flood water in the tunnel. The ceilings were low and in the dark she hit her head against the old Victorian brickwork. She reached up to feel moisture on her forehead and bringing her fingertips to her lips, found the sharp metallic taste of blood.

She knew where she was; she was in the labyrinth where they'd found Kelly Ingles just before Christmas. The poor girl had been left to die in one of the disused storage rooms of the old canal-side mill. Her torch was fading but she recognised the heavy wooden door at once – this was the room. Maxie pressed her shoulder against it but it wouldn't budge. She fell to the floor weeping and inside the room she could hear a faint cry. Maxie roared and planting her legs firmly for leverage, leant back against the door and pushed with all her might. It creaked open just enough for her to wedge through and stumble towards the bundle of blankets that Kelly had been left in.

‘Susan I’m here,’ she cried out as she tore the blankets aside. ‘Hold on, I’m coming.’

But there was no-one under the blankets and when Maxie woke from her nightmare to face a black night as dark as her dreams, her heart was pounding and her face was wet with tears.

Chapter Twenty-Eight

As Maxie went through the exhausting ritual of dressing for work a couple of nightmare-filled nights later, she could see just how dreadful she looked. No amount of make-up could hide her deeply sunken eyes, the result of a complete absence of sleep over these past nights. The dream haunted her and rather than face it, she tried desperately to stay awake for as long as she could. But no matter how hard she tried, Morpheus always took her in the end and he always took her back into those tunnels.

She trudged into her kitchen but had no energy or inclination to fix herself breakfast. She hadn't eaten for days and although even coffee stuck in her throat, it was the only thing keeping her going so she made herself a carry cup and took it out to the car. Maxie set the Satnav for a route she knew like the back of her hand but in her current state of mind, she welcomed a friendly computerised voice telling her what to do. It almost took her by surprise when she reached the car park as she couldn't actually remember any of the usual landmarks along the way or stopping at any traffic lights. However, she must have done or someone would have blasted a car horn and that would have woken her up.

She sat in the stationery car picturing herself being stopped for dangerous driving and being tested for drink or drugs. They wouldn't find anything but if they had a test for burnout it would be off the scale.

'Woah Professor,' said Sonny when they'd gathered in the cold case room. 'You look awful – have you been in a fight?'

She had hidden from view for most of the morning handling the admin and report writing required of her role but just prior to lunchtime, she had to face her team. At least they never skirted around issues.

'Kind of,' she answered. 'So where are we?'

The guys told her that they'd been through the births, deaths and marriages register so had maiden names to check so they'd hand them to Jean to look up on the databases.

'We're going to meet Craig,' said Joseph. 'He's taking us through the newspaper archives for things that haven't been digitised. We're entering your world.'

He smiled as he spoke and Maxie knew it was a gentle joke and she would normally have given a witty retort but she just wasn't in the mood so simply nodded. She turned her attention to Belle. 'I'm doing the interviews for the next podcast,' said Belle. 'Getting Mike's entourage in and talking about the pressures that made them take those drugs. I'm also going to get people looking for Rebecca.'

'I don't think you're going to get anything from the women,' said Maxie. 'I genuinely don't believe they knew what they were really buying or who was behind it.'

'Maybe,' Belle said, 'but we have to play out what we already have for the listeners – we said we'd involve them. Is there something you'd rather I asked?'

'Put out another appeal for sightings of Rebecca – in fact keep that high profile on social media channels and ask about the youth club – see if anyone can remember who used to run the trips,' Maxie said. 'They were like any school trip and there had to be a certain number of responsible adults – usually one of the parents volunteered.

'Guys,' Maxie said directly to Sonny and Joseph. 'You see if the youth club is mentioned in any of the archives. It would have been involved in community projects too and that's the kind of thing that would appear in local papers.'

'So we're looking for a responsible adult who sold speed to the kids in his care?' Joseph laughed, getting a glare from his professor.

'We're looking for a lead,' she said bluntly.

Having outlined her own plans – to meet with DS Dawson and find out more about David Wallace, the team went their separate ways.

Maxie watched as Andrew took in her appearance and tried to hide his instinctive reaction. Instead of saying anything, he kissed her on both cheeks then they both sat in the booth they'd met in last time.

'You look as if you need some TLC,' said Andrew with his face partly hidden behind the menu.

Maxie couldn't reply because of the lump forming in her throat but gave him a little smile.

Andrew lowered the menu and tried to look at her but she turned her head quickly and was steadfastly staring at the specials board. He gently reached out and turned her face towards his and as he did so, Maxie swallowed back the combination of tears and tiredness that threatened to spill out at such a caring touch.

'Beef bourguignon and green things,' was all he said as she met his eyes. 'We need iron if we're going to be burning the midnight oil.'

He ordered for both of them then poured out glasses of water. 'I wish it could have been wine,' he said clinking his glass against Maxie's, 'but we're driving this afternoon.'

Andrew talked through the details he was permitted to share and as he spoke, Maxie sipped at her glass. She couldn't remember water ever tasting so good – it seemed to be bringing her back to life with every drop. And Andrew's words were no longer just going over her head – they were starting to sink in. The fog she'd felt all morning was beginning to clear.

Maxie told Andrew what she'd found as they ate. Having been unable to face food for most of the week, the sensation of chewing each morsel slowly was almost meditative. She couldn't finish it all but Andrew was ready to help clear her plate. Maxie smiled at the easy way he reached over and stabbed at her potatoes with his fork.

'So you're now pretty sure Susan was involved in the sale of these drugs and although she may not have known it at first, the drugs weren't as innocent as they seemed,' he asked her. 'That's a pretty hard truth to take – how are you feeling about that?'

'I've thrashed about because of it,' Maxie said after she'd considered his question for a few moments. 'But as you say, when the truth knocks I have to let it in.'

'And your family? What do they think?'

Maxie sighed. 'I've been summoned to see them tomorrow so we'll see. I think they just want me to stop digging.'

'They're probably just concerned. It's obviously taking a toll on your health.' His words were gentle rather than critical and Maxie nodded an acknowledgement.

'I still have to know,' she whispered.

They turned down the pudding that was included in the fixed price meal and Andrew insisted that they drop Maxie's car at the station before heading off in his.

'Trust me,' he said. 'You won't want to be leaving a beauty like that where we're going.'

The glory of the Lancashire countryside slipped away as they turned towards the more neglected parts of the county and finally reached the Brookfields estate. It had a history that could be found in many parts of the country – back in the sixties, old terraced houses had been demolished and brand new high rises erected in their place. These new places had all the modern amenities a family could want but lacked the one thing they needed – community. With years of neglect and economic hardships a rot set in and crime started to take root. However the criminals who tried to create fiefdoms in places like this had underestimated the power of mothers. The very people who were overlooked were the ones to claim back their homes and estates. They fought to get facilities for their children and took great risks to keep the drug dealers from recruiting their kids. Maxie looked at the proudly clean windows of the shabby homes and saw their struggle. Families who could not afford the luxury of choice lived here and they would always face an ongoing battle – because discrimination against the poor was every bit as real as all other kinds.

They parked outside one of the blocks of flats and walked into the hallway. It smelt of bleach and urine which Maxie tried not to breathe in as they walked past scuff marks and graffiti that showed signs of having been scrubbed recently. The lift was working but when it arrived Maxie took one look inside and decided she'd rather walk.

'The thought of it breaking down and us being trapped in something that smells like a brewery skip gives me the shudders,' she said. 'I'm having enough nightmares as it is.'

They took the stairs slowly and grabbed a breather at each landing. 'So David Wallace's mum still lives here?' asked Maxie as she played for time to get her breath back.

'She does. She's not in the best of health and took the news of David's death pretty badly.'

'What about his dad?' asked Maxie.

'Therein lies the story,' said Andrew. 'The father was violent towards the mother, the son tried to intervene and got himself both a kicking and then thrown out of the house. He hasn't been seen for years but unbelievably, the father is still around and still causing trouble, even at his age.'

Maxie shook her head in despair as they started to climb again.

'Father used to call David a ponce for being good at school and liking all those rock bands with long hair,' continued Andrew.

'So the change in name was just to disassociate himself from his father?' asked Maxie.

'Yes – George was his grandfather's name and Fairview his grandmother's maiden name.'

'So why the reappearance now?' asked Maxie.

'That's what we have to find out.' He stopped and knocked at a freshly painted door with new brass furniture. 'This is it.'

A woman carrying a portable oxygen machine peered around a door chain and on seeing Andrew's badge, let them both in. Mrs Wallace struggled back to her living room and into her chair in front of a large TV. As Maxie watched her, she knew from the file that she'd had David very young so was only in her late sixties but looked at least a decade older.

'Can I get you something to drink?' asked Mrs Wallace with her arms poised on the chair as if she was going to attempt to push herself back up to standing.

Quickly, both Andrew and Maxie told her they were fine then sat down on the sofa beside her.

'Have you found out what happened?' asked Mrs Wallace.

Andrew told her gently that enquiries were ongoing and they'd let her know as soon as they possibly could. 'I've brought a colleague with me because she's looking into a case regarding someone that David might have known when he was a teenager,' he went on to explain, introducing Maxie.

'A professor,' said Mrs Wallace. 'My David could have been a professor – always was clever. His dad hated that, used to say he had an answer for everything.' Her words came with a deep raspy breath of sorrow.

'He was a good boy,' she continued after a moment of silence. 'When he saw how poorly I'd got he bought me that TV and one of those beds that lifts you up – like you see in the adverts. It's a godsend. Such a good boy – 'course his dad thought he was just trying to show him up, splashing the cash and everything.'

'Is Mr Wallace around at the moment?' asked Andrew.

'Lord no.' Mrs Wallace looked shocked at the question. 'He wouldn't have you lot in here asking questions. He's at the bookies so won't be back until he's drank all his winnings or drowned his sorrows.'

Maxie wanted to ask why on earth she was still with that awful sounding man but she knew better so simply paused and then passed Mrs Wallace her phone with the picture of David and Rebecca on it. The old lady broke into a smile as she recognised it. 'Oh he was so happy there,' she said. 'He loved his music.'

'Do you recognise the woman in the picture?' asked Maxie. 'Do you know whether she was David's girlfriend?'

Mrs Wallace shook her head and pointed at another teenage boy in the picture. 'That's who he was sweet on,' she said. 'And that's why his dad just couldn't accept him. It was a lot harder back then though, it wasn't as fashionable to be gay as it is now. My husband was so hard on him – said it was all my fault he was like that and told him that we wasn't having David bringing AIDS into the house.'

Andrew asked for the name of David's boyfriend – Mrs Wallace remembered that he was called Stephen but knew very little else about him.

Maxie took her phone back and looked at the young men in the image. How different their lives would have been compared to her students. She shuddered to imagine David growing up in such a prejudiced time as well as an abusive home and could now understand why he changed his identity so completely. The girlfriend he'd mentioned to the quiz team couldn't be found because she didn't exist – David had been bearing the scars of his upbringing to the very end, by still hiding his sexuality. His death may have opened up a lead to solving her sister's death but this man didn't seem to have anything to do with it. And yet he'd built a business dealing in the very products that Susan had been selling – was that just a coincidence?

Maxie realised that Andrew and Mrs Wallace were staring at her as she continued to gaze at the picture. 'I'm sorry,' she said shaking herself from her thoughts. 'I was just thinking that some parts of the good old days weren't that good at all were they?'

'They certainly weren't,' Andrew said. He thanked Mrs Wallace for her time and stood to leave.

Maxie shook her hand and took her arm as they made their way back to the front door. Maxie handed her a business card and asked Mrs Wallace to call her at any time if she thought of anything that might relate to Susan or Rebecca. The very poorly lady nodded then tucked the card under her blouse and into her bra.

'You didn't have an Avon round did you Mrs Wallace?' asked Maxie as they were saying goodbye.

'No love,' she said. 'Lord knows I needed the foundation to cover up the bruises but best I could afford was pound shop.'

Chapter Twenty-Nine

After leaving Mrs Wallace, Maxie and Andrew went back to her flat and spent a good part of the evening mulling over the possibility that she was on completely the wrong track in her cold case investigation.

'What if it's nothing to do with drugs or supplements or whatever we're calling my sister's sideline,' Maxie exclaimed. 'What if this case is about bigotry and homophobia? We need to talk to Mr Wallace – it sounds as if he has a violent streak.'

Although the motivation would have made no difference to the outcome, Maxie couldn't help but feel relieved, perhaps bordering on euphoric to think that her sister might once again have died an innocent victim and not the local dealer.

'We may know more about him but we still have no idea why David died,' Andrew said. 'We found the occupant of the other desk in the lock-up. He's a freelance web designer who only pops in once a month so only just found out about his client's death. There's nothing to suggest he was involved at all.'

'Then maybe it is a crime of love. Perhaps the teenage David was in a clandestine relationship with someone who was experimenting with their sexuality and he tried to rekindle it but that person is now happily married and is terrified that their past will come out.' The words spilled easily from Maxie as this preferred narrative started to make so much sense.

'Perhaps he bumped into this Stephen; it could have been a chance meeting,' she continued. 'They'd met on the street and the killer took David up the lane to somewhere quiet so they could talk.'

'David got the wrong idea and tried to embrace him,' said Andrew picking up the story. 'And the other guy panicked, reached for the first thing that came to hand and hit out at him. As we've always thought, it wasn't an intentional murder.'

Andrew had left late and that night Maxie actually slept without being awoken by nightmares. Her synapses were on fire as she breezed through the following day giving insightful lectures and challenging her students to dig deeper in their analysis. The old Professor Reddick was back and not even the thought of tomorrow's Open Day could put her off her stride.

'Good to see you looking so well again, Professor,' Dean said as they passed in the corridor. 'Is everything ready for tomorrow?'

She told him that it certainly was and that she personally would be guiding the prospective students and parents through a case file that the university had helped to solve. 'When I've finished with them, even the parents will want to enrol,' she told him.

After lectures she had a catch-up with her cold case students, who told her that everything was on course for interviewing Mike Priestly's entourage – although they'd all insisted on doing this anonymously – and that they'd send her the edited file before it aired to see if she wanted any further edits.

'I know I've already asked you to talk about the youth club,' said Maxie. 'Could you also find out if any of their friends were gay? Or if they knew of any students who were? Don't go in directly or air it without putting it past me, I'm working on the assumption that someone may have been experimenting but wouldn't want that known.'

'And they'd clam up if they thought it was going to come out now,' said Belle nodding her understanding.

'Did you discover anything from the newspaper archives?' Maxie asked Sonny and Joseph.

'That the internet was the best thing *ever* invented,' Joseph said with a groan. 'Honestly, it's no wonder crimes weren't solved back in the old days – we're going back to the archive purgatory later.'

Maxie laughed and told them that conviction rates hadn't changed that much even with all the technology they now had.

'That's only because confessions were beaten out of people,' Sonny said. 'I've watched *The Sweeney* – how was that show ever made? Everyone is corrupt.'

Maxie could have engaged in banter about the "golden days" of policing for the rest of the day in the mood she was in but she was heading down to her son's house and had to get a move on. She commended the team on their great work and left them to their investigations.

Maxie whizzed down the road with the radio on full volume and the heated seats comforting her against the thought of the early spring evening air. The nights were thankfully growing lighter and colour was starting to emerge in gardens and along roadsides everywhere. The suggestion of the cheery yellows of daffodils and pinks of cherry blossom had the effect of bringing optimism to the world and to this case. Maxie hadn't wanted to believe her sister was involved in anything nefarious and now she didn't have to. She knew this had hampered her willingness to investigate thoroughly; deep down Maxie really didn't want to find out a truth that was unpalatable.

She thought as she drove that although it was feasible for David to have been killed because of his homosexuality, why would anyone attack her sister because of that? Could it have been a hate crime because Susan was also gay? Maxie couldn't remember any particular boyfriends visiting their home but then again, she'd never allowed anyone she'd dated to meet her parents and get the inevitable twenty questions about their prospects and parents' occupations. But Rebecca had visited all the time so perhaps Susan's lover was hiding in plain sight. They were both regular attendees of the youth club and now David was too. Had this been the place they all felt safe? Maxie let her imagination run wild, picturing her sister as a gay rights activist declaring that they would hide no more – that she would host a party and everyone could be themselves. However, some factions weren't happy about that so caused the fracas that had roused their neighbours and later the same people came back to silence Susan. Maxie knew she was doing it again – sanctifying her sister. She had to stop this and focus on the few facts they had.

Maxie arrived at her son's flat as the sun was setting. She parked in one of the guest spaces just as Karl and her mother emerged from the building to look at her new purchase.

'Special,' exclaimed Karl as he edged Maxie out of the way and jumped into the driver's seat. 'It suits you.'

'Much more than that huge Jeep,' added her mother as she got in beside her grandson. 'I never knew why you got it, it was always Susan who wanted a Jeep – you were obsessed with sports cars.'

That comment astonished Maxie. 'No,' she replied. 'I always wanted the Jeep.'

'Not before she died you didn't,' said her mother very matter-of-factly. 'Now are you going to take us for a spin? I'll get in the back.'

Karl got in beside his mum and Maxie resumed her place behind the wheel, starting up the car then driving her passengers around the block.

'Oh isn't it quiet?'

'And smooth.'

'And it still has that new car smell,' said Maxie's mother. 'Do they spray it on in the showroom?'

Karl told her that was exactly what happened and the two of them continued to chatter until they were back in the parking space.

Maxie had other things on her mind throughout the little test drive and wondered how much of her own story was influenced by her sister. Had she really not wanted that Jeep? Had she not noticed her sister's sexuality? What else had evaded her supposed powers of detection? At least she was in the company of the one person who would probably know. She followed Karl and her mother back into his flat which was small but comfortable. Her son had accepted as many cast-offs as he could when furnishing it so it didn't look like a stereotypical man cave. A huge TV, gaming console and black leather sofa still had pride of place but at least there were coloured cushions and throws which softened their presence.

He even had a small dining table in the kitchen and although Maxie imagined that most days he ate from a tray on his lap, tonight he had actually set places for the three of them.

'Have you cooked?' asked Maxie incredulously. She doubted it but there was no mistaking the smell of something delicious emanating from the oven.

'Gran brought a lasagne but I did buy some garlic bread,' he replied with a wry smile.

'I thought you might need some home cooking,' added her mother as she put out some paper napkins.

Her mother's lasagne was good but very heavy. However saying no to her mother was simply not going to happen. Conversation was light as they ate but after everyone passed on pudding and coffee was served, Maxie had the sense that she was about to be interrogated.

Her mother scraped her chair back in order to face her daughter and reached out to grab her hands. 'So tell me what you've found out,' she asked.

Maxie could tell by the facial expressions of both her son and her mother that they planned to try to dissuade her from continuing the investigation, to "let bygones be bygones". She had no doubt that the words "it won't bring her back" were already forming on her mother's lips. So she launched with a piece of information they wouldn't have known from the local news – that the person killed at the care home was attacked by someone who had been at Susan's party. Her mother slumped back in her chair, shocked at the news.

'You mean they've hurt someone else?' she said.

'They've actually *killed* someone else, Mum,' Maxie clarified, refusing to underplay what had actually happened.

‘So you think these two crimes are linked even though they’re thirty years apart?’ asked Karl, pouring himself and his grandmother a glass of wine. Maxie had an early start in the morning for the Open Day so was planning on driving back that night.

‘I do and there are two possible links,’ said Maxie going on to explain the supplements sideline and the potential homophobia.

‘My auntie was a county lines runner,’ said Karl with an ironic snort of laughter. ‘I’d better not become a famous game designer – or maybe being one of the bad boys would improve my credibility.’

‘My daughter was no more a drug dealer than she was a lesbian,’ huffed Maxie’s mother, folding her arms as if to call the matter to a close. ‘Not that I would have minded the latter at all.’

‘With respect, Mum …’ Maxie started.

‘And we all know that actually means *with absolutely no respect*,’ the senior Reddick said.

‘I just meant to say that we don’t always know what our children prefer to keep secret,’ she continued. ‘Take Karl – moving to Manchester with an internship rather than going to uni – I knew nothing about it until it was announced.’

‘But let’s get back to Auntie Susan shall we?’ said Karl getting the focus away from himself. ‘You think this Rebecca was her girlfriend?’

Before Maxie had the chance to answer him, her phone rang. She didn’t recognise the number and was about to decline it but her instincts told her not to. ‘Mrs Wallace,’ she exclaimed, picturing her business card being tucked away for safety. ‘How can I help you? Have you thought of something?’

Karl and her mum sat silently with their mouths gaping slightly open as they watched Maxie take the call.

‘Slow down – who is? I’ll be there as soon as I can – lock the door, turn off the lights and don’t let him in,’ she said, simultaneously finishing the call, downing the last dregs of coffee and then declaring, ‘I have to go.’

Maxie darted out of the flat and down to the car, realising that her family was following and insisting that they were coming too. ‘It sounds like trouble and I’m not letting you walk into it alone,’ said Karl. ‘If this person has killed two people already we’re not giving them the chance to make it three.’

Maxie didn't have time to argue so let them cram themselves in as she set off as quickly as she could. Karl put the Brookfield address into the Satnav while Maxie drove, putting up two fingers to every speed camera that tried to slow her down.

'Mum,' said Karl looking at the dashboard. 'You haven't charged the car.'

'What?' Maxie was anxious and frustrated; she didn't want to hear about any obstacles.

'You haven't charged the car,' repeated Karl pointing at the gauge. 'We don't have enough range left to get there. You have to stop.'

'I can't,' shouted Maxie. 'I have to get there.'

Karl switched off the air conditioning, the phone charger and the heated seats. It wouldn't be enough and he told his mother. 'We're going to get stuck on the motorway. You have to stop.'

But Maxie simply put her foot down on the accelerator and drove even faster. Karl picked up her phone and found Andrew's number. He explained what was happening and where they were going, then let him speak to his mother. 'Karl is right, Maxie,' said Andrew. 'You can't make it that distance. I'll be there within half an hour and I'll do a call out for a local response team. Stop, charge up and then meet me.'

A warning light came on and Karl looked at his mother. 'It's freezing out there,' he said. 'And Gran will have to stand on the hard shoulder if we run out of charge on the motorway.'

A sign appeared for services in five miles and Maxie sighed with defeat. When they reached it, she signalled and pulled off going straight to one of the rapid charging spaces. While waiting she rang Mrs Wallace to tell her that the police were on their way; there was no answer. She rang again, no answer. And again. And again. And again.

Her phone rang and seeing Andrew's name she felt a tiny ray of hope that evaporated on his words, 'I'm sorry Maxie, we got there too late.'

Chapter Thirty

Andrew was awakened by the sound of Maxie bludgeoning through the living room.

'Sorry,' she said on seeing him lift his head from the makeshift bed on the sofa. 'I didn't mean to wake you.'

'That's okay,' he said through a yawn. 'I normally sleep through slamming doors and plates crashing. Why on earth are you up so early?'

'Got to get into work.' Her hand was trembling slightly as she put a slice of bread into the toaster but she clenched her fist and managed to steady it. 'It's Open Day.'

'You're going in? After everything you went through last night?'

Andrew had phoned for a response team and they'd got to the Wallace house within twenty minutes but they were too late. Andrew had phoned Jean and together they'd arrived shortly afterwards to find the woman they'd interviewed only a few hours earlier that day strangled in the bathroom where she'd locked herself for safety. As there was nothing more they could do – after all the cause of death was obvious and they knew the killer was her husband, who hadn't even been sober enough to hide his tracks. They'd found an empty bottle of cheap vodka in his jacket along with a fistful of torn-up betting slips so guessed that he'd come home angry and ready to take his losses out on his long-suffering partner. As Maxie listened to the report of what had happened, she knew she couldn't allow herself to imagine that Wallace had heard about her visit and that in some way she was to blame for this. Andrew and Jean reassured her there was nothing to suggest it and they had both seen this so sad scenario too many times in their careers. They left things to the crime scene team and then drove to the service station.

At the services they'd split up; Jean driving Karl and his grandmother back to Manchester in Andrew's car, while he brought Maxie back to her flat in the electric vehicle. It had been a very late and sombre night. They'd both had a couple of brandies on getting back but said very little. As Andrew had been over the limit, he was offered a place on the sofa which he more or less collapsed into after Maxie had retired.

'I have to keep going *because* of what we went through last night,' Maxie said, avoiding eye contact with the detective while slamming some butter on the piece of toast as if it had somehow misbehaved. She passed the inelegant offering to Andrew. 'I wasn't there when she needed me.'

Andrew tried to put his hand on hers but she shrugged it off, took one mouthful of coffee and then threw the rest of the cup in the sink. She reached for her coat and briefcase telling Andrew to have a shower if he wanted and to make sure the doors were locked. With that she was on her way.

Getting into the car she had mixed feelings. It had let her down when she really needed it; the Jeep wouldn't have done that. Then again, she wouldn't have set off in the Jeep with no fuel. A growing sense of constant failure was gnawing at her; she was finding both the past and the present an uncomfortable place to be. Maxie longed to just catapult herself into a future where life was easy and she'd learned from all the mistakes she was ever likely to make. The presenter on the radio reminded everyone that today was Friday the thirteenth but then told them not to worry as in Italy it wasn't considered unlucky.

'We're not in bloody Italy,' Maxie shouted back at him although she had difficulty in imagining how much worse than yesterday this day could possibly get.

News of Mrs Wallace's death and her relationship with the care home murder had reached the university although it was mainly her cold case students who could understand the full impact on the case and their professor. They approached her gently, offering condolences and any further support she might need.

'I just need you all to keep focussed on the investigation,' she said. 'Don't let any of these deaths go unpunished.'

The Open Day was running across several faculties so many members of staff and students were helping out and the place was buzzing. Maxie had planned that groups of would-be entrants would arrive in the main lecture theatre and would then be split into waves for a tour with a different member of the Criminology Department. They would see all the facilities that the university had to offer but at different times so as not to overwhelm the laboratories or library facilities – where some current students would still be working. Question and answer sessions about the campus, the social facilities and housing would be addressed by students themselves. Maxie knew that teenagers trusted other teenagers to give them the low-down on these issues more than any lecturer and so didn't try to guide or intervene in those conversations. At the end of the tour at lunchtime, they'd regroup in the lecture theatre to hear about career opportunities and unique features of the Lonsdale degree.

Professor Maxie Reddick and the work of the Applied Criminology Unit were one of those unique features and so for the final twenty minutes of the lecture, DCI McAlister joined Maxie at the lectern. She explained how the unit had been set up to research issues that would directly impact police policy and arrest rates.

'From emerging cybercrimes through to unconscious bias,' said McAlister, 'this Unit has supported the day-to-day work of my teams. Take for example, repeat offenders; you may not know this but most crime is committed by a minority of individuals. The work done by Professor Reddick and her team could help us identify repeat perpetrators and the likelihood of resolving multiple crimes at once – and I'm sure you can imagine just how valuable that would be to me and to society as a whole.'

From the far side of the room, Maxie could hear someone whispering as the DCI spoke. She turned to give them a stern "quiet please" glare and stopped in her tracks on seeing it was Mike Priestly sitting at the end of a row with a teenage girl who was probably his daughter and a woman in her early forties who Maxie guessed was his wife. Maxie had been so wrapped up in making sure the event went smoothly that she hadn't noticed their arrival. Mike looked up and caught her eye so she simply raised a finger to her lips in a friendly gesture. He gave her the thumbs up in return.

Questions followed the DCI's speech and she dealt with them like the professional she was. As the session was leading to a successful conclusion, a young man raised a hand and asked the final question. 'What opportunity is there to get involved in the podcast?'

Maxie introduced her cold case students who had positioned themselves on the front row. They explained their involvement and what they were learning from it.

'I always knew how to use the technology,' said Sonny. 'So the key output for me has been learning to weave all the insight into something compelling that people will want to listen to.'

'For me it's about the depth of analysis and sheer slog we need to undertake to get results,' continued Joseph. 'When you read case studies, they're inevitably already solved and so pretty clean cut.'

'And I'm seeing these cases as more than just studies,' added Belle. 'These are real people we're getting justice for.'

'Or not getting justice for.'

The whole lecture theatre turned towards the off-cuff comment and Mike Priestly shrugged his shoulders then mouthed an apology.

She couldn't help herself. Maxie turned and walked towards Mike brushing off the DCI who tried to hold her back.

'What do you mean by that?' Maxie asked as she stood directly over Mike.

'Sorry, just a little quip,' he replied. 'But I've just joked to Eve here that she shouldn't get involved in your ACU or whatever it's called. People who get close to you have a terrible tendency to end up dead.'

Mike looked out to the audience for a reaction to his "joke" but the room was filled with an awkward silence. DCI McAlister tried to pull the session to a close by picking up Maxie's notes and reading them aloud.

'We'd like to thank everyone for coming today,' she said. 'Please do email the university ...'

She didn't have time to finish the sentence. Maxie had dragged Mike to his feet by his collar. 'Say that again,' she growled through clenched teeth.

The foolish man did just that and as he spoke Maxie pulled back a hand and, with a strength she didn't know she had, slapped Mike as hard as she could across the face sending him flying backwards into his wife and child. The theatre occupants gasped and some of the teenagers starting recording the fracas which hadn't ended with the slap. As Mike cowered with his hands over his face, Maxie kept going – clenching her fists and dishing out pathetic little punches until she'd run out of energy. Sonny and Joseph pulled her off while Belle got the Priestly family out of the room and DCI McAlister insisted everyone else leave immediately. The room had emptied apart from Maxie's five aides when the dean came rushing in.

'Just get out of here,' he growled at Maxie, 'right now.'

Her face was blazing with the shame of having lost it so badly and so publicly and she simply couldn't trust herself to get behind the wheel in this state. Maxie needed to cool down so walked through the grounds of the campus and onto a back road that led into town. With each step she felt a little calmer but still couldn't quite believe what she'd just done. Maxie held her hands up and looked at them as if they weren't attached to her body. It would be easier to accept if they were capable of independent actions – some muscle memory having taken over and reacted to the provocation. If someone else had punched Mike Priestly she would have said she completely understood – he deserved it for what he'd said. But it wasn't someone else – it was her and it was in front of parents, students and the DCI. She had absolutely no idea how she was going to redeem herself this time.

After an hour's slow walk she reached a pub on the canal and ordered herself an orange juice. She hid in a corner in case any of the families who'd attended the open day walked in and noticed her. The orange juice made her feel queasy as it made its way to her churning stomach. She'd have liked something a bit stronger to settle her nerves but being caught drinking wouldn't do her any good either. Maxie called her cabbie and he was there within twenty minutes. She needed to confess her sins to someone who wouldn't judge so when they'd set off for her flat, Maxie wasted no time in telling him what had happened.

'Blimey,' said the cabbie whistling his astonishment. 'I would have paid to see that. Next time make sure you get yourself a deal with Sky Sports if you're going to start boxing.'

Maxie would have liked to laugh but simply couldn't. She managed a faint smile and asked him what he would do in her position.

'The only thing you really can do is grovel,' he replied. 'People will want to make you suffer but they can't make you feel any worse than you do yourself so let them know that. Grovel hard, get on your knees and apologise over and over again. Then take some time off and I guarantee, they'll have forgotten about it when you get back.'

Maxie wasn't sure his solution would work no matter how much she grovelled. She'd suspected Mike of being behind the dean's first warning and now she'd played directly into his hands. She could have kicked herself for being so stupid.

They pulled up outside her flat and as she reached into her bag to get her purse, she noticed Andrew was also pulling up. He had to have heard what had happened and was here either to offer comfort or to relay a message from the DCI. Maxie calmly paid her cabbie and thanked him for his advice.

'Don't let the beggars grind you down,' he called out the window as he drove off.

Maxie took a deep breath and walked towards the detective. He had a strange expression on his face and she couldn't make it out – fear? Embarrassment? Her friend certainly looked as if he'd rather be anywhere but right there, right now.

'I'm guessing you've heard about my meltdown,' said Maxie. 'I should have taken your advice and not gone in today.'

It was only then that she noticed Andrew was with a uniformed officer who now stepped out of the car. Maxie watched as Andrew inhaled, stood tall and said, 'Professor Reddick, I'm afraid we've had a complaint against you. I'm arresting you on the charge of assault and need you to come to the station with us.'

Chapter Thirty-One

How many times had her police procedures lecture covered this? Maxie turned to the left, the right and looked straight ahead as instructed. The pictures of her arrest would make it into the public domain sooner or later and she could imagine Mike Priestly and his friends using them for darts practice. How could she have been so stupid? This investigation was getting the better of her and now everyone could see that. There were still so many unanswered questions and in this situation Maxie knew she wouldn't be able to get to the bottom of it. In all likelihood she'd be debarred from the university and the cold case would almost certainly be wrapped up. If it did continue then Maxie would not be allowed anywhere near it.

She provided the fingerprints and DNA without comment then followed the sergeant processing her case to an interview room where she gave her statement admitting the assault and was left with only her thoughts for a couple of hours. Eventually an officer she didn't know came in to see her.

'We've established that Mr Priestly wasn't injured during the assault,' he said reading from his notes. 'And witness statements confirm that he did play a role in provoking the attack. Given the circumstances and your position, we have decided to release you with a caution which as I've no doubt you understand, is still a conviction for assault and will stand on your record.'

Maxie breathed a huge sigh of relief – it wasn't going to court. She was led back to the charge bar where her possessions were handed back to her. As she reached into the tray taking out her phone and university pass, Maxie felt a pang of remorse as she really didn't believe she'd be needing the pass any more.

She grabbed one of the taxis at the rank rather than calling her usual guy as she couldn't imagine polite conversation with anyone at the moment. She ran straight into her flat and threw off her clothes as she strode through the hall, launched herself into the shower and washed off the past hideous twenty-four hours. As the hot water started to calm her, Maxie sensed that her body and soul needed nurturing. She took her time to massage in copious amounts of shampoo then carefully condition her hair. Once wrapped in a soft towel, she eased the comb through her hair rather than tug at it and then smoothed a scented lotion over her body. She stroked the knuckles of her fingers which ached a little from the pounding they'd given Mike. It was a strange sensation that she'd never experienced before, but then again, she hadn't pummelled anyone before either. Dressing in a gentle cashmere tunic that felt like a hug, Maxie was ready.

Feeling like an addict on the twelve-step programme, Maxie sat down and made a list of the people she had to apologise to. Mike should have been at the top of that list but she simply couldn't bring herself to write his name – she was sorry she'd lost it and wished that she'd taken him down with a chilling retort instead but he deserved her anger. It was getting late, but Maxie began dialling. The DCI was first on her list, if only because the dean would ask whether she'd called McAlister. Whether she was genuinely unavailable or not, the detective chief inspector didn't pick up so Maxie left an extremely grovelling message. Next it was the dean and she stood up tall before pressing his contact details.

'How are you?' he asked, catching her slightly off guard with the concern in his voice.

'Embarrassed, humiliated, thoroughly ashamed of myself. I am so sorry, Dean, I don't know what came over me.'

'I think we both know what came over you,' came the kindly reply. 'You're too invested in this cold case and that affected your judgement. I did warn you that you were looking exhausted and asked you to take a step back.'

'I couldn't,' murmured Maxie. 'I have to know what happened and when I realised Mike was trying to have me thrown off this case by having a word with you, it just made me even angrier.'

'I don't know what you mean, Maxie,' he said. 'I'd never spoken to Mike before today when I assured him the matter would be properly looked into.'

'But he's a cricket buddy. I saw a photo of him accepting a trophy and you were in it.'

There was a moment's silence before he continued. 'I honestly don't know him Maxie. I'm on one of the committees so I do get dragged out for photos but I don't know all the members – there are nearly two hundred of us.'

Maxie could picture her brain as one of those old-fashioned telephone exchanges seen in black and white films where telephonists plug in wires to connect people. One of her wires had been unplugged but if it wasn't Mike who'd complained then who was it? She asked Dean.

‘I’m sorry,’ he said. ‘You know that has to remain confidential. Although you have to see the irony in all of this – you thought Mike was trying to scupper your efforts and he wasn’t, yet by goading you to attack him very publicly, he’s actually succeeded.’

Even Maxie couldn’t hold back from joining in a little snigger with him – gallows humour was still humour.

‘So where does this leave us?’ she asked, hearing the loud exhale on the other end of the phone.

‘As you probably realise, we have had to suspend you pending investigation,’ he said. ‘I imagine that you pleaded guilty and have been given a warning?’

Maxie confirmed that she had.

‘Then with a conviction for assault, it’s highly unlikely that your licence will be renewed,’ he continued. ‘Not impossible, with the extenuating circumstances, but we’re in a tricky position which won’t be resolved quickly. On the bright side, you have time to get well.’

‘Who will cover for me?’

‘Dr Leo Turner will take over your postgraduate responsibilities and I will share the undergraduate work out as much as I can.’ As he spoke, Maxie realised just how much of a done deal this already was.

‘Fortunately with the timing, it’s exam and module preparation that will take up most of the workload,’ she said. ‘And I’m glad to see Leo getting the opportunity he deserves – he’s a very clever guy.’

‘You taught him well,’ Dean replied tenderly.

‘Can I come in to get my personal possessions?’ asked Maxie. ‘And do a handover with Leo?’

‘Of course you can.’ The amicable tone lifted Maxie’s mood until the sentence was completed. ‘I’ve allocated from two to three on Sunday afternoon. The campus should be quiet then and Dr Turner has been asked to come in. After that date I’m afraid all emails and passes will no longer work and I would ask you not to come in again or contact any students until I have the decision of the Faculty Board.’

She’d read many anecdotes about people who’d been made redundant only to discover it was the best thing that had ever happened to them. They’d discovered their passion for music or travel and had carved out a whole new career for themselves. But the only thing Maxie felt like carving right now was a tombstone.

Here Lies Professor Reddick
Idiot

Could she even call herself Professor? Was she still one? Maxie supposed that technically while the university debated the issue, she still was but what would happen after the suspension? She'd be joining the leagues of people referred to in the past – "former" prime minister / England captain / professor or whatever dizzy heights they'd risen to. She still had her doctorate, that couldn't be taken from her just as an Olympian was always an Olympian. Although if the crime were serious enough even those awards could be stripped away. She'd already lost the title "sister" and it was beginning to feel as if every other part of her identity was starting to evaporate. Mother, she was at least still a mother. She called Karl and found him staying at his gran's.

'Thank God you're out,' he said. 'We heard what happened – it's all over social media – well the local pages anyway.'

'I guessed it would be,' she said. 'My humiliation is complete then. I am so sorry; I hope it doesn't embarrass you in any way.'

'It was a bit of a shock,' he said. 'Seeing videos of my middle-aged mother pummelling some poor bloke, especially when the punches were very, very girly. Don't worry – public opinion is on your side.'

'Really?' She knew that you could never predict what reaction the collective jury of social media would have or how long it would last.

'Yeah – view is that Mike is a smug prick and deserved all he got.'

'Oh I don't want that.' Maxie sighed. 'I don't want people taking sides or making this the focus of everything. It isn't about me or him, it's about finding out how Susan and David died. Those are the only things that matter here.'

She then spoke to her mother – assured her she was fine and promised that she'd get some sleep. Neither of those statements were true but they both knew that and Maxie was glad to see another call coming in so she could say goodbye.

'I don't think I should be talking to you guys,' she said answering a WhatsApp video call to her cold case students. 'I've been suspended.'

'We know,' Sonny said. 'Dean has told us that our desk research will stand as our final dissertation but we shouldn't pursue the actual investigation.'

‘I’m so sorry,’ said Maxie. ‘I hoped this would be a ground-breaking experience for you guys, one you’d never forget. But not for the wrong reasons.’

They all gave a little laugh which certainly eased the tension.

‘It has been ground-breaking,’ said Joseph. ‘I’ve learned more from this one case than any other project and I’m not ready to give up.’

‘You have to,’ said Maxie sternly. ‘You all have to.’

‘We may have to give up the study,’ said Belle, ‘but we can do what we like with our own time. Craig has employed us.’

The students went on to explain that since the video of her fight with Mike went viral, listener figures had gone through the roof and they were needed to field all the new information and additional marketing. ‘We’ve blown *Secret Sleuth* out of the water,’ added Sonny. ‘They were losing listeners with all the work we’ve done so they tried to stir up some scandal around your boxing match but it backfired and they’re basically out of the scene. Listeners want you back Professor but Craig thinks it might be too soon.’

‘And he’s right,’ said Maxie. ‘It would be.’

‘That’s why he’s given us part-time jobs as researchers and presenters,’ said Belle. ‘The university has no jurisdiction over what we do to pay our rent.’

The students looked euphoric and Maxie could see there would be no dissuading them. And technically Belle was right – students did all kinds of things to pay their way and some of them were far dodgier than hosting a podcast. She nodded her acceptance of what they’d said.

‘So we did the interview with Mike’s entourage,’ said Joseph. ‘It’ll air tonight and it’s pretty bland – nothing we didn’t already know – but what was more interesting was what they said when the interview was over.’

‘Yeah – we were still recording – not because we were trying to trap them, just because I hadn’t gotten round to turning things off,’ added Sonny.

Maxie asked what was said and her students promised to send the extra footage so she could listen to it herself. Within five minutes of finishing the call, Maxie was sitting back with her headphones on as the women she’d last seen on the dance floor spilled the beans.

‘I’m glad that’s over,’ said one voice. ‘It wasn’t too bad - I thought it would be like a court scene with us all having to confess what we took.’

'How do you Trish Harrington plead …' Another voice laughed. 'Guilty or not guilty?'

'Guilty of buying Avon products, but I wasn't going to tell them that,' said the first voice Maxie now knew belonged to Trish. 'It's totally linked with the drugs now and I never was part of that scene.'

'No-one would believe that though would they?' said another voice which Maxie assumed belonged to the final groupie Liz Dixon. 'No smoke without fire and all that.'

'Precisely, and I never knew it was any more than the slimming pills did you, Cheryl?'

'I had a suspicion,' said Cheryl. 'Mike certainly won more races when he'd had his *vitamins*.'

The girls laughed but Maxie felt a chill through her body. She knew in her bones that Mike was involved somehow but so far, she'd hit brick walls with every line of enquiry. Jean had told her that his fingerprints didn't match those at the care home and Dean had confirmed that it wasn't Mike who'd reported her. However he hadn't denied knowing who was dealing and now she knew why he was so keen to forgive and forget the sinners of the past – he was very likely one of them.

Chapter Thirty-Two

She almost wished there was a giant grandfather clock in her apartment. Time was passing so slowly and so *silently* that loud ticking hands and the occasional chime to mark the hour would be very welcome. The students had made it clear that they were going to continue work on the podcast and Jean had said that the cold case would run alongside the care home murder until the fingerprint had been identified, so the investigation was still live, it just didn't include her and she didn't know who she was if she wasn't involved in crime one way or the other.

She knew she had to follow up on Mike and his involvement but the thought of his self-satisfied smile if she blundered in with an inaccurate accusation was too much to bear. She had to have solid evidence of his precise involvement and be emotionally ready to tackle the guy when they next came face to face; and neither of those statements applied at present.

Maxie sipped at her coffee and grimaced; it had gone cold like the other two this morning. She didn't actually want any coffee, making it just filled the time. The door buzzer went and she almost leapt out of her skin at the sound of a potential visitor. She smoothed down her hair and slapped some colour into her cheeks before approaching the intercom. It was her mother, holding up a cake. Deflated that it wasn't someone connected with the investigation, Maxie nevertheless buzzed her in and held open the door until she arrived.

'I wasn't sure whether you'd been eating,' puffed her mother as she reached the top step. 'People in stressful situations go one way or the other – feast or famine.' She followed her daughter into the kitchen and put the shop-bought lemon drizzle down then headed for the kettle.

'I'm fine, Mum,' said Maxie. 'I promise not to fade away. I'm not really in the mood for cake – but please help yourself.'

Which is precisely what her mother did – pouring a cuppa, plonking a slice on a plate, sitting down beside Maxie and generally making herself at home.

'I was thinking about that man,' she eventually said wiping a crumb from her lips. 'The one you thumped. I think I remember him.'

Maxie blinked with astonishment and wanted to yell a hundred things at once ranging from "now you tell me" to "come on then, spill all." She didn't need to say anything as her mother continued.

'Susan loved her sport as you probably remember; not just playing but watching it too. If that school had had cheerleaders back then, I'm sure she would have been one. She and Rebecca always used to support the basketball team when they went to matches and I'm sure he played for them.'

Maxie remembered Mike saying exactly the same thing as they waited in the gym after the fire at the school.

'I never really took much notice but you could tell whether they'd won or lost by the mood the girls were in when they got home,' continued her mother. 'They started off doing very well and then I think they were promoted into a higher league and were always being beaten. I vaguely remember Rebecca telling Susan they could find better ways to spend their Saturdays. And then suddenly, the girls were all smiles again as the team were winning their matches.'

Maxie's mother looked triumphantly up at her as if she'd solved the case. 'Don't you see?' she said. 'They must have started doing well again because of these drugs you've been talking about.'

Maxie let her cogs whirr quietly until the overwhelming silence in the room broke her mother. 'What are you thinking?' she asked looking intently into her daughter's face.

'I'm wondering whether the memory is real,' Maxie said eventually. 'Or whether it's a construct designed to support me by telling me something that confirms my own narrative.'

'And in English?'

'Whether you're saying that because you know it's what I want to hear,' said Maxie.

'I wouldn't do that,' her mother said. 'Well I would but I haven't this time. They were doing badly and then they improved.'

'Can you remember the year or month?'

The elder Reddick shook her head but said she thought it was in Susan's upper sixth and imagined that the records would probably still exist somewhere. Maxie doubted they'd be easy to find as a lower league Lancashire school basketball team was hardly likely to have a well-documented or archived hall of fame. She could imagine the pain on her students' faces if she asked them to dig through yet more paper records to look for this.

'What's the matter?' asked her mother.

Maxie realised that she had slumped back in her chair and was projecting the despair she suddenly felt, knowing she could no longer simply brief her students and that they weren't even hers any more. She swallowed back the emotion. 'I'm just feeling lost right now. I'm not sure I can do this.'

Her mother reached out and took her daughter's hands in hers. 'Of course you can, it's what you do,' she said. 'And even back then you always maintained that you'd be the one to find out what really happened – even when your father and I wanted you to let it go.'

'It's fuelled me,' murmured Maxie. 'I'm beginning to wonder whether I built my whole career on grief. If Susan hadn't died, would I have been a hairdresser or an artist?'

'Good Lord I hope not,' said her mother smiling and lightening the mood. 'The whole of the county would have wonky fringes.'

Maxie laughed with her, then accepted a small slice of cake and a hot cup of coffee. After they'd chatted further, Maxie's mother declared that she had to get back home as they were expecting a delivery from the garden centre. 'One of those fire pits for the summer,' she said with glee. 'You'll have to come round – and bring Andrew.'

Maxie opened her mouth to say she didn't organise DS Dawson's social life but decided not to bother and just let her mother go. She still had a crime to solve.

In the absence of any other resources, Google would have to be her go-to investigation tool so she opened up her laptop and began. Although Maxie tried to keep the search terms as narrow as possible based on her mother's memory – *1993 basketball team Barwick* – it turned out there was actually a Barwick in the US and they were very prolific in the sport. Even attempting to restrict the search to UK-only resulted in pages of references to the town in Georgia rather than the one she actually wanted. She pushed the keyboard away, frustrated by it and sat with her elbows on the table, cupping her chin with her hands. No matter how much she tried to kid herself, she knew recent events had well and truly taken the wind out of her sails. She hadn't lost her brain power or her ability to analyse situations and yet here she was, stuck because Google wasn't playing ball. It was like she was grieving again but this time for herself rather than her sister and that would get her nowhere. Maxie knew she simply had to keep putting one foot in front of the other until she was eventually running again.

'Fake it till you make it, girl,' she declared to herself, pulling a notepad towards her. She'd make a list of potential sources and simply doing them and ticking them off would sustain her for now. Top of the list – *Rebecca.*

Susan's best friend was still managing to evade the police and everyone searching for her. Unless they were lying, her parents hadn't heard from her either. Maxie rang the number they'd given her yet again and predictably it went straight to message. The phone hadn't been switched on since Rebecca had vanished so the police had been unable to locate her at all. No cash withdrawals, no sightings, no phone usage and more importantly, no body. Maxie and the police believed that if harm had come to Rebecca, they would know about it by now. Instead they were all convinced she was in hiding and it seemed that that woman certainly knew how to go underground. Maxie left a message simply asking if she knew whether the school basketball team had another name – like the Barwick Bears or something. She didn't beg Rebecca to get in touch or promise security because she knew the police would be doing that.

Having ticked Rebecca off her list, Maxie went back to Google trying several other names involving animals – bears, badgers, bulldogs, buffalos – nothing worked. She guessed that the team hadn't been important enough for anyone to want to digitise their history but perhaps another team in the league had more devoted followers. Maxie searched for a local league and to her absolute delight, eventually found a WordPress site set up by a fan of the Lonsdale Lions.

The level of detail about the Lions was phenomenal and as Maxie clicked through the league results of every year since the team had been founded, she couldn't help but imagine the person who'd created all of this. She pictured someone rather nerdy, still living with his parents and with 1990s posters still adorning his bedroom walls.

It was a very stereotypical image and it was absolutely shattered when Maxie clicked the "about me" tab. There was a photo of a rather handsome forty-year-old with his wife and children. They were playing basketball in their garden and smiling broadly. A picture of health and happiness. Richard Grey was a sports historian and the author of several books about the sport. He'd been a Lion in his schooldays, hence the website and although there were references to matches against the Barwick Broncos – which Maxie decided she would never have guessed as it was such a stupid name – there simply weren't the details she needed.

Maxie saw that there was a contact page and her finger hovered over it for a few moments. He wasn't involved in any case or the university so there was no reason why she shouldn't just get in touch and ask if he remembered any more about Barwick but Maxie was slightly wary of getting such a contented-looking family embroiled in the mess she seemed to be creating. But it was all she had and so pushing her concerns aside, she typed out a message for Richard and left her mobile number too.

Maxie sat back wondering what Richard was actually doing today; whether he spent his Saturdays working on his website so would see her message immediately or whether he'd be out with his family. It was completely illogical to expect him to get back to her immediately but Maxie stared at the screen willing to get a notification of a response. Then she tutted to herself and shook her head. 'Honestly Maxine Reddick, have you lost your ability to think?' she said out loud as she pressed the "fixtures" tab on the website.

A Lions fan would be at the game today and having realised that, Maxie saw that it was a home fixture. Richard would very likely be there, taking photos and writing up a report of the game. She'd already decided that going out and doing something active would be far better than waiting by her email so she noted the address and closed the laptop. It felt good to know she was going out and that this was a completely fresh lead. It couldn't be closed down on her because no-one else knew about it yet.

Although she was already wearing jeans and a hoodie so probably looked sporty enough to go as she was, Maxie checked the team strips before she left, just to make sure she wasn't inadvertently wearing the opposition's colours. Happy that she looked suitably neutral, Maxie got into her freshly-charged car and headed towards the sports stadium getting there just as the teams were going out onto the court. It wasn't like a football match with thousands of spectators so it wasn't difficult to locate Richard. He was on a spectator row near the front, cheering on his son and taking pictures. Maxie guessed he wouldn't be happy to hold a conversation while the game was ongoing so watched along with everyone else, glad to have something to take her mind off events.

In the end, she quite enjoyed herself and along with the rest of the home crowd, leapt up with delight as the Lions secured a last-minute victory. The teams left the court to a standing ovation and Maxie saw that as the rest of the spectators departed, Richard remained in his seat writing notes. She took a deep breath and walked up to him, 'That was a close finish,' she said smiling at him.

'Too close,' he said, looking up at her. 'Last season that team were nowhere near as good as us and now they're almost whopping us. I don't think I've seen you here before.'

Maxie sat down beside him and explained that she'd just stumbled across his website so had decided to come down to watch a game. 'I was actually searching for the history of another team when I found your site,' she added. 'The Barwick Broncos?'

Richard nodded and said, 'I remember them.'

'I was told they were promoted and were doing badly then turned their game around.'

Richard frowned, obviously thinking back. He opened his phone and downloaded a document. 'Yeah – 1993 I think,' he said. 'From nowhere, they came second in the league that year.'

He showed Maxie the document and added that he seemed to remember they'd been in danger of relegation before that.

'What changed?' asked Maxie.

'Sorry,' Richard said. 'I don't really know. I guess they just got their act together. Although …' He paused and bit his lip as he thought. 'They may have had a new coach. I might be wrong but it rings a bell.'

'Do you have any details or photos of this coach?' asked Maxie feeling her heart beat faster at this new potential fact.

Richard shook his head and apologised again before adding, 'But if it helps, I get all my old photos from Sheppard & Sons. They've been official school and team photographers for decades and have archives to die for.'

Maxie could have kissed him.

Chapter Thirty-Three

Maxie kicked the wall beneath the photography shop window and growled in frustration. A passer-by walking her dog tugged the pooch out of her way and gave her a terrified look. Maxie apologised and pointed up at the closed sign. 'I'm only twenty minutes late – you'd think there'd be someone in locking up wouldn't you?' she said by way of explanation but the dog walker simply hurried away.

Then she noticed the situation was even worse than that. Like many small businesses who work Saturdays, Sheppard & Sons was also closed on Sundays and Mondays so Maxie had a whole sixty-five hours to wait before it reopened on Tuesday morning when she could question these people. That seemed an impossible length of time so she jabbed out the phone number on the sign which unsurprisingly went straight through to a message inviting her to call back on Tuesday – she couldn't even leave a request for a call back.

'How on earth do you get business if you don't even take messages?' Maxie yelled at her phone. 'You're taking this work-life balance thing a bit too far if you ask me.'

After yet another pedestrian had given her a very wide berth, Maxie calmed down slightly, realising that barking out her frustration was doing absolutely nothing to help the situation.

She got back in her car where she figured she could rant and rave as much as she liked without terrifying the neighbourhood and began the drive home. It had been such a hopeful moment and now it had been dashed – or delayed but right now that felt like the same thing. An anxious energy was building between her ribs and she simply couldn't let it settle or grow into either despair or anger. She had to do something.

Maxie switched on Classic FM hoping for some soothing symphony but it was something loud and bombastic which wouldn't help at all. Smooth FM however was playing a mellow medley of Carpenters' songs and while listening to those soft tones Maxie felt her heart rate come down considerably. Each tune was laced with melancholy and she could feel gentle tears on her cheeks as she drove along. She didn't feel sad and knew this was simply a release of emotion but driving with blurry eyes wasn't the wisest thing to do so seeing a hotel just ahead, Maxie pulled off and parked up.

She wiped her eyes and walked into the main building looking for a place to have coffee. It was buzzing and Maxie realised from all the formal dress and buttonholes that there was a wedding going on. Of course, she thought to herself; the photographer is closed on Sunday because they're probably at a wedding or event and Monday is the only chance they actually get to have a day off. She knew that they wouldn't be pleased to have her gate-crash the party but it wasn't the first time she'd done it and if she were subtle then she might be able to have a word.

Maxie asked the receptionist where she could have a coffee and followed her directions to a small bar being kept for non-wedding guests. She ordered a cappuccino and using the hotel's Wi-Fi, searched for Sheppard & Sons' social media pages.

They were well-maintained and up to date showing all the weddings, birthdays and engagements the photographers had recently attended. It looked as if the posts were added around a fortnight after the event and Maxie presumed this was done to ensure the happy couples were pleased with the pictures before they went public. Future events weren't signposted but Maxie could see that Sheppard & Son appeared to be booked for weddings at one particular hotel. She nodded thanks to the waitress who was delivering her coffee and rang the venue getting the news she really wanted to hear. Yes, there was a wedding tomorrow and yes, Sheppard & Sons had been booked for the official photos.

Maxie punched the air, downed her cappuccino quickly and strode back to her car triumphantly. It was only when she was checking her mirror to reverse out of the space that Maxie realised she'd walked through the hotel lobby with a frothy cappuccino moustache but the sight of it made her laugh out loud and boy that felt good.

Sure that tomorrow would bring some progress, Maxie settled calmly into the evening. She had a long bath then put on a face mask which forced her to lie still for another fifteen minutes but she wanted to look presentable when she arrived at the hotel – not like a woman who'd lost her job and her dignity. She went through her wardrobe and picked out a royal blue coloured dress suit that she used for official university events like fundraising lunches. It was smart yet not too formal and with a brightly coloured scarf looked perfect for a spring wedding. Happy that she'd prepared for the next day, she sat down on the sofa with a glass of wine and pulled up the most recent episode of the podcast.

It was the recording featuring Mike's entourage and as her students had given her the most interesting sound bite it told her little that she didn't already know. Nevertheless, she couldn't help but feel a surge of pride and warmth as she listened to them interviewing the women and sharing potential leads. They ended the episode presenting some of the loose ends where they needed the audience's help and went back to the scene described by the newly married groom who saw two people leaving Maxie's old house and one person standing in the doorway.

'Our witness was sure that this took place just before Susan was found dead so it's vital we track down these people,' said Belle.

'Were you there? Even if you're afraid to come forward because you had no involvement in the case, we'd love to hear from you,' added Joseph.

'Because in this case, ruling anyone out really is a step forward,' concluded Sonny in what was obviously a scripted ending.

Maxie could picture them all in the studio with Craig and ached to be with them sharing theories and developing each episode but knew that for now at least, she had to keep a low profile.

Still fighting the very possible lapse in mood, Maxie quickly shook that notion out of her head and pressed play on the podcast episode that featured the information from the groom. She listened as he spoke.

'It was my wedding day. When you played all those songs that were top of the charts back then, it brought everything flooding back. It was that one song – "Back for Good" by Take That.

'We were sitting in the back seat of the limo which was taking us from our wedding to our hotel for the night,'

'So you were driving to the hotel – what happened next?'

'As I said, we were in the back and I had my head leaning against the window. I had my arm around my wife and her head was resting on my shoulder. The Love Hour *was on and the radio was playing that song. I felt the happiest I had ever felt. You know when people describe love as something warm and fuzzy? Well that's exactly how it was.*

'We drove down Glenshiels Road and that's when I saw them. The light was on in the hall and the front door was open.'

'We're talking about Susan's house here aren't we?' prompted Belle. 'How can you be sure of that?'

'The pictures you posted and the fact that it's beside a junction. We'd paused at that junction and I looked out the window. There was a man

dragging a woman back down the path away from the house. He had hold of her by the arm and I remember being truly saddened by that and vowing never to let anyone treat my wife like that.'

'And the light in the hallway, you said the door was open? Was anyone standing there?'

'Yes. I only saw a silhouette but I'm sure it was a woman.'

Maxie switched it off. She remembered listening to that man waxing lyrical about his love for his new bride and wanting to shake him, ask him why he didn't get out of that car and investigate, why he had simply sat back and watched a man dragging a woman down a path? For once in this investigation she'd actually restrained herself but if they'd been talking to him more recently, Maxie very much doubted she'd have been able to hold herself back.

The silence of her thoughts was interrupted by the phone ringing and to Maxie's delight she saw it was Andrew. 'I didn't think you were allowed to contact me,' she said immediately on picking up the call. 'Although I am so glad to hear your voice – being the outcast is no fun at all.'

Maxie rattled off the day's findings but resisted telling him that she planned to crash a wedding in the morning as she knew what his response would be. She talked non-stop until she heard Andrew say, 'Maxie? You know this voice that you're so glad to hear? Could you let it get a word out?'

They both laughed and Maxie apologised for her over-exuberance. 'Please,' she said. 'To what do I owe this immense honour?'

'Well it's not happy news unfortunately,' he said in a dour tone. 'I just wanted to let you know that the funeral of Mrs Wallace and her son is next week and I thought you might want to pay your respects.'

'Thank you,' Maxie said as that melancholy crept into the room again. 'I obviously didn't know them but they seemed to have had a tough time at the hands of the husband and father. Do you think it'll be well attended?'

'I get that impression,' Andrew said. 'Her sister is arranging everything and she's rounding up support from the neighbours and gay rights groups. There are no flowers just donations to the local shelters for families escaping abusive relationships.'

'That's good. Send me the details and I'll make a donation.'

Andrew promised that he'd email them and was saying goodbye when Maxie interrupted. 'Andrew – I know I can't ask you about your investigation, but is it overstepping to call Jean for an update on the cold case? Will I get her into any trouble?'

Andrew sighed and Maxie could just picture him running his hands through his hair as he often did. 'Your mum is now the main liaison point being the next of kin so if she hasn't been contacted then I doubt there are any new developments,' he said. 'Unofficially – I know Jean would love to hear from you – as a friend and totally unconnected to the case of course.'

'Oh, of course,' Maxie said, getting the hint. 'Well in that case, I might ask my friend round for a glass of wine.'

Andrew laughed and as he said goodbye, warned Maxie not to get the cold case officer tipsy.

She checked the clock before dialling – it was before nine so Maxie calculated that wasn't too late and on hearing Jean's delighted greeting as she picked up, felt very glad she'd called. 'I was worried I'd never hear from you again,' Jean said. 'And I didn't want to make the first move.'

'I know what you mean,' Maxie said. 'There are eggshells everywhere and I'm frightened to take any steps in case I shatter them all. How are you?'

Jean said that she was well and was working as hard as she could on the case but the leads were drying up. Their best chance was finding David Wallace's killer so she was keeping close tabs on DS Dawson. Maxie explained the new lead she had and wondered whether Jean would like to accompany her to the wedding tomorrow.

'Oh I'm sorry,' said Jean. 'As much as I'd love to see you, I just don't think I can be seen with you yet. I know that sounds awful but if the DCI thinks I'm going against orders …'

Maxie said she understood completely.

'Have you been listening to the podcast?' asked Jean in an obvious attempt to move the conversation on. 'I think your students are doing a marvellous job – you taught them well.'

'They are – but I won't take credit for natural talent,' said Maxie. 'I think young people know how to use media in a way we never will. I was actually just replaying that interview with the newly wed.'

'Listening to *The Love Hour* on his way from the wedding – I remember that show,' Jean said. 'So slushy, all those people dedicating songs to their Honey Buns and Cutie Pies. We're still searching for those people to come forward but if they had anything to do with it, I very much doubt they will.'

It struck Maxie like a punch from a prizefighter. Of course, how could she have missed the obvious?

'Jean,' she said. 'Do you have remote access to the witness statements right now?'

The investigator said that she did so Maxie asked her to check one of them. They hung up while Jean went off to search for it and in those ten minutes, Maxie chewed the nail of her index finger down to a tattered stub.

'Got it,' said Jean on the call back. She skim read the statement. 'Heard the cries, went round, dragged you from the scene while his wife waited for the emergency services.'

Maxie shook her head in despair and disbelief. 'The groom got the timing wrong,' she said. 'The show is on for a couple of hours and he wasn't describing a scene just before Susan's death. He was listening to the end of the show and describing my neighbour Mr Kennedy coming to drag me from the house with Mrs Kennedy staying behind. I don't know how I missed that.'

Maxie sighed deeply and felt tears prickling the corners of her eyes. She blinked them back knowing that it was humiliation and defeat she felt and she simply had no more time for self-pity.

'You just wanted to believe that there was a lead,' said Jean gently. 'We all do that – hang on to something even when our instincts are telling us we shouldn't.'

'But it's not a lead is it? Just another dead end.'

Chapter Thirty-Four

After they'd spoken for another hour or so, Maxie had returned to her constructive frame of mind and eventually agreed with Jean that it was better to have loose ends tidied up rather than dangle false hope in front of them. She knew she was simply smarting because she hadn't realised it earlier – there was no mysterious external force at play here and it would have been a highly unlikely scenario anyway. So although an enormously emotional Sunday lay ahead where she'd be clearing out her desk and handing over her university pass, Maxie had slept surprisingly well and was now ready to face things head on.

The day itself helped keep thoughts of the afternoon out of the way; it was the type of beautiful spring day that every bride dreams of and the daffodils formed a glorious terrestrial sunbeam along roadsides and in gardens. They seemed to glow especially bright in the hotel where the wedding was taking place – a lovely old manor house with gardens worthy of a Jane Austen novel. The photographer had an easy job in this setting. Maxie had arrived extremely early hoping to catch either Sheppard or Son setting up but it wasn't to be. When she enquired at reception whether the photographer had arrived, she was told that he had and was with the wedding party taking the pre-ceremony shots. The confused look on Maxie's face prompted the receptionist to add, 'You know – the bride having her veil arranged by the bridesmaids, the mother of the bride putting on her hat, the groom having a drink with his best man – that kind of thing.'

'It sounds like the groom is having the better time of it,' Maxie said smiling. She hadn't had any photos like that taken at her wedding and remembered the photographer despairing as she didn't really want many official ones either. She'd said that she would remember the day anyway and in truth, she hadn't looked back at the photographs much – even when she was still married. Perhaps you had to have a romantic aptitude to go in for such a thing.

Unable to do much except wait, Maxie found a quiet corner, ordered coffee and watched the hubbub build. Her contemplations were disturbed by a text from her mother warning her that her father had found out about the investigations and was going to call. Within less than a minute, that's exactly what her dad did.

'Maxine, what's going on sweetheart? I'm hearing all sorts,' he said with a wobble in his voice.

She wasn't prepared for this and in that moment, couldn't think straight – she simply didn't know what to say so went with, 'Hello Dad, gorgeous day isn't it?'

'If you're leading with the weather then it must be bad,' he said, causing Maxie to smile a little as he knew her so well.

She explained they'd found a fingerprint during a recent crime, told him its connection to their house and how that had led to the reopening of the investigation by the cold case team. It was all technically true but managed to skirt around the fact that Maxie had both insisted on and led the new inquiry until recently.

'A fingerprint at a care home? Which one? I'll see if any of our friends visit it or know it,' her father said with a little more surety as if this was something he could fix. 'If it's just one of our old pals checking in on a relative then you'll have wasted a lot of police time.'

Maxie recalled that wasting police time or that of any of the emergency services was one of the greatest sins according to her dad. Her mother used to say that he'd hop to hospital with a broken leg rather than call an ambulance.

'Well if it is one of your pals, then they've killed someone so I'd give them a wide berth,' she replied realising how harsh she sounded but unable to stop herself. 'And finding out what really happened that night isn't a waste of time. Surely you don't think that?'

Maxie could hear her dad exhale deeply. 'I don't know,' he said with that original frailty resurfacing. 'I hear you think there might be drugs and all sorts involved? I don't want to think of our Susan like that. I've come to terms with the notion that she just might have fallen coming down to open the door. Accidents do happen.'

He said those last words as if he'd trotted them out hundreds of times as the sad explanation for the loss of his eldest daughter. It was a neat but tragic story and Maxie knew that he was doing his best to console her when he added, 'And no-one blames you at all, I hope you know that.'

There was little point in continuing the conversation. Her father had buried his head in the sand when they'd lost Susan and he wasn't going to change. All Maxie could do was promise that if she found out anything, he would be the first to know. As she said goodbye she contemplated what different people her parents had become after the incident. Whereas her dad had retreated into a smaller but safer space, her mum had decided that as life could end at any moment then she was going to live it. It had affected them all in different ways and it was only now that Maxie could see that so clearly.

She was jolted from her thoughts by the appearance of a man aged around mid-thirties carrying camera equipment and hurriedly making his way to the room where the ceremony would be taking place. Maxie grabbed her bag and hotfooted it after him.

'Mr Sheppard?' she called as she entered a room set out with chairs either side of a makeshift aisle bedecked with elaborate pale pink rose garlands and a spectacular wedding arch at the head.

'Wow,' exclaimed Maxie as she was stopped in her tracks by it all. 'This is fabulous, but you wouldn't want to have hay fever in here.'

The photographer glanced at her but continued with his work and Maxie could see he was looking for the best angle to capture the happy couple and assessing the light.

'I'm afraid to say that I've been stalking you,' Maxie continued as she got no reaction. 'I went to your shop and saw you were closed so visited your social media pages and established that you usually worked here. Then …'

The man looked up at her with a harassed expression on his face. 'Look,' he said. 'I'm really busy – what do you want?'

Maxie spoke as quickly as she could, telling him she needed school photographs from the nineties and had been told Sheppard and Son were the people to approach.

'So you're not with this wedding party?' checked the photographer. When Maxie confirmed that she wasn't, he plonked himself down on a chair and ran his fingers through his hair looking stressed out. 'It's my dad you need to speak to,' he said. 'I'm the "and Son" part of the equation. He had all the school contracts and can probably find what you're looking for. I'll ring him.'

And he immediately did just that. The fact that the call was answered quickly, the request relayed accurately and the son was nodding to whatever he was being told filled Maxie with hope.

'Good news,' said the son. 'Dad can help and will be at the shop tomorrow for you. He'll open the side door so don't be put off by the closed sign.'

The beaming smile Maxie had put on with the start of that response faded slightly when she realised she was getting nothing today. 'And he's not free any earlier?' she asked tentatively. 'Like later today?'

The photographer guffawed. 'Get my dad off a golf course on a Sunday? Not even if you were Helen Mirren – and he *really* likes her.'

He stood up and got back to checking a light meter. When Maxie didn't budge he turned and said, 'You need to go. If anyone thinks I'm less than 110 per cent on this job then it's curtains for me.' He pulled an imaginary noose around his neck to make the point.

'Bridezilla?' asked Maxie as she made to go.

'Even worse – Mother-of-the-groom-zilla.' The photographer turned back to his work.

Back in the hotel reception, guests had started arriving and the place was buzzing. Once again Maxie felt as if she were standing outside looking through a pane of glass at people enjoying themselves. For these people, the day ahead was planned out with meticulous timing. They belonged here whereas she had just one task to perform now and she was dreading it. After that she feared every day would loom empty both of people and purpose. It was the strangest feeling, she thought as she strolled out to the car park, as without her job and the routine of university life she had no idea how she'd fill her days. She couldn't work, visit the police station, record a podcast – nothing that had been her life was now available to her. It didn't matter whether she drove home right now or got on a plane to Brazil – people might be curious but they wouldn't miss her.

Maxie got into her car and looked at herself in the rear-view mirror. If this situation was going to continue and if the suspension was made permanent then Maxie knew she had to decide what she wanted to do with her life. She'd become that cliché – a person who lives for their job. As she started the car and pointed it towards the university for what could be the very last time, she realised that she'd loved that job and didn't know who that woman in the mirror was without it.

Leo was waiting for her and embraced her in a tight hug. 'I am so sorry for what is happening,' he said. 'It's so unfair, I would be nowhere without you.'

Maxie pulled back from the hug and looked at him fondly; the angst he was feeling was written all over his face.

‘Thank you, Leo,’ she said. ‘I wish that were true but I punched a parent and in front of the DCI! Honestly, if I’d wanted to get myself sacked, I really couldn’t have planned it better.’

Leo gave a snotty snort of laugh then apologised profusely as he whipped out a handkerchief. They walked towards the faculty door where Leo was about to open it for Maxie but she stopped him.

‘One last swipe,’ she said pressing her staff pass at the key fob and delighting at the fact that a green light appeared and the door clicked open.

That familiar smell and sense of order enveloped Maxie as they walked through the corridors. She stopped at a graduation photograph of last year’s students not particularly to look at it, just to touch the walls. Straight, sure walls that led to her office and her former life.

‘And as for you,’ she continued after clearing her throat. ‘You have always been a first-rate academic and you don’t need me or anyone else to get you to the highest echelons. Remember that and just go for it.’

They reached her door and through the glass partition, she saw that Leo had arranged a surprise for her. Belle, Sonny and Joseph stood around her desk and in the centre was an enormous cake.

‘You’ll get into so much trouble for this,’ she told Leo as she walked in and hugged each student. ‘But thank you so much.’

‘We thought you deserved a leaving do,’ said Joseph. ‘Although sorry it’s only coffee – we know how much you like a glass of wine.’

‘My bad reputation precedes me wherever I go,’ Maxie said laughing. ‘This is just perfect.’

Maxie cut the cake as they sat around her desk and they ate enjoying an amicable banter about professions Maxie could pursue now she was “free” of the university as her students put it.

‘Prizefighter is the obvious one that springs to mind,’ said Leo.

‘Nightclub bouncer,’ added Sonny. ‘You could get in for free then.’

‘They wouldn’t need a bouncer at any nightclub that would have me,’ said Maxie. ‘The sight of my dance routines would close the place down.’

After a period of jollity the room started to go quiet. Leo put down his paper plate, wiping his mouth with one of the Wonder Woman napkins the students had supplied.

‘I can tell you’re all aching to talk shop so I’ll just go and check my emails,’ he said. ‘I’ll be back in forty minutes.’

Maxie nodded her thanks then waited until he was out of earshot and could honestly report that he knew nothing about the case save what was in the public domain.

'So I have a potential lead on the drugs that were circulating,' said Maxie. 'I've a meeting with a photographer to find out who the team coach was when the school was performing well.'

'We've been looking into that too,' said Belle. 'Joseph has become pretty sharp on the old microfiche and has looked up the league tables. They were nowhere, then got really high in the league during 93 but after spring 94 they were in the pits again.'

'When we think the drugs stopped circulating,' added Joseph. 'Your sister would have still been in the sixth form up to the summer of 94 but not the autumn term – she'd left by then.'

He stopped there and Maxie nodded saying she knew the timescales fit. She told them she would see if there were any pictures of their games around that time.

'The reports don't mention a new coach?' she asked and all her students shook their heads.

'Also,' said Sonny, 'after the episode where we mentioned the youth club, we got an anonymous message which just told us to look closer.'

Maxie frowned. 'Nothing else?'

'Nope, but I have replied and am trying to coax more out of this person. I'll also do some specific posts to try and find other people who went there.'

The team finished updating each other and then began to box up Maxie's personal effects while she focussed on downloading her research and personal papers from the desktop.

'I'm going to need these for my next job application,' she told the students with an air of levity that was entirely faked.

Leo popped his head around the door. 'Are you ready Professor Reddick?' he asked emphasising her title.

Maxie stood tall and said she was. She picked up one of the boxes and walked out of her office to a round of applause from her four now ex-students.

Chapter Thirty-Five

She'd been sitting in the coffee shop opposite the photographers for over forty minutes waiting for the owner to arrive. There'd been no point in waiting at home; the carpet would have been threadbare with all the impatient treading. Far better to get out and wait nearby which is what Maxie was doing now. And by happy coincidence, this place sold absolutely fabulous almond croissants. When the assistant arrived at the table to clear her crockery, she contemplated ordering a second pastry but was saved from the calories by a silver-haired man getting out of a sports car and opening the side door of Sheppard and Sons. She gave the assistant a tip, gathered up her things then ordered a couple of the croissants to go. Maxie guessed he'd have coffee in his office but didn't want to arrive empty-handed, after all he had been very obliging in agreeing to meet her today.

Maxie walked slowly across the road, trying to give the poor guy some time to at least take his jacket off. She checked her watch and when she was sure he'd had a full five minutes she knocked at the door and within a few seconds, a rather handsome guy with a deep tan that was most likely the result of all that time on the golf course, sparkly blue eyes and silver hair, answered. He accepted her gift with a smile, introducing himself as Ted and welcomed her in; Maxie followed him to the back of the shop as she contemplated giving up the hair dye herself and embracing the silver. She doubted she'd look this good; probably more like one of the witches in Macbeth.

'So you're interested in old Barwick school photos,' said Ted as they stopped and stood in front of a wall of shelves.

'Yes,' she said. 'Specifically sports events from autumn 1993 to summer 1994.'

'Good, I like specifics,' replied Ted as he moved to the lower left-hand shelves. 'If you don't mind getting dusty then you can take a box and look through with me. Just please put every file back exactly as it was.'

Delighted to have the chance to do some of the searching, Maxie threw off her jacket and literally rolled up her sleeves. She took the box Ted handed her to one side of the table and began looking through its contents. For such a specific timeline, there were an awful lot of pictures and Maxie blew out her cheeks as she realised that.

'You didn't think I'd have this many,' Ted said with a laugh, catching her expression. 'Sorry – I tend to keep things. I always mean to digitise them but I haven't quite worked out whether that would mean I've to get permission under the data protection act – you know, for storing images of people. And I'd far rather be enjoying my retirement than bothering with all that stuff.'

'I don't blame you,' Maxie said. She could now see that the filing system was pretty good. The largest file denoted the month, and within that, each type of event was collated – among them new appointees and sports. Maxie told Ted she was interested in the basketball team so he suggested that he do the big sort to get to the specific files she might need and then Maxie look at the photos to see if there was anyone she recognised. It was a good plan so they got into a rhythm, sitting side by side quietly sorting then studying each and every picture.

'Woah,' declared Maxie picking up one photo and holding it up to get better light. 'I think I might have something here – can I borrow that magnifying sheet?'

Ted handed her the one he'd been using, then stood behind her, moving the angle poise lamp on the desk to ensure she had as much light as possible.

The photograph clearly showed a young Mike Priestly standing under a basketball hoop celebrating with the rest of the team. The reverse gave a date of Saturday November 27, 1993 and a scribble saying GZ.

'What does that mean?' asked Maxie pointing to it.

'That it appeared in the Gazette,' replied Ted.

Maxie took a photo of the picture, messaged it to Sonny then called him immediately after and asked him to look through the archives to see if there was any story attached to it. He told her he was on his way to a lecture but would do it as soon as he could. Maxie apologised and realised how quickly she'd forgotten that other peoples' lives were carrying on as normal. She told her student not to worry about it and that she'd ask Craig for his help. Her podcast co-presenter wasn't thrilled to be asked to do an archive search but agreed if Maxie promised to get back and record another episode as soon as possible.

'Your notoriety might not be great for the university,' he said, 'but it does wonders for our followers.'

'Once a hack always a hack.' Maxie laughed and promised that she would return when she could.

'I've found some more pictures from that season's games,' Ted said as she finished the call. 'Are any of these useful?'

Maxie studied them closely; she recognised the names and faces of the team members but they didn't really give her anything new until one photo focussed not on the team but the crowd cheering behind the staff bench. She sunk back in the chair and pressed her hand over her mouth as the emotion threatened to overcome her.

'What is it?' asked Ted.

'My sister,' whispered Maxie pointing to Susan and Rebecca in the front row of the crowd, laughing and cheering as if life would go on forever.

When she explained Susan's death, Ted nodded and told her he remembered hearing about it at the time. He suggested they pause and have a coffee before continuing but Maxie needed to keep going. She picked up the photo and studied the faces on the staff bench. They were such small images and each person wore a team baseball cap which slightly obscured their features but under the magnifying sheet, Maxie spotted someone she knew. There, folding his arms, looking away from the camera and smiling at the two girls was a very young Tom.

'I don't bloody well believe it,' she exclaimed. 'The two of you were in this together.'

Ted happily agreed to get her a larger copy developed and let her take the original for now. Keeping far calmer than she actually felt, Maxie helped tidy the room and thanked the photographer for his help.

Back in her flat, Maxie checked the LinkedIn profiles of both Tom and Mike, knowing what she'd find – that everything but their most recent postings had been deleted. It didn't matter, she'd made extensive notes on everyone at the beginning of this case and no-one could take them away from her. She dug them out and verified a fact that had meant nothing to her at the time – Tom had been on his teacher-training placement year at Barwick from autumn 1993 to summer 1994 before moving out of the county to take a permanent position after graduating.

Maxie rang Craig to establish whether he'd had the chance to search the archives. He had and was emailing the story that went with the photograph. Maxie refreshed and refreshed her screen until eventually it popped into her inbox:

"Halloween Trick for Polforth but Treat for Barwick"

It stated how Barwick had continued its amazing winning run, beating the league leaders in a frenzied high-scoring game where the Barwick players ran rings around their opponents. Whether knowingly or not, the journalist had commented that someone *"has sprinkled magic dust on this team recently"*.

It wasn't evidence and Maxie doubted that any would still exist but she had to follow it up. Facing Mike Priestly was not something that she relished and equally imagined he would refuse to meet her. Tom had been very nice and extremely helpful when they'd first met but perhaps he hadn't taken her seriously back then. Now with all the attention she and her students had created, he might not be so accommodating. And another thought had now raised its ugly head – had Tom or Mike been the ones to start the fire? Had they been trying to get rid of the photos that Fiona had found? Maxie knew they'd already been interviewed about it but had denied any involvement and there'd been no reason at the time to question that. But they had to be asked again and it had to be done through official channels for either man to play ball.

She made the call to Jean, explained everything and asked if the investigator could bring them in for questioning. 'I'll give it a go under the guise of helping us to clear up a loose end,' she said. 'But they won't be obliged to meet me. Why don't you ask DS Dawson?'

'Their prints aren't at his primary crime scene and I know they've already been questioned over the fire so there'd be no reason to,' said Maxie. 'I'm not sure he'd think my suspicions a good enough excuse to get them back in but you are still looking at Susan's case and this could be relevant.'

Jean agreed to try and get both men in saying that she'd aim for the end of the day but couldn't promise anything. Maxie put down her phone and sighed.

Her instincts were telling her that even if both Tom and Mike confessed to taking performance-enhancing drugs, it wouldn't get her any closer to knowing what happened to Susan. One of her students had done some research into their use in sport and so she knew it was quite commonplace and most importantly, not illegal if for personal use. She desperately hoped she wasn't going to discover that Susan was their supplier and therefore the only one actually committing a crime. Her dad wouldn't thank her for discovering that.

If only Rebecca would get in touch. Maxie rang her number again and as usual got no reply. Then she sent Andrew a quick text asking if there had been any sightings of her but again there hadn't and finally she called Mrs Henderson but got her husband who told her bluntly to stop pestering his family.

Her phone rang and seeing it was Andrew she perked up a little expecting some news. There was none, he was simply ringing to arrange to meet her after the upcoming funeral. They agreed to arrive separately and stay apart during the proceedings in case any press were there but then they'd have coffee somewhere. After the call, Maxie walked to her bedroom and looked through her wardrobe to choose a dress. She needed to be as unobtrusive as possible so black was the only option. Taking out a dress, coat and some shoes, she hung them on the door and looked at the sombre outfit. This combination of clothes could only ever mean sorrow.

The next call was from Jean who had both good and bad news; Tom and Mike had agreed to come in and answer some questions on the condition that Maxie wasn't there.

'But I need to question them,' she urged.

'I'm sorry, it can't happen,' Jean said. 'But come down beforehand and I'll sneak you in – you can watch the interview from the observation room.'

Maxie knew she had no choice in the matter so said she'd write up her thoughts and questions for Jean then do as she was told.

Come the hour, Maxie arrived at the station early and was bundled into the observation room before anyone could see her. Twenty minutes later, she watched Jean invite the men into the interview room and offer them coffee. She looked at the body language of Mike and Tom as Jean began sorting the papers in her file. Tom's foot was tapping rapidly showing his nerves whereas Mike relaxed confidently with his arms behind his head. Even if he were innocent, to Maxie this seemed an arrogant pose. If she had been in that room, she'd probably have punched him again.

'As you know,' began Jean, 'I am investigating a cold case – the death of Susan Reddick in 1995. Someone you both knew.'

'I'm not sure that I did really know her,' said Tom.

Jean raised her eyebrows and slid the photograph over to him. 'We've learned that you actually did your teacher training in Barwick,' she continued, 'and that as this picture shows, you were involved with the basketball team. Mike here was a member while Susan Reddick and her friend Rebecca were both big fans. The photo shows you smiling at Susan.'

Mike looked over at the photo. 'It shows him smiling at the crowd,' he said. 'It doesn't mean he knew all their names.'

'Very true,' Jean said with a smile. 'I've also looked into your time at university, Tom – you were a bit of a star on the athletics field weren't you?'

Maxie hadn't known this so Jean had obviously been following up on Tom's history.

'What has this got to do with your cold case?' asked Tom. 'It sounds as if I'm being accused of something.'

'Not at all,' said Jean. 'I'll cut to the chase. You went from being a mid-ranking athlete at school to a top performer on the track at university. You arrive on a placement at Barwick and they go from being a middle-of-the-road basketball team to beating the league champions. There are rumours of drugs – not just on the field, but off too and specifically, it is rumoured that Susan was selling these. What can you tell me about this?'

'Nothing whatsoever,' asserted Mike pushing the photograph back towards her and standing up. 'Now if we're actually here just to verify some crazy theory Professor Reddick has then we'll be on our way. We had *nothing* to do with her sister's death.'

With that he tugged at Tom's arm and they both marched out of the room.

Maxie waited until she'd heard them stride past the door and then opened it slightly to peek out. Mike looked furious whereas Tom had a weary gait. She let them turn a corner and then followed at a safe distance. Outside, they parted ways with Mike getting into his car and Tom walking towards the park. *Perfect*. She waited until he'd sat down on a bench with his arms on his knees and his head hanging down before sitting down quietly beside him.

'I imagined you wouldn't be far away,' said Tom without looking at her. 'Are you recording this?'

'No,' she said softly. 'Tell me what happened.'

Tom sighed and looked up, facing forward and not towards Maxie. 'I loved sports but wasn't great – not bad but not great,' he said. 'Puberty hit, I got fat and my performance on the track was even worse. I was reading all these articles about fat metabolisers and performance enhancements – I pretty much loathed my body then so got hold of some and that was it. I felt good so trained harder and then started winning things. They turned my life around and I loved them. I went from being the fat kid to the powerhouse – you have no idea how good that felt.'

Maxie looked at him and wished she could reach out to squeeze his hand because she did know exactly how that felt.

'So when I arrived at Barwick, I found a team in the same place I was – down and out,' continued Tom. 'I saw their parents on the sidelines shaking their heads in dismay each week and the spectator numbers dropping so I decided to do something. I gave them a little of what I'd taken.'

'And they started winning,' said Maxie.

'Yep – then the crowds returned, they were being applauded during assembly and having their choice of girlfriends. It was all good.'

'So how did Susan get involved?' asked Maxie.

'One of the team told her that they were taking supplements,' said Tom. 'That's what I always called them and I think I was trying to kid myself they were nothing more than vitamins. Anyway, the girls started hearing that I had these weight-loss pills and of course they wanted them too. Susan had an Avon round so was visiting their houses anyway so I used to give her the bulk order and she'd distribute them.'

'Who supplied them?'

'Mail order from the back of a bodybuilding magazine,' said Tom. 'They were easy to get hold of and we all made a bit of money from them.'

'But Susan stopped selling them?'

Tom nodded. 'She did. She was worried that it might not look good for her teaching career if someone found out.'

'So you had this stock of supplements and no-one to sell them?' prompted Maxie.

'Susan wasn't my only "associate"', replied Tom. 'I'm ashamed to say that I had a few teenagers selling for me. I'd get them whatever they wanted but then it all turned sour when that girl became ill after the party. I was pretty terrified. I didn't want my career to go up in smoke so I just decided to stop. Some guys weren't happy about it and one in particular said that he should get what they'd ordered but I wouldn't do it. I was sure I'd be struck off and never allowed to teach, honestly I was scared witless that I'd be found out.'

Maxie recalled the Kennedy's report of the party and imagined that guy might be the one who'd said Susan owed them something, maybe they blamed her for the source drying up. 'Then Susan died and no-one was asking about Amy any more,' she said sighing.

She watched Tom nod slowly then turn towards her. 'Your sister's death took the focus off me and the team,' said Tom. 'But I promise you that I had absolutely nothing to do with it and really don't know what happened. And I assure you there was no secret drugs ring going on – just a bunch of teenagers trying to look buff.'

'But the fire at the school – you know what happened there don't you?' Maxie struggled to stay calm as she fixed her gaze on Tom.

He nodded.

'We didn't know which photos she had so Mike set light to the whole box that she'd unearthed.' He hung his head. 'We didn't know she was still in there.'

Everything about his tone and stance rang true. Maxie could see that this man was telling the truth. Neither he nor Mike wanted this aspect of their personal history known but they hadn't killed her sister.

'Did you call the dean to say I was neglecting my students?' she asked, suddenly remembering she hadn't figured out the culprit yet.

'Mike asked me to,' he said, colouring-up in shame. 'I know someone on the student board and I reported that a parent had made a complaint to me.'

'Will you call the dean and tell him it was false?' asked Maxie in the hope this would make a difference to her suspension.

'Of course I will.'

They sat silently side by side. Maxie was going through everything they thought they'd uncovered during this investigation; a mysterious couple caught leaving who turned out to be her and her neighbour, an ominous drugs ring that was nothing of the sort. Was she ever going to find out what really happened?

'What are you going to do with all of this?' asked Tom.

'You've both committed crimes but I'm only here to find out what happened to Susan. I'd suggest you turn yourselves in but I can't force you – although personally I'd love to see Mike behind bars.' She smiled, picturing his smug face in the striped convict suit seen in cartoons.

'Yeah,' replied Tom. 'I was quite happy to see him promoted out of my school.'

Maxie stood and held out her hand which Tom took and shook. 'Do only good things from now onwards,' she said.

'I promise,' Tom said. 'And I hope you find what you're looking for.'

Chapter Thirty-Six

'That's better,' said Andrew as they stood side by side behind a tree and out of sight of the main party. 'It doesn't feel right for a funeral to happen in bright sunshine.'

The sky had waivered all morning; a bright blue backdrop hosting fulsome grey clouds threatening to burst forth and now finally, they had. Maxie was glad to be able to put up an umbrella and hide herself even more. She and Andrew had ended up having to stand together only a couple of feet apart because of the size of the crowd that had gathered. Despite the fact that there was no focus on her whatsoever, she couldn't help but flinch every time a photographer raised a lens; she simply did not want her current local notoriety to distract from the proceedings.

Andrew nudged her as a large taxi pulled up and Jacqueline Morton got out. Both their eyes widened in astonishment as the care home manager went to the back of the cab and helped an elderly gentleman out into a wheelchair.

'We have to find out,' whispered Maxie, walking towards them and standing nearby as the proceedings for mother and son progressed.

Now impatient to talk to Jacqueline, the service seemed to take an interminable length of time. Mrs Wallace's sister Petra led a joining of hands around the internment plot as they said the Lord's Prayer followed by a series of non-religious blessings. Maxie had been to funerals where everyone had stood trying to be brave and it had always seemed such an alien thing to do. There was none of that here – the people gathered, hugged, embraced, stood with their heads tipped together and their fingers entwined as the raindrops soaked through them. Someone wished David and his mother peace and freedom from fear in the next life and Maxie found herself joining the "Amen", meaning it utterly and completely. She approached Petra – a woman who'd lost both a sister and nephew to tell her the service had been wonderful and then turned back towards Andrew.

As the crowd dispersed, the detective formally approached Jacqueline and asked her relationship with the deceased. Although Maxie couldn't ask anything, she could listen and heard her say that the man in the wheelchair, Albert George Younghusband, had been Mrs Wallace's father. His grandson had never visited him in the home and with a fading mind he had not recognised the man lying dead in their grounds as his own family. It was also clear he really didn't understand that today he was burying that grandson and his daughter. Mrs Wallace's sister joined them and kissed the top of her father's head but it was evident he had no clue who she was either. Jacqueline left with her patient and the sister turned towards Maxie.

'I know you lost your sister too,' Petra said with a look of deep empathy. 'So you'll know exactly how today feels. I don't want you to even think of blaming yourself for any of this, only one man killed my sister and hopefully he'll rot in jail now. I hope they find your sister's killer soon and you finally get some peace.'

She walked on as Maxie whispered a thank you. The compassion in this stranger's voice struck her deep in the chest and all she could do was stand with her heart pounding until everyone was gone. Almost everyone – a solitary figure approached the graveside shortly after everyone had left.

'It's Mrs Henderson,' Andrew whispered to her.

Rebecca's mother placed a small bunch of daffodils at the graveside then stood up, looking all around. Happily the trees with their fresh abundance of leaves did hide them so they weren't spotted. They could watch as Mrs Henderson dropped her head in sadness and walked away.

'I think she was hoping Rebecca might be here,' said Andrew. 'Let's wait and see if she turns up.'

It was still pouring with rain but getting wet wasn't an issue to Maxie if there was even the slightest chance of Rebecca reappearing. The pair got as close to the tree trunk as they could for shelter, using the umbrella to guard against the droplets from the leaves. Huddled together like this began to feel like a scene from an Enid Blyton novel and Maxie said so, getting a small snort of laughter from Andrew.

After around forty minutes, their efforts were rewarded. A figure, clad in an oversized black parker and boots, light-footed it to the graveside, securing a bunch of bright blue anemones and a card underneath a painted stone. Andrew darted out from his hiding position and went after her but soon returned.

'She just vanished,' said Andrew, breathless, as he got back to Maxie. 'She must know some hiding places in here because there is no way she could have got back to the road in that time.'

'There are plenty of them,' said Maxie pointing at all the large ancient memorials that skirted the newer burial site. 'Anyway, we have something – this is the card she left.'

Andrew took it and read it out loud, '*"Your truth will soon shine, Maxie x",*' he said. 'So the message is obviously for you rather than from you.'

'She knew I'd be here,' Maxie said, looking around and hoping to see Rebecca's face pop out from behind a tree or tombstone. 'And she wants us to wait.'

'Wait here?' asked Andrew, taking out an evidence bag and wrapping up both the message and the stone.

'I doubt it, I think she means for me to wait until she contacts me,' Maxie said. 'But I suppose it wouldn't do any harm to give her a few moments to reappear.'

'Then can we do it somewhere dry?' he asked.

They walked to the chapel and stood in the doorway. They could see the graveside from here but as time ticked by there was no sign.

'It's interesting that she left a message for you but not her mother,' continued Andrew checking his watch. 'I'm guessing Rebecca was watching the funeral so would have seen her mum here. Why do you think that is?'

'Could be she's been in touch with her already using a new phone,' Maxie said. 'Or perhaps she wants me to know she's innocent.'

'You believe she knows what actually happened,' added Andrew.

'I hope so. Right now I really cannot think of anyone else who would know.'

The spring rain shower stopped as quickly as it started, leaving the grounds of the cemetery looking bright, fresh and revived. As Andrew had said when they'd arrived, this really did seem at odds with the place but Maxie remembered back to Susan's funeral which had been a gloriously sunny day. Her father had looked up at the sun and told her youngest daughter that Susan was up there smiling at them because heaven was actually a lovely place to be. He hadn't believed it any more than she did and he burst into such sorrowful tears as he finished the sentence. Her sister wasn't in a place like this; neither of her parents could countenance the idea of a teenager dwelling amongst all these ancient souls and so had taken her ashes to the seaside, scattering them over the dunes that she had loved playing in as a child. For years after that Maxie met up with her parents and they'd visit the spot and have ice-creams from the parlour that Susan had adored. It had never felt right – marking the anniversary of a tragic death with a sugar cone, no matter how reminiscent it was of her sister. Sure enough, after their divorce and parting of ways, her parents stopped doing it and instead bought a memorial bench looking over the sea. It was only then that Maxie realised the whole ice-cream shenanigans was for her benefit – to cheer her up and stop her from blaming herself every single year. It would take more than that.

Andrew had to visit Rebecca's parents; after all, there'd been a sighting of her daughter so at least they knew she was alive and well – he was obliged to tell them this despite the fact he suspected they already knew. Maxie followed him to their house in her car, but ignored his instruction to stay where she was and stood behind him as he knocked. Maxie needed to see their expressions when they heard the news. Mrs Henderson had scrubbed off any make-up by the time they arrived and answered wearing an apron over her black dress. Andrew asked if he could come inside but the fragile looking woman shook her head and asked if he could say what he had to right here. Maxie could see that Rebecca's mother was extremely uncomfortable uttering these words and suspected they were her husband's instructions.

'We're just here to let you know that we've had sight of Rebecca and that she looks well,' said Andrew.

Mrs Henderson clutched her hand to her chest and exhaled a huge sigh so Maxie could see that this was news to her. Rebecca's mother stumbled backwards onto the staircase but still held out a hand to stop Andrew who tried to cross the threshold and help her.

'She went to David's funeral after everyone had left,' continued Maxie. 'She left a painted stone – does it mean anything to you?'

Andrew held out the stone, now in an evidence bag to her. Mrs Henderson looked at it and softly stroked it. Then she bit her lip and pushed the stone back towards the detective.

'Never seen it before – take it away,' she said sharply.

'Do you have an alternative number for her Mrs Henderson? One she may have given no-one else?' asked Andrew.

'No, no I don't.'

Although her body language suggested that she certainly did know something, Maxie could see they wouldn't get any information from Rebecca's mother at this point so thanked her and gave her a squeeze on the arm. The detective reiterated that her daughter was still wanted for questioning and that if she got in touch, Mrs Henderson had to tell the police. He got a nod in response and a thank you for letting her know about Rebecca.

'And this obviously applies to your husband too,' added Andrew as Mrs Henderson got up from the stairs, straightening her apron.

'I'll tell him,' she said closing the door on them slowly but firmly.

As they walked back to the cars, Maxie got a call from Jean. She put it on speaker so Andrew could hear too as the excited investigator said, 'A new lead, we know where Rebecca got the money from to vanish.'

They were told to meet her at The White Horse where Maxie had first reencountered her sister's best friend and when they arrived both Jean and a member of Andrew's team were there taking statements from the landlord.

'So what's going on?' asked Andrew.

'After the appeal for information, Jake here got in touch didn't you?' Jean said. 'Would you like to repeat what you've just told us?'

Jake sighed and rolled his eyes. 'I gave Bex a couple of grand to disappear,' he said languidly. 'She said she needed to go away for a while but couldn't use any of her cards because you lot would trace them.'

'Did she say where she was going?' asked Andrew.

'Oh yeah, of course.' Jake laughed. 'A woman wants to disappear from someone but before she goes she tells a publican where she's running to!'

Maxie had to hold back a smirk and instead composed a serious expression as she faced the landlord directly. 'Okay, so it was a stupid question but Rebecca was my sister's best friend and I am terrified for her,' she said. 'Please tell us how this whole loan came about – everything and anything.'

'I've seen you in here before,' said Jake sizing her up. 'You were by the jukebox with Bex.'

Maxie confirmed that was her and got everyone to sit down together around a table where, ignoring the stickiness, Maxie folded her arms upon it and told Jake to start.

'She's in here all the time,' he said. 'Does some shifts if we're short-staffed and is basically part of the furniture, plus we've hooked up a couple of times. A while back she said that something had happened and she needed to get away. She'd had a row with a bloke a week or so beforehand so I presumed it was to do with that.'

Andrew showed Jake pictures of all the men related to the case and Jake pointed out David. 'It was him,' he said.

Maxie stood open-mouthed as Jake confirmed what he'd just said then continued his account. 'It was just after some school reunion – she'd been gabbing about that, not sure whether to go or not but decided to give it a go and came in here beforehand for some Dutch courage. Later that night she cornered me and told me she had to leave.

'Everyone knows that you guys find people when they withdraw cash so she asked if I could lend her some to get by. I was expecting it to be a hundred quid not two grand but she left me all her cards and showed me that she had enough in the bank to repay me when she could access it. I took it out of the safe, gave her a couple of sweatshirts and one of my old parkas then never saw her again.'

'I understand that you were trying to protect Rebecca by not contacting us so why do it now?' asked Jean.

Jake rubbed his head before speaking. 'Wish I could say it was for some Good Samaritan reason,' he said. 'But I need that money back. Cards and accounts without the PIN number are useless and it's been weeks – for all I know she could be dead.'

The pragmatism of his words and expression shocked Maxie. She'd seen him as Rebecca's knight in shining armour at the beginning of this conversation but could now see the relationship for what it was.

'Did she promise you interest on this loan?' she asked, getting a nod in response.

They left without telling him that Rebecca was happily still alive but assuring him that the money in her accounts still hadn't been touched.

'Would I count as an official creditor if … if she did die?' he asked.

'Only if your arrangement is in writing,' said Andrew, leaving the landlord with a contact number and a sarcastic look.

Chapter Thirty-Seven

'She has a couple of grand so at least she's probably had a roof over her head,' said Jean. 'I hate to think of any woman having to sleep rough although I know thousands do.'

Andrew and his colleague had returned to the station while Maxie and Jean found a somewhat nicer pub to have something to eat. Maxie snuggled into a chair near a radiator, glad to have some warmth on a day that had so far kept her chilled to the bone.

'Not many places would accept cash though,' Maxie said. 'It can't be a long-term rental or Airbnb so I suspect it's a small B&B. And it can't be that far away if she doesn't have her car and hasn't appeared on any public transport CCTV.'

'It would be easy enough to evade them with a bottle of hair dye and a pair of glasses,' said Jean. 'Just don't wear a baseball cap and keep your head down – that's a giveaway.'

They both laughed at the clichéd image often seen on cop shows. 'How would you disappear if you needed to?' asked Maxie as the food arrived and they began to tuck in.

'I would dye my hair black and get those glasses for a start,' Jean said. 'And I'd wear very different clothes – possibly a hijab or something else very religious – people tend not to stare at the devout. I might also put something in my shoe so I had a permanent limp – from a distance if you saw this woman approaching you'd look straight past her.'

'Looking like that you could hop on a bus immediately and get as far away as possible before anyone even started looking,' continued Maxie. 'But you have to buy the dye, glasses and hijab somewhere.'

'True,' said Jean. 'We know Rebecca got away quickly that night and possibly had help from someone else in the pub. I suspect Andrew will be looking into that now he knows she went there. She's the linchpin.'

Jean's words echoed in Maxie's head as they parted ways and each went home. It had been a long and eventful day which had revealed so much they hadn't known. Rebecca was the linchpin – the one person who knew what had happened and if she didn't then she knew enough for everyone else to be able to put together the pieces.

She made herself a cup of coffee and pulled out her notes. Caffeine at this time of night would destroy any hope of sleep for her but Maxie didn't want to sleep. She wanted some of the answers and felt that this day was holding them just out of sight.

She scribbled as she thought. Jake's account had given them an even more tangled web to navigate but that's what she had to do. Maxie's own involvement began with David's death but Rebecca's role in this case started before that. She'd been seen with him and they'd been arguing. She'd walked off and David was dead within days. Killed while possibly visiting his grandfather – who had known Mr Younghusband was resident there? Both Mr and Mrs Wallace for sure but there'd been enough DNA collected when Mrs Wallace was killed to know that neither of them had killed their son despite the father's violent and homophobic nature. Did Rebecca know David would be at the care home? It was the kind of thing that would be said during conversation so it was entirely feasible. Rebecca had been ruled out of David's death but if DNA and fingerprinting hadn't existed then she would have been the prime suspect – present at Susan's party and a known associate of David's. But they did exist and so they knew she couldn't have wielded the bat because it wasn't her fingerprint on it. Had she asked someone else to do it? Jake had helped her out with money, was that all he had done? Andrew hadn't charged him with wasting police time and hadn't taken fingerprints but he had to now be wondering the same as she was. Although it was late she rang him and asked.

'Yep, got them – nope, no match,' was Andrew's reply. 'Although as that doesn't relate to the cold case you're not supposed to be working on, you didn't hear it from me.'

Maxie knew they'd been sailing close to the wind today; if they hadn't both been attending the funeral she would never have been able to tag along at the pub. Rebecca's message to her would enable Andrew to stay close if only to check that the woman everyone wanted to question hadn't made contact.

She chewed a fingernail wondering which stone hadn't been properly turned yet. Rebecca, Susan and David couldn't be connected by something recent; it had to have been something in their childhood. She picked up the picture she'd taken to Mrs Wallace and remembered that the podcast still had an anonymous caller to follow up. At this hour, she couldn't justify calling Craig but if she messaged him and he was still awake, he might just read it. Sure enough Maxie saw the little ticks on the message that told her it had been received and read then waited for Craig to call, which he did.

'Do you ever sleep?' were his first words.

'I could ask the same. Did I wake you?'

'Not quite, what can I help you with?'

Maxie asked whether the anonymous caller who'd told them to look closer at the youth club had rung back.

'Not as far as I know,' he said. 'Joseph is the one following that up although I do know he has some facts about the place. Stuff like it ran from 1987 to 1994, held dances and camping trips – that kind of thing. I can't really see it leading anywhere. You must remember it.'

'It wasn't really my kind of thing,' Maxie said. 'I remember Susan talking about it when she was younger but I don't think it loomed large in her life. I'll ask Joseph to see what he thinks.'

'Please wait until the morning to call him,' pleaded Craig.

Maxie really didn't want to have to wait that long but knew it would be completely inappropriate to ring in the middle of the night so reassured Craig that she'd wait.

'One more thing before you go,' he said. 'The listeners are baying to hear from you again. How about an update this Saturday?'

Maxie sighed, pausing to collect her thoughts. She loved the podcast but now the microphone was focussed on her, she wasn't sure what to do. 'There's nothing to say,' she replied after a moment. 'Every single lead we've had has led nowhere and I'm not sure the listeners want to hear that. People like crimes to be solved and the bad guys to be caught. That's what TV tells them and so that's what they believe.'

'Belle thinks that there could be an angle in dealing with unresolved issues, interviews with families who've never got justice – how people like you feel,' said Craig. 'She says there's a whole body of academic research into this.'

Maxie couldn't help but raise a smile at those words – her students were doing exactly as she would have done for any other case – find an angle that kept it alive. She had to go along with it.

'Okay,' she said. 'I promise you I'll think about it and get back to you in the morning.'

Come morning the first thing Maxie did was to call Joseph and ask about the anonymous contact. 'He or she hasn't been back in touch,' he said.

'To be honest, after a few attempts I gave up – may just be one of those cranks who likes to stir things.'

'Maybe but the youth club remains one of the few paths not pursued and so far this person is the only one who has raised it. Do you think they'd respond if I asked them?'

'Worth a try but they'd have to be convinced it was you. Why don't you record a short video message and get it to me then I'll pass it on?' said Joseph.

Maxie agreed and as soon as she closed down the call she opened up the camera and, without make-up, combing her hair or even thinking about what she was going to say she pressed record. 'Hi, I'm Professor Maxine Reddick and I usually host *Criminal Thoughts* with Craig Johnston. You got in touch recently to tell us to look closer into the youth club but no-one seems either willing or able to talk about it. Please, please get back in touch and I will give you my personal number so you can tell me what you know. I promise you need never reveal your identity.'

Maxie was aware she shouldn't have made that final promise just in case she ever needed this person to give evidence with what they knew. She'd face that issue if and when it arose. She sent the video to Joseph who gave her a thumbs up when it had been forwarded on.

The morning loomed empty as Maxie opened up her laptop. One of the good things about no longer being an active member of the university was the lack of emails but this was also the very thing that emphasised her ongoing situation. There was one official-looking message from the dean; Maxie clicked on it to read a very formal letter letting her know the date her suspension would be reviewed. It wasn't for months so lifting the suspension by the autumn term would be tight. The sense of failure weighed heavy and as she sat with it, noticing how it made her feel, she considered that this would be worth talking about on the podcast – it wasn't dynamic but it was honest and would probably touch a number of people.

The shrill ring of her phone made her jump and the excited voice of Joseph pulled her right back to the moment. 'It's a he and he'll talk to you,' he exclaimed.

Maxie took the details and promised to record the call if she were allowed. Buoyed with both nerves and excitement she walked around the kitchen trying to calm herself; it felt like the last chance saloon and she had to get this right. If she was dressed professionally she'd feel professional so the first thing Maxie did was to have a shower and put on a wrap dress that she had often worn to work. With make-up and hair that would have sufficed in a TV studio she sat back down and placed her phone on the table. On speaker she dialled the number she had been given and waited for an answer.

A timid male voice narrated his tale as Maxie sat silently listening. 'I wasn't one of the cool kids; I was a bit weedy not good at sports or anything really. And I knew I was different but at thirteen or fourteen you don't exactly know why and it wasn't talked about in the kind of home I grew up in. Whenever my gran asked whether I had a girlfriend yet, my mum would say "oh there's plenty of time for that" and I hoped there was. Not that any girl would look twice at me and my acne – pizza face they used to call me – but when I looked at them I felt nothing anyway. Not like how I felt when I watched the football team.

'It was my dad who said I needed to be mixing more and got me into the youth club. It was okay at first – it seemed to be where all the misfits went. I made a couple of friends and started to realise what being a teenager was actually about so when it was announced that there'd be weekends away at the youth hostels I jumped at the chance.

'That's where it happened. They used to ask for parent volunteers to supervise us and the mum would sleep in a room beside the girls' dorm while the father slept near the boys. One night I was woken up by our parent volunteer and told to follow him. We went into his room and he locked the door. He told me that he'd been watching me and that I would make a great youth worker one day because I was kind and caring. I was really flattered; no-one had really ever told me I was good at something so when he offered me some rum and coke to toast my bright future, I accepted it. It was strong but I tried not to show it. Then he leaned over and kissed me. I didn't stop him, I'd never been kissed like that and wasn't sure what I was supposed to do. Then he took my hand and put it inside his pyjama bottoms. It was horrible but I got an erection and he noticed. He said he was glad I was enjoying myself and then …'

The caller broke down into tears as Maxie had already done. She waited until he spoke. 'There were others like me, especially boys like me whose fathers wanted their sons toughened up. We couldn't tell anyone at home and he could spot us a mile off. I don't think this has anything to do with your sister, I just want that bastard to pay for what he did.'

'Do you remember his name?' Maxie asked very gently.

‘I’ll never forget it,’ came the reply.

Maxie’s jaw dropped as the caller named his abuser – Roy Henderson.

It explained everything.

Chapter Thirty-Eight

Knowing that neither action would bring results, Maxie nevertheless called both Rebecca and her mother immediately. Predictably there was no reply from either but she had to find them as quickly as possible.

'Rebecca,' said Maxie leaving her message. 'Please call me and tell me where you are, I know what happened. I know why you're hiding but call me, please, just call me. I can help.'

The next call was to Jean.

'I know what happened, Jean,' said Maxie. 'Can you pick me up? We might have some miles to cover and I can't afford to risk running out of power. I'll explain when you get here.'

Jean said she'd be over within half an hour which gave Maxie time to send through the interview with the anonymous caller to her students and Craig, then have a group video call with them.

'It's really horrible,' said Belle. 'Imagine keeping that bottled up for all these years, it could really destroy your life.'

'You think he also abused David?' asked Sonny.

'I'm sure of it,' Maxie said. 'David went on those trips and had exactly the sort of background that he preyed on – boys whose fathers were bullies and had nowhere to turn. And I'm sure they weren't the only two.'

'So we have his permission to tell his story as long as one of us reads it out so he can't be recognised?' said Joseph. 'I don't think we should present this as an adjunct to the cold case, it needs to be recognised in its own right.'

'I agree,' said Sonny. 'And we should ask anyone who experienced the same thing to come forward.'

'Remember we cannot name him yet,' said Maxie. 'We're not starting a trial by podcast.'

They agreed to work out the details of the episode and surrounding campaign with Craig then update her later in the day.

'Where will you be?' asked Craig.

'I honestly don't know,' Maxie said. 'I have an idea where to start looking but none as to where I'll end up.'

'Be careful,' warned Craig. 'Don't do anything stupid … or illegal.'

'I won't thump him,' said Maxie. 'I want justice not a countersuit.'

The intercom buzzed just as Maxie was ending the call so she picked up a coat and ran down the stairs to Jean. As the two women rushed towards the car, Maxie couldn't help but think of her sister and Rebecca referring to themselves as *The Professionals*. She and the cold case investigator were more *Cagney and Lacey* but it felt good to be working alongside someone as focussed on solving the case as she was.

'Did you bring the stone?' asked Maxie as she belted up. Jean passed the painted stone that had been left at the graveside.

'I've had to sign it out so Andrew will know that we're up to something,' Jean said. 'Now where to?'

Maxie's only shot at finding Rebecca was believing that this stone painted with bluebells actually meant something. From Mrs Henderson's reaction to it, she could tell it had been recognised but for some reason Rebecca's mum hadn't acknowledged it. Maxie decided to take a punt that Petra might have some idea. She told Jean this and gave her the address of the charity where David's Aunt Petra worked. Maxie had no idea whether the woman would be in the office today but was convinced she would help if she could.

A forty-minute drive feels like ninety minutes when every second counts and with each red traffic light or cautious learner driver, Maxie could feel the tension in her rise. She'd promised Craig she wouldn't thump this guy when she saw him but with each delay that promise looked more and more precarious. Jean's phone rang in its holder and Maxie saw DS Dawson's name come up.

'Where on earth are you two?' he asked.

'How did you know I would be with Jean?' replied Maxie.

'Who else would be purloining evidence without informing the investigating officer?' he said with a heavy tone of sarcasm. 'Now what are you up to and does it have anything to do with my murder case?'

Maxie paused and thought about holding out on Andrew but she knew Jean would get into trouble and Cagney would never do that to Lacey. She told the detective about the anonymous caller and the abuse that had taken place, then said they were on their way to try and find Rebecca. 'I think she knows what happened and will try to keep her mother safe before turning her father in. He's a violent man.'

'Which is precisely why you should not be pursing him,' Andrew said. 'I'll get a car to pick him up. You two should stand down now.'

Maxie ended the call and looked over at Jean. 'He's not technically your boss is he?' Jean shook her head. 'Then it seems foolish to turn the car around now when we're nearly there.'

The cold case investigator smiled and put her foot down.

Maxie made a silent heavenly *thank you* as they walked into the office of Mothers Against Hatred and saw Petra talking to a colleague. She took a breath then walked up to her. 'We met at the funeral,' she said with a hand outstretched.

'Yes, I know who you are but I don't think we've been formally introduced – I'm Petra Younghusband, David's Aunt. It looks as if you want to talk.'

'Somewhere private if that's possible,' Maxie said.

They followed Petra into a tiny office, stacked high with flags and banners that obviously came out for protest marches. They both turned down the offer of a coffee but Maxie accepted some water; the thought of telling this woman the truth of their joint situation suddenly drying her throat to Saharan levels. Without naming the abuser she told Petra what had happened at the youth club and that she thought one of his friends had discovered the truth and was now hiding out. Maxie delivered the news as gently as she could but Petra's face drained of colour a little more with each word.

'I think this stone might be a clue,' said Maxie. 'It was left for me to find at David's funeral – does it mean anything to you?'

Petra took hold of it and ran her hand over it as if it contained some remnant of her nephew. She nodded.

'Yes,' she said. 'I have a caravan near the Lake District and it's from my front porch – I like making them. The bluebells in the woods there are spectacular and David used to love them. He took a friend there once – a girl. Becky – I think that's what her name was. That's who you're looking for isn't it?'

Maxie glanced over at Jean before giving a slight nod. They didn't really know this woman but had to trust her. 'Can you give us the address of the caravan?' asked Jean.

'No and it's quite hard to find with just the Satnav,' said Petra grabbing a coat and bag. 'But I can take you there.'

Jean shook her head and said it wasn't possible, that this was an official investigation and she would not put anyone else at risk but Petra was having none of it. She told them they had no choice and to argue any further was just delaying things.

The three women climbed into Jean's car and pointed it northwards on the motorway. Miraculously it wasn't busy or besieged by roadworks but Jean would not break the speed limit, responding to the frustrated protests, that if they were stopped by an unmarked car it would cost them time and very possibly her job. Mile by mile ticked by; they didn't make small talk but Maxie wanted to know more about David.

'Did he ever mention the youth club weekends?' she asked.

'Not as such,' Petra said. 'I remember my sister being unsure that he actually enjoyed them but she said his father insisted that he go. My hideous brother-in-law believed they would make a man of his son.'

'So David was effectively forced back to his abuser time and time again,' said Maxie imagining how terrified and helpless the poor teenager must have felt.

Andrew rang Jean's phone again and Maxie pressed accept. 'Are you going to tell me where you're heading?' he asked.

'We're just …' started Maxie.

'Don't even think about lying,' said Andrew. 'Jean's car has an anti-theft device and I can see you're heading north – so I'll ask again, where are you going?'

Jean took over the call and informed the detective that the cold case investigation had uncovered an address where Rebecca might be lodging. They were on their way to it and would send him the precise details after the call.

'Have you picked up that pervert?' shouted Petra from the back seat.

'Who on earth do you have with you?' asked Andrew.

Maxie glared at Petra then explained who she was; she could picture Andrew shaking his head in despair.

'Jean,' he said. 'I am asking you to stand down. I will call Cumbria police and get them to check out the address. You are three civilians and I will not let you put yourselves in harm's way. I'm sure when I do speak to your commanding officer, they will agree with this.'

'Have you brought the suspect in?' pressed Maxie.

'No,' confessed Andrew. 'He wasn't at the house so might well be where you're heading. Stand down.'

'I'm sorry,' said Maxie. 'We're a damn sight closer to that caravan than the Cumbrian police. If I have to call Uber, I'm going.' She ended the call and switched the phone off.

Having exited the motorway, the roads twisted and turned through the undulating hills of the southern lakes. They were beautiful but remote and Maxie soon discovered that she needn't have bothered switching off the phone as there was absolutely no mobile signal here.

'Not far now,' said Petra. 'Take the next right.'

Jean signalled and slowed down. Maxie could see that she was slightly wary of these narrow country lanes and knew she'd feel the same. She glanced in the mirror and noted that the car behind wasn't being held up by them as they were also turning right.

Within fifteen minutes they saw the entrance to a small park in a fabulous valley surrounded by hills. They located Petra's caravan and parked up. Petra ran up to the door and tried the handle which was locked; she fiddled with the numbers on a key-safe underneath the porch – it opened but there was no key.

'Have you kept the same combination all these years?' asked Maxie.

'David's birthday,' replied Petra. 'He was my only nephew.'

Maxie opened a bin lid and saw some fresh rubbish so peered through the windows and rapped on them. 'Rebecca, it's Professor Reddick,' she called out. 'If you're in there come out. We know what happened, you're safe.'

There was movement just below eye level; Maxie got up onto her tiptoes to be able to see the floor just below the window. 'I can see you,' she said. 'Let us in, we'll take you to safety.'

The lock turned and the door opened. A distraught looking Rebecca and her mother stood to one side to let the three women in. Maxie walked straight towards Rebecca and hugged her tight.

'I'm so sorry,' wept Rebecca. 'All these years and I didn't know. I'm so, so sorry.'

Maxie held her for what seemed like a lifetime. The two women clung to each other and wept every tear in their bodies until Rebecca had told her the whole sorry story. After all these years, discovering her sister's killer felt bittersweet. She had never anticipated that in doing so, Rebecca would find out her father was a murderer.

'We should get back,' said Jean. 'We have to make this entire case official.'

She walked everyone towards the car as Petra locked up the caravan. Their silence was disturbed by a rustle in nearby shrubs and a sudden rush of movement. Roy Henderson ran out and grabbed the arm of his daughter, dragging her down to the ground.

'You're not ruining my life after all I've done for you,' he yelled as he straddled her and pinned her to the ground, raising his fist in a punch.

Thwack.

Roy Henderson collapsed sideways and Rebecca pushed him off quickly before running into her mother's arms. Maxie turned to look in the direction of the noise and saw Petra with a bluebell painted stone raised above her head, ready to strike again if required.

Chapter Thirty-Nine

'Thank you for joining us on *Criminal Thoughts* and this, our final episode of *My Sister's Killer*,' said Craig. 'In this concluding episode, we will be telling you what we can about the case of Susan Reddick. We are able to say that the prime suspect has been apprehended but obviously we cannot name them before the case goes to trial. For that reason, some of the names in today's episode have been changed. We are joined today by the entire cold case team and a special guest who we will refer to as Susan's friend. Friend — thank you for coming; we know that this case must have been very difficult for you.'

Rebecca nodded slightly then cleared her throat before saying, 'It has,' in a barely audible whisper.

Craig moved the microphone closer to her and asked if she'd like to start with her memories of Susan as a teenager.

'We probably shouldn't really have been friends, we were so different.' Rebecca's voice was still very low. 'She was so organised, knew exactly what she wanted from life and was going to get it. But she was great fun too. We went to gigs, parties, basketball tournaments and when I got a bit too drunk, she always got me home.'

Rebecca looked up at Maxie with tears in her eyes. 'We might have been the same age but she was like my big sister too sometimes.'

Maxie swallowed hard; hearing about her sister from someone who knew her better than she did was hard.

'She could talk to anyone,' continued Rebecca getting more confident. 'That's why she was so good at the Avon stuff and the supplements. She could suggest the slimming pills might help without saying you were fat.'

She snorted before adding, 'She even told me I needed a brain power supplement without me realising what she was saying – I guess that proved I needed it.'

Rebecca laughed and lightened the tone of the room.

'Anyhow, she didn't think all that stuff was dangerous at all – she used to say that they were most likely just multi-vitamins and her customers were experiencing a placebo effect. At that last party – that's what she was handing out, just to prove her theory. She wanted to prove to people that they could have a good time without the drugs.'

'Amy's brother, Paul appeared on this podcast and said she jumped when she saw him turn up that night – do you know why that might be?' asked Maxie.

'I'm guessing she was horrified to see Amy rather than her brother,' replied Rebecca. 'That woman was getting stuff from everywhere and always went too far. The sort of person you really didn't want at your house party.'

Maxie raised her eyebrows towards Craig and he nodded. They both knew they'd have to edit some of that before the episode aired but right now, they had to let Rebecca talk.

'So how did David get involved in the supplement business?' continued Maxie.

'I knew Susan was making a fair whack so I asked her to let David in on it,' replied Rebecca. 'He hated his dad so much and needed money to get away. He wanted to get his mum away too but she wouldn't go. Stockholm syndrome I guess.'

'So David became the sales person in Brookfield?' asked Maxie getting a nod in response. 'What happened when Susan decided to stop selling?'

'She'd read something about slimming pills containing speed not multi-vits and although she had no proof of that, she wasn't going to risk her whole future so she threw them down the toilet. She told the guy she bought them from that they needed to stop or she'd report him.'

'Did you know who the dealer was at the time?' asked Jean.

'No I didn't – Susan said his identity had to remain top secret.'

'But Susan threatened to expose him and when she did that, it threatened David's livelihood and his dream of escaping,' said Maxie.

'To start with yes and he had a row with her at the party about it,' continued Rebecca. 'But then he found out the supplements were just being bought from a brochure and so started buying them himself. He tried to get me to continue with Susan's patch after she died but I just couldn't. I pictured her up there with her arms folded in disapproval – you know like she used to.'

Maxie smiled as she remembered that particular look – she used to get it a lot from her big sister.

'But we know now that David stuck to the supplements business and actually made a pretty good living from it,' said Joseph. 'We're always being sold some magic pill or the other by influencers and he cashed in on that. Do you have any idea why he was keeping that business secret?'

'His dad,' replied Rebecca. 'He really didn't want that man anywhere near his life.'

'The prime suspect who is in custody is actually your father isn't he? Are you okay to move on to his involvement in this?' asked Maxie.

'He's not my father any more,' Rebecca said through a clenched jaw. 'He never was my real dad and now mum and I are changing our names, we want nothing to do with him.'

'That was one of the complications in the case,' said Joseph. 'Because although your prints and DNA were on file from the investigation into Susan's death, there was no familial match to the ones from either crime scene because the prime suspect was not your natural father. As there'd been no reason to suspect your stepfather, his own prints were never taken.'

'He volunteered to act as a parent supervisor on the youth club weekends away and before long was abusing those people he was supposed to be protecting,' Belle said. 'He knew which parents wouldn't believe their kids, so preyed on them.'

At this, Rebecca ran out of the studio crying and Jean went after her as they paused the recording. After a few moments Jean popped her head in to say they were taking a walk around the block and to continue without them.

'David Wallace was one of those kids,' continued Sonny as they resumed. 'His dad was a homophobic bully and would probably say that it was all David's fault if he knew. David kept quiet and suffered, leaving home as soon as he could.'

'On the night of my sister's death, we know from Susan's friend that David came to the party at my house,' said Maxie. 'Mr Kennedy our neighbour has also identified the teenage David as the boy he saw. We know that David had a photo of the prime suspect with his hand on a young boy's thigh – that boy was the brave anonymous caller who exposed him. That caller told us about the photo and said that David was giving it to someone who always did the right thing even when it irked him. He was talking about my sister.'

Maxie swallowed and signalled to the others that she couldn't continue. Craig picked up the narrative.

‘However, David also made the fatal mistake of telling the prime suspect he had the photo and who would be safeguarding it. We know from the police that the prime suspect said in his confession that he hadn’t planned to hurt Susan but he had to find out if David was telling the truth. Susan apparently started telling him he should be ashamed of himself and that she’d be reporting him as soon as her parents got home. The prime suspect pushed her and she hit her head on the stairs.’

‘He claims that he didn’t intend to hurt Susan,’ continued Maxie with a croak in her voice. ‘But he didn’t try and help either. He moved Susan’s body as he rummaged through her dressing gown pockets and then ransacked the house but he didn’t call an ambulance.’

Maxie bit her lip as tears began to form. Craig reached over and squeezed her hand.

‘If David suspected Friend’s stepfather was guilty of involvement in Susan’s death, he said nothing; perhaps he didn’t think he’d be believed, and he would very likely get no support at all from his own abusive father. Instead, he ran. He stayed away from Barwick and made a success of his life,’ said Belle picking up the baton. ‘But one day he decided to stop running and make the prime suspect pay for what he’d done. He knew his revelation would hurt others so wanted to forewarn them.’

Jean and Rebecca walked back into the studio and signalled that they were okay to continue.

‘Tell us what happened when you met David earlier this year,’ said Sonny.

Rebecca blew her cheeks out before saying, ‘He said he wanted to come home. He wanted to move his business here and look after his mum but had to keep everything secret until he’d got her away – in case his dad found him.

‘When he told me about my stepfather, I was completely and utterly horrified. I knew he was a bully from the way he treats my mum but I never, ever suspected this. I told David that I would help him in any way I could but begged for time to get my mother away from that monster. He agreed and said that he had to see his elderly grandfather first anyway to make sure that he wouldn’t be impacted by it all coming out. That was the last time I saw him.’

‘But he never saw his grandad and he never got the chance to report his abuser,’ said Maxie. ‘Your stepfather spotted David by chance and followed him to the care home. Seeing that the teenage boy he knew had turned into a brave adult intent on justice, your stepfather grabbed the first thing to hand and took a swing at him.'

Jean now addressed Rebecca. 'You couldn't shy away from what you suspected had happened but still feared for your mother.'

'I couldn't help David but as long as no-one suspected my stepfather, then Mum was safe. That night at Mike's party'—Rebecca raised her eyes to Maxie—'I could see you would be looking into the past, Maxie, and from what I'd read online, I knew you wouldn't stop until you got answers. I couldn't face you again and say I knew nothing so I hid. I stole a driving licence from a handbag in the pub, hired a car with the cash I got from Jake and the next morning headed for the caravan park I'd been to with David. I knew it was remote but had to check it out, then I'd come back down for Mum when he wasn't around.'

'This has been a tough case – particularly tough emotionally,' said Craig as he rounded up the show. 'We may have answers but they haven't always been what we wanted to hear. I'd like to thank Susan's friend and Professor Reddick for allowing us to share this case with you.'

The show ended with a thank you to everyone who had contacted them to provide information and paid tribute to the very brave person who'd come forward to say that the prime suspect had also abused them.

All of the team were completely and utterly wrung-out emotionally as the recording came to an end. Rebecca said goodbye and told them she had to get back to her mother while the others adjourned to a bar and raised a glass to a successful conclusion of the cold case.

'To Sonny, Joseph, Belle – you've been exceptional. If you choose a career in criminology you'll go far,' said Maxie, clinking their glasses in turn. 'And to Jean Carruthers – thank you for risking everything to help solve this case.'

'It's been my privilege to work with you,' Jean said.

'You'd think we'd be on a high having caught the bad guy,' said Sonny. 'But it's not like that is it?'

'Not always,' Maxie acknowledged. 'There's a huge body of academic research into the emotions of relatives of killers and those who abuse as well as the emotional impact on the investigating officers. It's worth looking into.'

'Once a professor, always a professor,' said Craig, trying to raise a smile from the group but failing.

The mood was sombre and no-one really felt like celebrating so when Andrew walked into the bar, Craig, Jean and the students made their excuses to leave.

Andrew ordered a round and sat down opposite Maxie, pushing a glass of wine towards her.

'All good?' she asked, taking a sip. 'There's no chance of bail is there?'

'None at all,' said Andrew. 'And Petra isn't going to face charges either.'

'Good.'

'So what now for you?' he asked after a couple of minutes' silence between them.

'I don't know,' Maxie said, dourly. 'The mystery is solved, my parents know Susan died standing up for someone and Petra's organisation is going to dedicate a flowerbed to my sister in the local park.'

'That's nice of them,' said Andrew.

'It is,' she said. 'I'm not sure how I would have handled finding out Susan was a drug dealer or worse.'

'Well she wasn't and you don't have to worry about that any more. But I asked what was next for *you*.'

Maxie shrugged her shoulders. 'My department and the ACU is in the capable hands of Dr Leo Turner and my podcast works much better with its injection of new blood. I've kind of made myself … obsolete …

'But I think it's time,' continued Maxie after a pause. 'I think I've stayed here because I haven't wanted to stray too far from Susan. I've been released now and feel the urge to explore new horizons.'

'Surely you're not leaving me,' said Andrew swallowing hard. 'We've worked well together – I'd miss your disobedience and love of a great curry.'

Maxie laughed. 'I wouldn't worry,' she said. 'You know what Schwarzenegger always says in those Terminator films you love.'

Maxie raised her glass to the detective and after laughing they shouted in unison:

'I'll be back.'

* The end *

Thank You

Dear Reader,

Thank you so much for choosing *My Sister's Killer* – I do hope you enjoyed it and it kept you guessing until the very end. I've adored writing this series and I'm so happy to hear from readers who tell me that they love Professor Maxie Reddick because I love her too. She's certainly a unique individual and even keeps me guessing with what she'll do next! This is the third book in the series so if you haven't had the chance to read the others, I'd urge you to give them a go – I'm sure they'll have you gripped.

Finally, I just wanted to say that reviews really do matter to any author, so when you get the chance, I'd love you to post a review wherever you bought the book. It's great to hear from you and, of course, good reviews help other readers find the series – so they're very much appreciated!

Helen

x

About the Author

Helen Bridgett lives in the North East of England. Outside of writing feel good fiction, Helen loves the great outdoors and having a good laugh with friends over a glass of wine. Helen lives with her husband and their chocolate Labrador, Angus; all three can often be found walking the Northumberland coastline that inspired her first novel, *Summer at Serenity Bay*.

To find out more about Helen, follow her on social media:

Twitter: www.twitter.com/Helen_Bridgett
Facebook: www.facebook.com/HelenBridgettAuthor

More Ruby Fiction

from

Helen Bridgett

One by One

Book 1 in the Professor Maxie Reddick Files

When practising what you preach is easier said than done …
Professor Maxie Reddick has her reasons for being sceptical of traditional policing methods, but, in between her criminology lecturing job and her Criminal Thoughts podcast, she stays firmly on the side lines of the crime solving world.

Then a young woman is brutally attacked, and suddenly it's essential that Maxie turns her words into actions; this is no longer an academic exercise – this is somebody's life.

But as she delves deeper, the case takes a sickening turn, which leads Maxie to the horrifying realisation that the attack might not have been a one-off. It seems there's a depraved individual out there seeking revenge, and they'll stop at nothing to get it … little by little … one by one.

Visit www.rubyfiction.com for more details.

Wrong Sort of Girl
Book 2 in the Professor Maxie Reddick Files

A young woman has gone missing. It's nearly Christmas. Why does hardly anyone seem to care?

Kelly Ingles' case should have been one to tug on the public's heartstrings: a young woman missing in the run-up to Christmas.

But Kelly wasn't perfect – she liked to party, enjoyed a drink, didn't always make the best decisions. And when evidence of her drunken antics appears online, it becomes clear that Kelly might not just have been in the wrong place at the wrong time; she might also be the wrong sort of girl to encourage public sympathy.

It's a case that's right up Maxie Reddick's street. As a criminology professor, she's made it her mission to challenge unconscious biases within the criminal justice system – the sort of biases that cause girls like Kelly to slip through the cracks.

But can she get the police and public on board before it's too late?

Visit www.rubyfiction.com for more details.

Summer at Serenity Bay

What happens when you send a group of celebrities to a tiny seaside village?

Advertising executive Chloe Walsh thought she was visiting her friend Roisin to get away from it all, but little does she know her kooky friend has a master plan to breathe some life into her sleepy seaside village through a new wellness retreat – and she needs Chloe's skills.

So starts a community effort to put the retreat, Serenity Bay, on the map. Everyone from Andy at the Surf Shack to Tony at the chocolate shop is involved – even Roisin's Gran has a few ideas!

But Chloe strikes gold almost too soon, attracting the attention of a major production company. Now a colourful group of celebrities are preparing to descend on Serenity Bay to film a reality TV show. Is the village ready for the fun and scandal that are bound to follow?

Visit www.rubyfiction.com for more details.

Christmas at Serenity Bay
Sequel to Summer at Serenity Bay

A peaceful Christmas in Serenity Bay? Think again!
Chloe Walsh's skills as location manager for the beautiful seaside village she calls home have come up trumps again, and Serenity Bay is now the setting for cosy crime drama *The Montgomery Mysteries*, starring amateur sleuth Dominic Montgomery and his crime-solving dog, Agatha.

But Chloe is in a race against time. Filming has to finish before the village Midwinter Festival but schedules are tight – and a mystery saboteur is intent on slowing things down even further. Not only is Chloe facing problems with the shoot, she also has some personal conundrums to solve – a diva actor has commandeered her flat, her mum is having a late mid-life crisis, plus she has no idea what to buy for her Christmas-obsessed boyfriend!

Can Chloe sort out her life and save Christmas for an entire village?

Introducing Ruby Fiction

Ruby Fiction is in imprint of Choc Lit Publishing.
We are an award-winning British independent publisher, creating a delicious selection of fiction.

See our selection here:
www.rubyfiction.com
Ruby Fiction brings you stories that inspire emotions.

We would love to hear how you enjoyed *My Sister's Killer*. Please leave a review on the store where you purchased this novel or visit www.rubyfiction.com and give your feedback.

Ruby novels are selected by genuine readers like yourself. We only publish stories our Tasting Panel want to see in print. Our reviews and awards speak for themselves.

Could you be a Star Selector and join our Tasting Panel?
Would you like to play a role in choosing which novels we decide to publish? Do you enjoy reading women's fiction? Then you could be perfect for our Tasting Panel.

***Visit here:* www.choc-lit.com/join-the-choc-lit-tasting-panel**

Keep in touch:

Sign up for our newsletter for all the latest news and offers:
www.spread.choc-lit.com

Follow us on Twitter: **@RubyFiction** and
Facebook: **RubyFiction**

Stories that inspire emotions!

Printed in Great Britain
by Amazon

18390545R00141